LAY HER AMONG THE LILIES
James Hadley Chase

Vic Malloy of Universal Services is once again trolling in waters so turbulent they make a maelstrom look like a millpond. The churning starts when Vic's assistant retrieves an envelope Vic had stuffed into an old trench coat and forgotten about. The envelope contains $500 and is a retainer from a potential client—a client he never followed up with. Now months have passed without a response from Universal Services and the case is as cold as a dead mackerel. Embarrassed by his sloppy oversight, he attempts to make amends for his mistake, but his efforts quickly lead to a dead end . . . literally. His prospective client, Janet Crosby, died of a "heart attack" the very day she wrote and mailed the check. The accompanying letter requested Universal Services to investigate her half-sister, Maureen, whose wild and wanton behavior was causing the family considerable concern. The trouble is Maureen— now having inherited a pile of cash—has been sequestered while she recovers from a mysterious ailment. Vic quickly discovers that there are more gears turning behind the scenes than a few family squabbles. Having more twists and turns than a minotaur's maze, *Lay Her Among the Lilies* affirms that James Hadley Chase is indeed the *King of Thrillers*.

James Hadley Chase (René Brabazon Raymond) was born in London on Christmas Eve, 1906, and started his career as a bookseller. Seeing that the hard-boiled thrillers were selling especially well, he decided to write his own—*No Orchids for Miss Blandish*. It was the start of an incredible run of nearly 100 novels. Dozens of Chase thrillers have been made into feature films and stage plays.

JHC

Lay
Her
Among
The Lilies

James Hadley Chase

Introduced by Randal S. Brandt

Bruin Crimeworks

Printed in the USA
ISBN 978-1-7349759-2-5
Published July 2020
Bruin Books, LLC
Eugene, Oregon, USA
www.bruinbookstore.com

For inquiries: bruinbooks@comcast.net

Introduction

James Hadley Chase's California Dream

FROM the opening lines of *Lay Her Among the Lilies*, James Hadley Chase sets an archetypal mid-20th century California scene: "It was one of those hot, breathless July mornings, nice if you're in a swimsuit on the beach with your favorite blonde, but hard to take if you're shut up in an office as I was . . . Sunshine, hot and golden, made patterns on the office rug." What could be more Californian—in particular, Southern Californian—than beaches, blondes, and golden sunshine? Over his career, California was one of Chase's favorite settings to employ in his novels. But his California is a dream place, based more on his imagination and second-hand knowledge of the Golden State than on reality.

In his day, James Hadley Chase could rightfully claim the title "King of the Thriller Writers." Starting in 1939, he wrote at a breakneck pace, churning out an average of two to three books per year, culminating in ninety published novels by the time of his death, at age 78, in 1985. In order to avoid the appearance saturating the thriller market, he wrote under a variety of pseudonyms, including James L. Docherty, Ambrose Grant, and Raymond Marshall. But, even his best-known moniker was a pseudonym. Chase was born as René Lodge Brabazon Raymond on December 24, 1906 in London, England. His father, Colonel Francis Raymond, who was a veterinary surgeon and had served in the colonial Indian Army, hoped he would pursue a career in science. Young René had other ideas, though. At the age of 18 he left home and took up a career in bookselling. He also kept a keen eye on the happenings in the United States. Prohibition, followed by the Great Depression, gave rise to American gangster culture centered in the city of Chicago. With his experience in the book trade and the popularity of the American pulp magazines, he could see that the appetite for gangster stories was huge. So, with the help of maps and an American slang dictionary, he wrote *No Orchids for Miss Blandish* and published it as by James Hadley Chase in 1939.

That book was also the beginning of Chase's literary love affair with the United States. Even though he never lived in the U.S the majority of his books have American settings. In fact, he only ever made two brief visits—one to Miami and the other a stop while en route to Mexico. And, of his American settings, California clearly held a place close to Chase's heart. Of his ninety novels, twenty-three of them are set in California. Florida checks in at second place with fourteen novels set in the Sunshine State.

Lay Her Among the Lilies, originally published in 1950, was the third and final novel—following *You're Lonely When You're Dead* (1949) and *Figure It Out For Yourself* (1950)— in a trilogy featuring private investigator Vic Malloy. Malloy heads an agency called Universal Services in a fictional California coastal town called Orchid City. He has a "leg-man," Jack Kerman, and an administrative assistant named Paula Bensinger, whom he calls the "backbone" of the operation (and in fact lent Malloy the money to start the agency in the first place). The plot kicks into gear when Paula hands Vic an envelope that had been languishing unopened in the pocket of a forgotten trench coat for the past fourteen months. Inside is a letter from socialite Janet Crosby asking Vic for a meeting to discuss her younger sister, Maureen, who is being blackmailed, along with a five-hundred-dollar retainer. Vic quickly discovers that his prospective client is dead. She died of a heart attack on the very day she posted the letter. Faced with the prospect of returning the much needed cash he decides, instead, to try to earn it by looking into the matter of why a young, seemingly healthy, woman would drop dead of a heart ailment.

Orchid City is located on the West Coast, somewhere between Los Angeles and San Francisco—it is, in fact, just off the "Los Angeles and San Francisco Highway"—but definitely has a Southern California vibe. Several of the street names, including Hollywood, Westwood, Hawthorne, and "Wiltshire," could have been lifted directly from a map of Los Angeles. Curiously, he also names an area of Orchid City "Coral Gables," which evokes South Florida. Chase's superficial knowledge of California geography is exposed when, later in the investigation, Malloy and Kerman drive up to San Francisco. Although neither distances nor driving times are given, they make the trip up and back within the scope of just a few hours. And, for an unexplained reason, they cross the San Francisco-Oakland Bay Bridge (called simply "Oakland Bay Bridge" in the novel) in and out of the city rather than sticking to the coast up the Peninsula.

Certainly some of Chase's second-hand knowledge of California came from fellow crime writer Raymond Chandler. Chase and Chandler had careers that were intertwined in more ways than one. In 1939, they both published their debut novels, *No Orchids for Miss Blandish* and *The Big Sleep*. Of course, Chandler's career was the more celebrated, even from its earliest days. Chase, like countless writers after him, was influenced by Chandler. In fact, Chase was perhaps too influenced by Chandler. After the publication of his 1945 novel *Blonde's Requiem*, Chase had to issue a public apology to Chandler for lifting plot elements from 1940's *Farewell,*

My Lovely.

Chase clearly let *The Big Sleep* influence him while writing *Lay Her Among the Lilies*. Superficially, both titles refer to death, but in rather benign terms, and both are told in the first person from the point of view of an honest private investigator. Although the character of Vic Malloy bears no more or less resemblance to Philip Marlowe than any of the countless wisecracking gumshoes that both preceded and followed him, there are other clues that lead one to suspect that Chase had *The Big Sleep* on his mind. Chase's plot centers around two sisters, the mature, responsible Janet and the young, wild, and blackmailed Maureen, who are echoes of Chandler's Vivian Regan and Carmen Sternwood. There is also a reference to actor Humphrey Bogart, who just a few years prior had taken a memorable turn as Marlowe on the silver screen.

Chandler and *The Big Sleep* may also offer an explanation for the name of Chase's fictional California city. To a Californian, the idea of any place in the state called "Orchid City" is absurd. While it is true that species of orchids can be found throughout the United States, orchids are most commonly associated with tropical regions—something California most definitely is not. If Chase had wanted to name a city in California after a flower, "Poppy City" would have made much more sense. So why Orchid City? Chase may have simply been evoking the title of his best-known novel (and its "sequel," *The Flesh of the Orchid*), or it may have been a nod to another popular fictional detective, Nero Wolfe, who was a famous orchidophile. But, when looking at *Lay Her Among the Lilies* through the lens of *The Big Sleep*, another plausible explanation emerges.

At the opening of *The Big Sleep*, Marlowe is summoned to the Sternwood mansion, where he meets with General

Sternwood in an overheated greenhouse filled with orchids. Chandler's descriptive skill, through the first-person narration of Philip Marlowe, is on full display.

> *[I]t was really hot. The air was thick, wet, steamy and larded with the cloying smell of tropical orchids in bloom . . . The plants filled the place, a forest of them, with nasty meaty leaves and stalks like the newly washed fingers of dead men.*

The association of orchids with death continues as Sternwood and Marlowe talk.

> *"I seem to exist largely on heat, like a newborn spider, and the orchids are an excuse for the heat. Do you like orchids?"*
> *"Not particularly," I said.*
> *The General half-closed his eyes. "They are nasty things. Their flesh is too much like the flesh of men. And their perfume has the rotten sweetness of a prostitute."*

In this context, Orchid City—a place that has its fair share of death and "rotten sweetness"—is an apt appellation.

On its surface, James Hadley Chase's vision of California is one of golden sunshine. But, just below that surface is darkness, and the invented Orchid City is revealed to be a town where dreams devolve into nightmares of sadism and murder.

Randal S. Brandt
Curator of the California Detective Fiction Collection
The Bancroft Library, University of California, Berkeley
August 12, 2020

LAY
HER
AMONG
THE LILIES

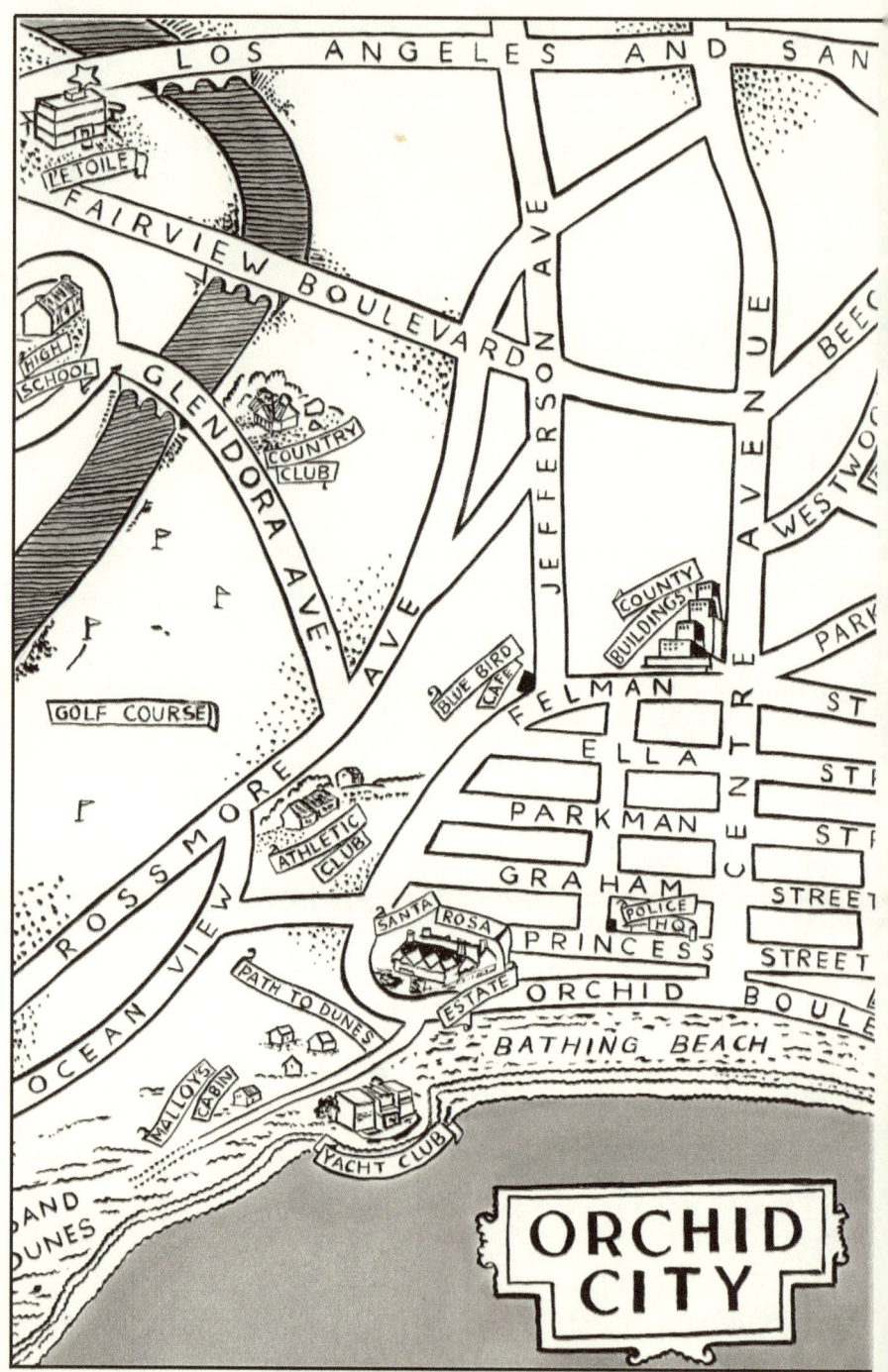

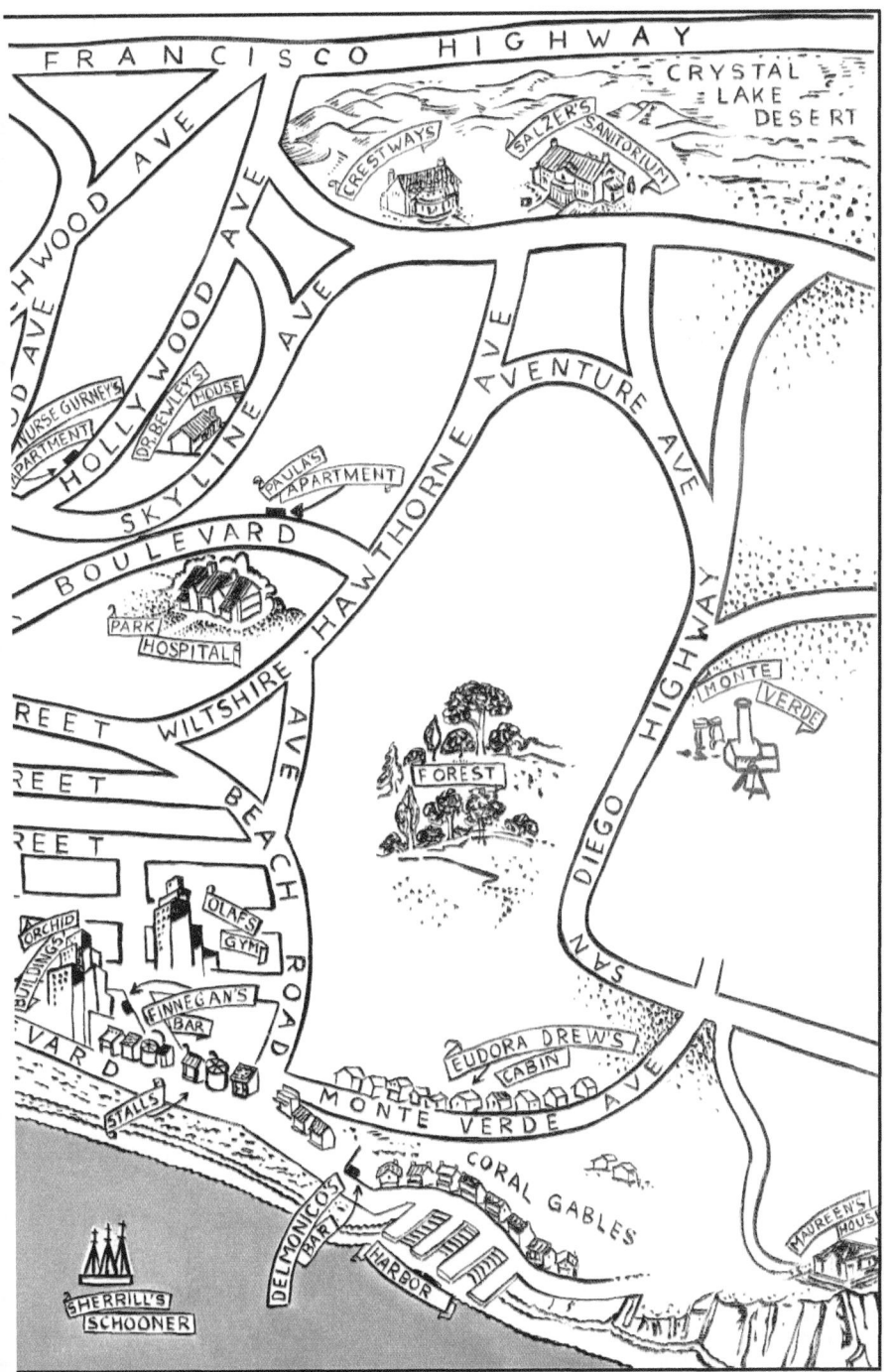

Chapter One

1

IT was one of those hot, breathless July mornings, nice if you're in a swimsuit on the beach with your favorite blonde, but hard to take if you're shut up in an office as I was.

The sound of the mid-morning traffic on Orchid Boulevard, the drone of aircraft circling the beach, and the background murmur of the surf drifted in through the open windows. The air-conditioning plant, hidden somewhere in the bowels of the Orchid Buildings, coped efficiently with the rising temperature. Sunshine, hot and golden, made patterns on the office rug Paula had bought to impress the customers, and which always seemed to me too expensive to walk on.

I sat behind the flat-topped desk on which I had scattered a few old letters to convince Paula if she should come in suddenly that I was working. A highball, strong enough to crack concrete, hid behind a couple of impressive-looking law books, and clinked ice at me whenever I reached for it.

It was now just over three and a half years since I founded Universal Services, an organization which undertook any job from exercising a pet poodle to stamping on a blackmailer feeding on a client's bankroll. It was essentially a millionaire's service, as our rates came high, but then, in Orchid City, millionaires were almost as numerous as grains of sand on a beach. During those three and a half years we had fun

and games, made a little money and had a variety of jobs—
even murder we had taken in our stride.

For the past few days business had been as quiet as a
spinster eating a bun in a lecture-hall. The routine stuff was
coming in all right, but Paula Bensinger took care of that. It
was only when something out-of-the-way reared its head
that I and my leg-man, Jack Kerman, went to work. And
nothing out-of-the-way had reared its head, so we were just
sitting around waiting and punching holes in a bottle of
Scotch and making out to Paula we were busy.

Sprawled out in the armchair reserved for clients, Jack
Kerman, long, lean and dapper, with a broad streak of white
in his thick black hair and a Clark Gable moustache, rubbed
the frosted glass of his highball against his forehead and
relaxed. Immaculate in an olive-green tropical suit and a
yellow and red striped tie, his narrow feet gaudy in white
buckskin shoes with dark green explosions, he looked every
inch a fugitive from the pages of *Esquire*.

Out of a long, brooding silence, he said, "What a dish!
Take her arms off and she'd have knocked Venus for a loop."
He shifted into a more comfortable position and sighed. "I
wish someone had taken her arms off. Boy, was she strong!
And I was sucker enough to think she was a pushover."

"Don't tell me," I pleaded, reaching for my highball. "That
opening has a familiar ring. The last thing I want to hear on a
morning like this is an extract from your love-life. I'd rather
read Krafft-Ebing."*

"That old goat won't get you anywhere," Kerman said
scornfully. "He wrote all the nifty bits in Latin."

"And you'd be surprised at the number of guys who

---

*Richard von Krafft-Ebing (1840-1910) was an Austro-German doctor who
specialized in the study of human sexuality. His most famous work is *Psychopathia
Sexualis*, where he coined the terms *sadism* and *masochism*. In context, Vic is
referring to a highbrow "dirty book."

learned Latin just to find out what he said. That's what I call killing two birds with one stone."

"That brings us right back to my blonde," Kerman said, stretching out his long legs. "I ran into her last night in Barney's drug store."

"I'm not interested in blondes," I said firmly. "Instead of sitting around here talking about women you should be out trying to hustle up new business. Sometimes I wonder what the hell I pay you for."

Kerman considered this, a surprised expression on his face.

"Do you want any new business?" he asked eventually. "I thought the idea was to let Paula do all the work, and we live on her."

"That's the general setup, but once in a while it mightn't be a bad idea for you to do something to earn your keep."

Kerman looked relieved.

"Yeah, once in a while. For a moment I thought you meant now." He sipped his highball and closed his eyes. "Now this blonde I keep trying to tell you about. She's a cute trick if ever there was one. When I tried to date her up, she said she didn't run after men. Know what I said?"

"What did you say?" I asked, because he would have told me anyway and if I didn't listen to his lies, who was going to listen to mine?

Kerman chortled.

"'Lady,' I said, 'maybe you don't run after men, but a mousetrap doesn't have to run after mice, either.' Smart, huh? Well, it killed her. You needn't look so damned sour. Maybe you have heard it before, but she hadn't and it knocked her dead."

Then before I could hide the highball the door jerked

open and Paula swept in.

Paula was a tall, dark lovely, with cool, steady brown eyes and a figure full of ideas—my ideas, not hers. She was quick on the uptake, ruthlessly efficient, and a tireless worker. It had been she who had encouraged me to start Universal Services and had lent the money to tide me over for the first six months. It was entirely due to her ability to cope with the administrative side of the business that Universal Services was an established success. If I were the brains of the setup, you could call her the backbone. Without her, the organization would have folded in a week.

"Haven't you anything better to do than sit around and drink?" she demanded, planting herself before the desk, and looking at me accusingly.

"What is there better to do?" Kerman asked, mildly interested.

She gave him a withering stare and turned her bright brown eyes on me again.

"As a matter of fact Jack and I were just going out to beat up some new business," I said, hastily pushing back my chair. "Come on, Jack. Let's go and see what we can find."

"And where are you going to look—Finnegan's bar?" Paula asked scornfully.

"That's a bright idea, sourpuss," Kerman said. "Maybe Finnegan will have something for us."

"Before you go you might like to look at this," Paula said, and flourished a long envelope at me. "The janitor brought it up just now. He found it in one of the pockets of that old trench coat you so generously gave him."

"He did?" I said, taking the envelope. "That's odd. I haven't worn that trench coat for more than a year."

"The cancellation stamp bears you out," Paula said with ominous calm. "The letter was posted fourteen months ago. I suppose you couldn't have put it in your pocket and forgotten all about it? You wouldn't do a thing like that, would you?"

The envelope was addressed to me in a neat, feminine handwriting, and unopened.

"I can't remember ever seeing it before," I said.

"Considering you don't appear to remember anything unless I remind you, that comes as no surprise," Paula said tartly.

"One of these days, my little harpy," Kerman remarked gently, "someone is going to haul off and take a slap at your bustle."

"That won't stop her," I said, ripping open the envelope. "I've tried. It only makes her worse." I dipped in a finger and thumb and hoisted out a sheet of notepaper and five one-hundred-dollar bills.

"Suffering Pete!" Kerman exclaimed, starting to his feet. "Did you give that to the janitor?"

"Now don't you start," I said, and read the letter.

CRESTWAYS,
FOOTHILL BOULEVARD,
ORCHID CITY.

May 15th, 1948

Will you please make it convenient to see me at the above address at three o'clock tomorrow afternoon? I am anxious to obtain evidence against someone who is blackmailing my sister. I understand you undertake such work. Please treat this letter as confidential and urgent. I enclose five hundred dollars as a retainer.

JANET CROSBY

There was a long and painful silence. Even Jack Kerman hadn't anything to say. We relied on recommenddations to bring in the business, and keeping five hundred dollars belonging to a prospective client for fourteen months without even acknowledging it is no way to get a recommendation.

"Urgent and confidential," Paula murmured. "After keeping it to himself for fourteen months he hands it to the janitor to show to all his little playmates. Wonderful!"

"You shut up!" I snarled. "Why didn't she call up and ask for an explanation? She must have guessed the letter had gone astray. But wait a minute. She's dead, isn't she? One of the Crosby girls died. Was it Janet?"

"I think it was," Paula said. "I'll soon find out."

"And dig up everything we've got on Crosby, too."

When she had gone into the outer office, I said, "I'm sure she's dead. I guess we'll have to return this money to her estate."

"If we do that," Kerman said, always reluctant to part with money, "the press may get wind of it. A story like this will make a swell advertisement for the way we run our business. We'll have to watch our step, Vic. It might be smarter to hang on to the swag and say nothing about it."

"We can't do that. We may be inefficient, but at least let's be honest."

Kerman folded himself down in the armchair again. "Safer to let sleeping dogs lie. Crosby's something in oil, isn't he?"

"He was. He's dead. He was killed in a shooting accident about a couple of years back." I picked up the letter opener and began to punch holes in the blotter. "It beats me how I came to leave the letter in my trench coat like that. I'll never hear the end of it."

Kerman, who knew Paula, grinned sympathetically.

"Slosh her in the slats if she nags," he said helpfully. "Am I glad it wasn't me!"

I went on punching holes in the blotter until Paula returned with a fistful of newspaper clippings.

"She died of heart failure on May 15th, the same day she wrote the letter. No wonder you didn't hear from her," she said as she shut the office door.

"Heart failure? How old was she then?"

"Twenty-five."

I laid down the letter opener and groped for a cigarette.

"That seems mighty young to die of heart failure. Anyway, let's have the dope. What have you got?"

"Not a great deal. Most of it we know already," Paula said, sitting on the edge of the desk. "Macdonald Crosby made his millions in oil. He was a hard, unlovable old Quaker with a mind as broad as a tightrope. He married twice. Janet, the elder daughter by four years, was by his first wife. Maureen by his second wife. He retired from business in 1943 and settled in Orchid City. Before that he lived in San Francisco. The two girls are as unalike as they can be. Janet was studious and spent most of her time painting. Several of her oils are hung in the arts museum. She seems to have had a lot of talent, a retiring nature, and a sharp temper. Maureen is the beauty of the family. She's wild, woolly, and wanton. Up til Crosby's death she was continually getting herself on the front page of the newspapers in some scandal or other."

"What kind of scandal?" I asked.

"About a couple of years ago she knocked down and killed a fellow on Centre Avenue. Rumor has it she was drunk, which seems likely as she drank like a fish. Crosby squared the police and she got off with a heavy fine for dangerous driving. Then another time she rode along Orchid Boulevard on a horse without a stitch on. Someone betted her she hadn't the nerve, but she did it."

"Let me get that straight," Kerman said, sitting up excitedly. "Was it the horse or the girl who hadn't a stitch on?"

"The girl, you dope!"

"Then, where was I? I didn't see her."

"She only got about fifty yards before she was pinched."

"If I'd been around she wouldn't have got that far."

"Don't be coarse, and be quiet!"

"Well she certainly sounds like a grand subject for blackmail," I put in.

Paula nodded.

"You know about Crosby's death. He was cleaning a gun in his study, it went off and killed him. He left three-quarters of his fortune to Janet with no strings tied to it, and a quarter to Maureen in trust. When Janet died, Maureen came into the whole vast estate, and seems to be a reformed character. Since she lost her sister she hasn't once been mentioned in the press."

"When did Crosby die?" I asked.

"March 1948. Two months before Janet died."

"Convenient for Maureen."

Paula raised her eyebrows.

"Yes, Janet was very upset by her father's death. She was never very strong, and the press said the shock finished her."

"All the same it's very convenient for Maureen. I don't like it, Paula. Maybe I have a suspicious mind. Janet writes to me that someone is blackmailing her sister. She then promptly dies of heart failure and her sister comes into her money. It's too damned convenient."

"I don't see what we can do," Paula said, frowning. "We can't represent a dead client."

"Oh yes we can." I tapped the five one-hundred-dollar

bills. "I have to either hand this money back to the estate or try to earn it. I think I'll try to earn it."

"Fourteen months is a long time," Kerman said dubiously. "The trail will be cold."

"If there is a trail," Paula said.

"On the other hand," I said, pushing back my chair, "if there's anything sinister about Janet's death, fourteen months provides a pleasant feeling of security, and when you feel secure you're off your guard. I think I'll call on Maureen Crosby and see how she likes spending her sister's money."

Kerman groaned.

"Something tells me the brief spell of leisure is over," he said sadly. "I thought it was too good to last. Do I start work now or wait until you get back?"

"You wait until I get back," I said, moving towards the door. "But if you've made a date with that mousetrap of yours, tell her to go find another mouse."

2

CRESTWAYS, the Crosby's estate, lurked behind low, bougainvillea-covered walls above which rose a tall, clipped, Australian pine hedge, and back of that was a galvanized cyclone fence topped with barbed wire. Heavy wooden gates, with a Judas window set in the right-hand gate, guarded the entrance.

There were about half a dozen similar estates strung along Foothill Boulevard and backing onto Crystal Lake desert. Each estate was separated from its neighbor by an acre or so of a no-man's-land of brushwood, wild sage, sand, and heat.

I lolled in the pre-war Buick convertible and regarded the wooden gates without much interest. Apart from the scrolled sign on the wall that declared the name of the house, there was nothing particularly different about it from all the other millionaire estates in Orchid City. They all lurked behind impregnable walls. They all had high wooden gates to keep out unwelcomed visitors. They all exuded the same awed hush, the same smell of flowers and well-watered lawns. Although I couldn't see beyond the gates, I knew there would be the same magnificent swimming pool, the same aquarium, the same rhododendron walk, the same sunken rose garden. If you own a million dollars you have to live on the same scale as the other millionaires or else they'll think you are punk. That's the way it *was*, that's the way it *is*, and that's the way it'll always be—if you own a million dollars.

No one seemed to be in a hurry to open the gates, so I dragged myself out of the car and hung on to the end of the bell chain. The bell had been muffled, and rang timorously.

Nothing happened. The sun beat down on me. The temperature hoisted itself up another notch. It was too hot even for such a simple exercise as pulling a bell chain. Instead, I pushed on the gate which swung open creakily under my touch. I looked at the stretch of lawn before me that was big enough for tank maneuvers. The grass hadn't been cut this month, nor for that matter the month before. Nor had the two long flower beds on either side of the broad driveway received any attention this spring, nor for that matter last autumn either. The daffodils and tulips made brown patterns of untidiness among the dead heads of the peonies. Shriveled Sweet William plants mingled with unstaked and matted delphiniums. A fringe of straggling grass disgraced the edges of the lawn. The asphalt driveway sprouted weeds. A neglected rose rambler flapped hysterically in the lazy breeze that came off the desert. An unloved, uncared-for garden, and looking at it I seemed to hear old man Crosby fidgeting in his coffin.

At the far end of the driveway I could see the house: a two-story, coquina-built mansion with a red tile roof, green shutters and an overhanging balcony. Sun-blinds screened the windows. No one moved on the green tile patio. I decided to walk up there rather than wrestle with the gates to bring in the Buick.

Halfway up the weed-strewn driveway I came upon one of those arbor things covered with a flowering vine. Squatting on their heels in the shade were three Chinese men shooting craps. They didn't bother to look up as I paused to stare, just as they hadn't bothered for a long, long time to look after the garden: three dirty, mindless men, smoking yellow-papered cigarettes with not a care in the world.

I tramped on.

The next bend in the driveway brought me to the swimming pool. There had to be a swimming pool, but not necessarily one like this one. There was no water in it, and weeds grew out of the cracked tile floor. The concrete surround was covered with a brownish, burned-up moss. The white awning which must have looked pretty smart in its day had come loose from its moorings and flapped querulously at me.

At right angles to the house was a row of garages, their double doors closed. A little guy in a pair of dirty flannel trousers, an undershirt and a chauffeur's cap sat on an oil drum in the sun, whittling wood. He looked up to scowl at me.

"Anyone at home?" I asked, searching for a cigarette and lighting it when I found one.

It took all that time before he worked up enough strength to say: "Don't bother me Jack. I'm busy."

"I can see that," I said, blowing smoke at him. "I'd love to sneak up on you when you're relaxing."

He spat accurately at a tub of last summer's pelargo-
niums from which no one had bothered to take cuttings, and
went on with his whittling. As far as he was concerned I was
now just part of the shabby landscape.

I didn't think I would get anything useful out of him, and
besides, it was too hot to bother, so I went on to the house,
climbed the broad steps and leaned my weight on the
doorbell.

A funereal hush hung over the house. I had to wait a long
time before anyone answered my ring. I didn't mind waiting.
I was now in the shade, and the drowsy, next-year-will-do
atmosphere of the place had a kind of hypnotic influence on
me. If I had stayed there much longer I would have begun
whittling wood myself.

The door opened, and what might have passed for a
butler looked me over the way you look someone over who's
wakened you up from a nice quiet nap. He was a tall, lean
bird, lantern-jawed, grey-haired, with close-set, yellowish
eyes. He wore one of those wasp-colored vests and black
trousers that looked as if he had slept in them, and probably
had, no coat, and his shirt sleeves suggested they wanted to
go to the laundry but just couldn't be bothered.

"Yes?" he said distantly and raised his eyebrows.

"Miss Crosby."

I noticed he was holding a lighted cigarette, half-con-
cealed in his cupped hand.

"Miss Crosby doesn't receive now," he said, and began to
close the door.

"I'm an old friend. She'll see me," I said, and shifted my
foot forward to jam the door. "The name's Malloy. Tell her
and watch her reaction. It's my bet she'll bring out the
champagne."

"Miss Crosby is not well," he said in a flat voice, as if he were reading a ham part in a hammier play. "She doesn't receive anymore."

"Like Miss Otis?"

That one went past him without stirring the air.

"I will tell her you have called." The door was closing. He didn't notice my foot. It startled him when he found the door wouldn't shut.

"Who's looking after her?" I asked, smiling at him.

A bewildered expression came into his eyes. For him life had been so quiet and gentle for so long he wasn't in training to cope with anything out of the way.

"Nurse Gurney."

"Then I'd like to see Nurse Gurney," I told him, and leaned some of my weight on the door.

No exercise, too much sleep, cigarettes, and the run of the cellar had sapped whatever iron he had had in his muscles. He gave way before my pressure like a sapling tree before a bulldozer.

I found myself in an over-large hall, facing a broad flight of stairs which led in a wide, half-circular sweep to the upper rooms. On the stairs halfway up was a white-clad figure: a nurse.

"All right, Benskin," she said. "I'll see to it."

The tall, lean bird seemed relieved to go. He gave me a brief, puzzled stare, and then catfooted across the hall, along a passage and through a baize-covered door.

The nurse came slowly down the stairs as if she knew she was good to look at and liked you to look at her. I was looking all right. She was a nurse right out of a musical comedy; the kind of nurse who sends your temperature chart haywire every time you see her. A blonde, her lips scarlet, her eyes blue-shaded—a very nifty number, a symphony of curves and sensuality; as exciting and as alive and as hot as the flame of an acetylene torch. If ever she had to nurse me, I would be bedridden for the rest of my days.

By now she was within reaching distance, and I had to make a conscious effort not to reach. I could tell by the expression in her eyes that she was aware of the impression she was making on me, and I had an idea I interested her as much as she interested me. A long, tapering finger pushed up a stray curl under the nurse's cap. A carefully plucked eyebrow climbed an inch. The red painted mouth curved into a smile. Behind the mascara the green-blue eyes were alert and hopeful.

"I was hoping to see Miss Crosby," I said. "I hear she's not well."

"She isn't. I'm afraid she isn't even well enough to receive visitors." She had a deep, contralto voice that vibrated my vertebrae.

"That's too bad," I said, and took a swift look at her legs. Betty Grable's might have been better, but not by much. "I've only just hit town. I'm an old friend of hers. I had no idea she was ill."

"She hasn't been well for some months."

I had the impression that as a topic of conversation Maureen Crosby's illness wasn't Nurse Gurney's idea of fun. It was just an impression. I could have been wrong, but I didn't think so.

"Nothing serious, I hope?"

"Well, not serious. She needs plenty of rest and quiet."

If she had had any encouragement this would have been her cue for a yawn.

"Well, it's quiet enough here," I said, and smiled. "Quiet for you, too, I guess?"

That was all she needed. You could see her getting ready

to unpin her hair.

"Quiet? I'd as soon be buried in Tutankhamen's tomb," she exclaimed, and then remembering she was supposed to be a nurse in the best Florence Nightingale tradition, had the grace to blush. "But I guess I shouldn't have said that, should I? It isn't very refined."

"You don't have to be refined with me," I assured her. "I'm just an easygoing guy who goes even better on a double scotch and water."

"Well that's nice." Her eyes asked a question, and mine gave her the answer. She giggled suddenly. "If you have nothing better to do . . ."

"As an old pal of mine says, 'What is there better to do?'"

The plucked eyebrow lifted.

"I think I could tell him if he really wanted to know."

"You tell me instead."

"I might, one of these days. If you would really like a drink, come on in. I know where the scotch is hidden."

I followed her into a large room which led off the hall. She rolled a little with each step and had weight and control in her hips. They moved under the prim-looking white dress the way a baseball thrown with finger-spin moves. I could have walked behind her all day watching that action.

"Sit down," she said, waving to an eight-foot settee. "I'll fix you a drink."

"Fine," I said, lowering myself down onto the cushion-covered springs. "But on one condition. I never drink alone. I'm very particular about that."

"So am I," she said.

I watched her locate a bottle of Johnnie Walker, two pint-size tumblers and a bottle of Whiterock spring water from the recess in a Jacobean Court cupboard.

"We could have ice, but it'll mean asking Benskin, and I

guess we can do without Benskin right now, don't you?" she said, looking at me from under eyelashes that were like a row of spiked railings.

"Never mind the ice," I said, "and be careful of the White-rock. That stuff can ruin good whisky."

She poured three inches of scotch into both glasses and added a teaspoonful of Whiterock to each.

"That look about right to you?"

"That looks fine," I said, reaching out a willing hand. "Maybe I'd better introduce myself. I'm Vic Malloy. Just plain Vic to my friends, and all good-looking blondes are my friends."

She sat down, not bothering to adjust her skirts. She had nice knees.

"You're the first caller we have had in five months," she said. "I was beginning to think there was a jinx on this place."

"From the look of it, there is. Straighten me out on this, will you? The last time I was here it was an estate, not a blueprint for a wilderness. Doesn't anyone do any work around here anymore?"

She lifted her shapely shoulders.

"You know how it is. Nobody cares."

"Just how bad is Maureen?"

She pouted.

"Look, can't we talk about something else? I'm so very tired of Maureen."

"She's not my ball of fire either," I said, tasting the whisky. It was strong enough to raise blisters on the hide of a buffalo. "But I knew her in the old days, and I'm curious. What exactly is the matter with her?"

She leaned back her blonde head and lowered most of the scotch down her creamy-white, rather beautiful throat. The way she swallowed that raw whisky told me she had a talent for drinking.

"I shouldn't tell you," she said, and smiled. "But if you promise not to say a word."

"Not a word."

"She's being tapered off a drug jag. That's strictly confidential."

"Bad?"

She shrugged.

"Bad enough."

"And in the meantime when the cat's in bed the mice will play, huh?"

"That's about right. No one ever comes near the place. It's likely to be some time before she gets around again. While she's climbing walls and screaming her head off, the staff relaxes. That's fair enough, isn't it?"

"Certainly is, and they certainly can relax."

She finished her drink.

"Now let's get away from Maureen. I have enough of her nights without you talking about her."

"You on night duty? That's a shame."

"Why?" The green-blue eyes alerted.

"I thought it might be fun to take you out one night and show you things."

"What things?"

"For a start I have a lovely set of etchings."

She giggled.

"If there's one thing I like better than one etching it's a set of etchings." She got up and moved over to the whisky bottle. The way her hips rolled kept me pointing like a gundog. "Let me freshen that," she went on. "You're not drinking."

"It's fresh enough. I'm beginning to get the idea there are things better to do besides drinking."

"Are you? I thought perhaps you might." She shot more liquor into her glass. She didn't bother with the Whiterock this time.

"Who looks after Maureen during the day?" I asked as she made her way back to the settee.

"Nurse Fleming. You wouldn't like her. She's a man-hater."

"She is?" She sat beside me, hip against hip. "Can she hear us?"

"It wouldn't matter if she did, but she can't. She's in the left wing, overlooking the garages. They put Maureen there when she started to yell."

That was exactly what I wanted to know.

"To hell with all manhaters," I said, sliding my arm along the back of the settee behind her head. She leaned towards me. "Are you a manhater?"

"It depends on the man." Her face was close to mine, so I let my lips rest against her temple. She seemed to like that.

"How's this man for a start?"

"Pretty nice."

I took the glass of whisky out of her hand and put it on the floor.

"That'll be in my way."

"It's a pity to waste it."

"You'll need it before long."

"Will I?"

She came against me, her mouth on mine. We stayed like that for some time. Then suddenly she pushed away from me and stood up. For a moment I thought she was just a kiss-and-goodbye girl, but I was wrong. She crossed the room to the door and turned the key. Then she came back and sat down again.

3

I PARKED the Buick outside the county buildings at the corner of Feldman and Centre Avenue, and went up the steps into a world of printed forms, silent passages and old-young clerks waiting hopefully for dead men's shoes.

The births and deaths registry was on the first floor. I filled in a form and pushed it through the bars to the red-headed clerk who stamped it, took my money and waved an airy hand towards the rows of files.

"Help yourself Mr. Malloy," he said. "Sixth file from the right."

I thanked him.

"How's business?" he asked, and leaned on the counter, ready to waste his time and mine. "Haven't seen you around in months."

"Nor you have," I said. "Business is fine. How's yours? Are they still dying?"

"And being born. One cancels out the other."

"So it does."

I hadn't anything else for him. I was tired. My little session with Nurse Gurney had exhausted me. I went over to the files. The C file felt like a ton weight, and it was all I could do to heave it on to the flat-topped desk. That was Nurse Gurney's fault, too. I pawed over the pages and after a while came upon Janet Crosby's death certificate. I took out an old envelope and a pencil. She had died of malignant endo-carditis, whatever that meant, on 15th of May 1948.

She was described as a spinster, aged twenty-five years. The certificate had been signed by a Doctor John Bewley. I made a note of the doctor's name, then turned back a dozen or so pages until I found Macdonald Crosby's certificate. He had died of brain injuries from gunshot wounds. The doctor had been J. Salzer; the coroner, Franklin Less ways. I made more notes, and then, leaving the file where it was tramped over to the clerk who was watching me with lazy curiosity.

"Can you get someone to put that file back?" I asked, propping myself up against the counter. I'm not as strong as I thought I was."

"That's all right, Mr. Malloy."

"Another thing, who's Dr. John Bewley, and where does he live?"

"He has a little place on Skyline Avenue," the clerk told me. "Don't go to him if you want a good doctor."

"What's the matter with him?"

The clerk lifted tired shoulders.

"Just old. Fifty years ago he might have been all right. A horse-and-buggy doctor. I guess he thinks trepanning is something to do with opening a can of beans."

"Well, isn't it?"

The clerk laughed.

"Depends on whose head we're talking about."

"Yeah. So, he's just an old washed-up croaker, huh?"

"That describes him. Still, he's not doing any harm. I don't suppose he has more than a dozen patients now." He scratched the side of his ear and looked owlishly at me. "Working on something?"

"I never work," I said. "See you some time. So long."

I went down the steps into the hard sunlight, slowly and thoughtfully. A girl worth a million dies suddenly and they call in an old horse-and-buggy man. Not quite the millionaire touch. One would have expected a fleet of the most expensive medicine men in town to have been in on a kill as important as hers.

I crawled into the Buick and stepped on the starter. Parked across the way against the traffic, was an olive-green Dodge limousine. Seated behind the wheel was a man in a fawn-colored hat, around which was a plaited cord. He was reading a newspaper. I wouldn't have noticed him or the car if he hadn't looked up suddenly and, seeing me, hastily tossed the newspaper on to the back seat and started his engine. Then I did look at him, wondering why he had so suddenly lost interest in his paper. He seemed a big man with shoulders about as wide as a barn door. His head sat squarely on his shoulders without any sign of a neck. He wore a pencil-lined black moustache and his eyes were hooded. His nose and one ear had been hit very hard at one time and had never fully recovered. He looked the kind of tough you see so often in a Warner Bros tough movie, the kind who make a drop-cloth for Humphrey Bogart.

I steered the Buick into the stream of traffic and drove East, up Centre Avenue, not hurrying, and keeping one eye on the rearview mirror.

The Dodge forced itself against the West-going traffic, did a U-turn while horns honked and drivers cursed, and came after me. I wouldn't have believed it possible for anyone to have done that on Centre Avenue and get away with it, but apparently the cops were either asleep or it was too hot to bother.

At Westwood Avenue intersection I again looked into the mirror. The Dodge was right there on my tail. I could see the driver lounging behind the wheel, a cheroot gripped between his teeth, one elbow and arm on the rolled-down window. I pulled ahead so I could read his registration number and committed it to memory. If he was tailing me, he was making a very bad job of it. I put on speed on Hollywood Avenue and went to the top at sixty-five. The Dodge, after a moment's

hesitation, jumped forward and roared behind me. At Foot-
hill Boulevard I swung to the curb and pulled up sharply.
The Dodge went by. The driver didn't look in my direction.
He went on towards the Los Angeles and San Francisco
Highway.

I wrote down the registration on the old envelope along
with Doc Bewley's name and stowed it carefully away in my
hip pocket. Then I started the Buick rolling again and drove
down Skyline Avenue. Halfway down I spotted a brass plate
glittering in the sun. It was attached to a low, wooden gate
which guarded a small garden and a double-fronted bungalow of Canadian pine wood; a modest, quiet little place,
almost a slum beside the other ultra-modern houses on
either side of it.

I pulled up and leaned out of the window. But at that
distance it was impossible to read the worn engraving on the
plate. I got out of the car and had a closer look. Even then it
wasn't easy to decipher, but I made out enough to tell me
this was Dr. John Bewley's residence.

As I groped for the latch of the gate, the olive-green
Dodge came sneaking down the road and went past. The
driver didn't appear to look my way, but I knew he had seen
me and where I was going. I paused to look after the car. It
went down the road fast and I lost sight of it when it swung
into Westwood Avenue.

I pushed my hat to the back of my head, took out a packet
of Lucky Strikes, lit up and stowed the package away. Then I
lifted the latch of the gate and walked down the gravel path
towards the bungalow.

The garden was small and compact, and as neat and as
orderly as a barrack-room on inspection day. Yellow sun-
blinds, faded and past their prime, screened the windows.
The front door could have done with a lick of paint. That

went for the whole of the bungalow, too.

I dug my thumb into the doorbell and waited. After a while I became aware that someone was peeping at me though the sun-blinds. There was nothing I could do about that except put on a pleasant expression and wait. I put on a pleasant expression and waited.

Just when I thought I would have to ring again I heard the kind of noise a mouse makes in the wainscoting, and the front door opened.

The woman who looked at me was thin and small and bird-like. She had on a black silk dress that might have been fashionable about fifty years ago if you lived in isolation and no one ever sent you *Vogue*. Her thin old face was tired and defeated, her eyes told me life wasn't much fun.

"Is the doctor in?" I asked, raising my hat, knowing if anyone would appreciate courtesy she would.

"Why, yes." The voice sounded defeated, too. "He's in the garden at the back. I'll call him."

"I wish you wouldn't. I'd as soon go around and see him there. I'm not a patient. I just wanted to ask him a question."

"Yes." The look of hope which had begun to climb into her eyes faded away. Not a patient. No fee. Just a healthy young husky with a question. "You won't keep him long, will you? He doesn't like being disturbed."

"I won't keep him long."

I raised my hat, bowed the way I hoped in her better days men had bowed to her, and retreated back to the garden path again. She closed the front door. A moment later I spotted her shadow as she peered at me through the front window blinds.

I followed the path around the bungalow to the garden at the back. Doc Bewley might not have been a ball of fire as a healer, but he was right on the beam as a gardener. I would have liked to have brought those three Crosby gardeners to look at this garden. It might have shaken up their ideas.

At the bottom of the garden, standing over a giant dahlia was a tall old man in a white alpaca coat, a yellow panama, yellowish-white trousers, and elastic side-boots. He was looking at the dahlia the way a doctor looks down your throat when you say 'Ah-aa,' and was probably finding it a lot more interesting.

He looked up sharply when I was within a few feet of him. His face was lined and shriveled, not unlike the skin of a prune, and he had a crop of coarse white hair sprouting out of his ears. Not a noble or clever face, but the face of a very old man who is satisfied with himself, whose standards aren't very high, who has got beyond caring, is obstinate, dull-witted, but undefeated.

"Good afternoon," I said. "I hope I'm not disturbing you."

"Surgery hours are from five to seven, young man," he said in a voice so low I could scarcely hear him. "I can't see you now."

"This isn't a professional call," I said, peering over his shoulder at the dahlia. It was a lovely thing, eight inches across if it was an inch, and flawless. "My name's Malloy. I'm an old friend of Janet Crosby."

He touched the dahlia gently with thick-jointed fingers.

"Who?" he asked vaguely, not interested—just a dull-witted old man with a flower.

"Janet Crosby," I said. It was hot in the sun, and the drone of the bees, the smell of all those flowers made me a little vague myself.

"What of her?"

"You signed the death certificate."

He dragged his eyes away from the dahlia and looked at me.

"Who did you say you were?"

"Victor Malloy. I'm a little worried about Miss Crosby's death."

"Why should you be worried?" he asked, a flicker of alarm in his eyes. He knew he was old and dull-witted and absentminded. He knew by keeping on practicing medicine at his age he ran the risk of making a mistake sooner or later. I could see he thought I was going to accuse him of making that mistake now.

"Well, you see," I said mildly, not wanting to stampede him, "I've been away for three or four years. Janet Crosby was a very old friend. I had no idea she had a bad heart. It was a great shock to me to hear she had gone like that. I want to satisfy myself that there was nothing wrong."

A muscle in his face twitched. The nostrils dilated.

"What do you mean—wrong? She died of malignant endocarditis. The symptoms are unmistakable. Besides, Dr. Salzer was there. There was nothing wrong. I don't know what you mean."

"Well, I'm glad to hear it. What exactly is malignant endocarditis?"

He frowned blankly, and, for a moment, I thought he was going to say he didn't know, but he got hold of himself, stirred his old withered memory and said slowly as if he were conjuring up a page from some medical dictionary, "It's a progressive microbial infection of the heart valves. Fragments of the ulcerating valves were carried by the blood stream all over her body. She hadn't a chance. Even if they had called me in sooner, there was nothing I could have done."

"That's what's worrying me doc," I said, and smiled to let him know I was on his side. "Just why did they call you in? You weren't her doctor, were you?"

"Certainly not," he said, almost angrily. "But it was quite proper to call me in. I live close by. It would have been unethical for Dr. Salzer to have issued the certificate."

"Just who is Dr. Salzer?"

He began to look vague again, and his fingers went yearningly towards the dahlia. I could see he wanted to be left alone, to let his brain sleep in the peaceful contemplation of his flowers, not to be worried by a husky like me who was taking up his time for nothing.

"He runs one of those crank sanatoriums right next door to the Crosby estate," he said finally. He's a friend of the family. His position is such he couldn't ethically issue a certificate. He is not a qualified practitioner. I was very flattered they asked for my help."

I could imagine that. I wondered what they paid him.

"Look, doc," I said. "I'd like to get this straight. I've tried to see Maureen Crosby, but she isn't well. I'm going away, but before I go I want to get a picture of this thing. All I've heard is that Janet died suddenly. You say it was heart trouble. What happened? Were you there when she died?"

"Why, no," he said, and alarm again flickered in the dim eyes. "I arrived about half an hour after she was dead. She had died in her sleep. The symptoms were unmistakable. Dr. Salzer told me she had been suffering from the disease for some months. He had been treating her. There was nothing much one can do with such cases except rest. I can't understand why you're asking so many questions." He looked hopefully towards the house to see if his wife wanted him. She didn't.

"It's only that I want to satisfy myself," I said, and smiled again. "You arrived at the house, and Salzer was there. Is that it?"

He nodded, getting more worried every second.

"Was there anyone else there?"

"Miss Crosby. The younger one. She was there."

"Maureen?"

"I believe that's her name."

"And Salzer took you to Janet's room? Did Maureen come, too?"

"Yes. They both came with me into the room. The—the young woman seemed very upset. She was crying." He fingered the dahlia. "Perhaps there should have been a post-mortem," he said suddenly. "But I assure you there was no need. Malignant endocarditis is unmistakable. One has to consider the feelings of those who are left."

"And yet, after fourteen months, you are beginning to think there should have been a postmortem?" I put a slight edge to my voice.

"Strictly speaking there should have been, because Dr. Salzer had been treating her, and as he explained to me, he is a Doctor of Science, not Medicine. But the symptoms . . ."

"Yeah . . . are unmistakable. One other thing, doc. Have you ever seen Janet Crosby before? I mean, before she died?"

He looked wary, wondering if I were springing a trap.

"I've seen her in her car, but not to speak to."

"And not close enough to notice if she showed any symptoms of heart trouble?"

He blinked.

"I didn't get that."

"I understand she was suffering from this disease for some months. You say you saw her in her car. How long ago was this that you saw her? How long before she died?"

"A month, maybe two. I don't remember."

"What I'm trying to get at," I said patiently, "is that with this disease she would have shown symptoms you might have recognized if you had seen her before she died."

"I don't think I should."

"And yet the symptoms are—unmistakable?"

He licked his thin lips.

"I really don't know what you're talking about," he said, and began to back away. "I can't give you any more of my time. It is valuable. I must ask you to excuse me."

"That's all right, doc," I said. "Well, thanks. I'm sorry to have disturbed you. But you know how it is. I just wanted to put my mind at rest. I liked that girl."

He didn't say anything but continued to back away towards the rose beds.

"There's just one other thing, doc," I said. "How was it that Dr. Salzer signed Macdonald Crosby's certificate when he was accidentally shot? Wasn't that unethical for a non-qualified quack to do that?"

He looked at me the way you look at a big spider that has fallen into your bath.

"Don't worry me," he said in a quavering voice. "Ask him. Don't bother me."

"Yes," I said. "That's a good idea. Thank you, doc, I will."

He turned and moved off down the path towards his roses. From the back he looked even older than he was. I watched him pick off a dead rose and noticed his hand was very shaky. I was afraid I had spoiled his afternoon.

The small bird-like woman was standing on the porch of the front door when I arrived back at the house. She looked hopeful but pretended not to see me.

"I'm afraid I've taken up a lot of the doctor's time," I said, raising my hat. "He tells me it is valuable. Would five dollars cover it?"

The tired eyes brightened. The thin face lit up.

"That's very thoughtful of you," she said, and looked furtively down the garden at the old bent back and the yellow

Panama hat.

I slipped the bill into her hand. She snapped it up the way a lizard snaps up a fly. I had an idea the old man at the bottom of the garden wouldn't ever set eye on it. At least I hadn't spoiled *her* afternoon.

4

I PUSHED open my office door and marched in. Jack Kerman was dozing in the armchair by the window. Paula was sitting at my desk working on one of her hundreds of card indexes—indexes that kept our fingers on the pulse of Orchid City, that told us who was who, who was in town and who had left town, who had married who, and so on. Although she had four girls working continuously on the cards, she insisted on keeping the keycards up to date herself.

She moved out of the desk chair as I tossed my hat at Kerman, waking him. He gave a startled grunt, rubbed his eyes and yawned.

"What's it like—working?" he asked. "Or haven't you started yet?"

"I've started," I said, and sat down, reached for a cigarette, lit it, shot my cuffs and plunged into the tale. I gave them all the details with the exception of my session with Nurse Gurney. I skirted over that knowing Paula wouldn't have approved and Kerman would have got too excited to think straight. "Not much," I concluded, "but enough to make me think it's worthwhile going on with. Maybe there's nothing wrong, maybe there is. If there is, the less commotion we make the better. We don't want to tip anyone off just yet."

"If this guy in the Dodge was tailing you, it seems to me someone's tipped off already," Kerman pointed out.

"Yeah, but we can't be sure of that. Maybe my face interested him. Maybe he was practicing to be a detective." I reached for the telephone. "Give me police headquarters," I told the exchange girl.

"You got his number?" Paula asked, fluttering through the stack of cards in her hands.

"Checking it now," I said. "Give me Lieutenant Mifflin," I went on when an unenthusiastic voice announced police headquarters. There was a plop on the line, and Mifflin's gritty voice asked, "Hello?"

Tim Mifflin was a good tough cop, and we had worked together off and on for some time. Whenever I could I helped him, and whenever he could he helped me. He had a great respect for my hunches when playing the horses, and by following my tips he had had the luck to make himself a little folding money.

"Malloy here," I said. "How are you, Tim?"

"What do you care?" he snapped. "You've never been interested in my health and you never will be. What do you want this time?"

"Who owns an olive-green Dodge, license number, O.R.3345?"

"The way you use headquarters for financial gain slaughters me," Mifflin said. "If Brandon ever finds out what I do for you he'll screw me."

"Well I won't tell him so it's up to you," I said, and grinned, "and another thing—talking about financial gain, if you want to make yourself a piece of change, put your shirt on Crab Apple for a win. Tomorrow, four-thirty."

"You really mean my shirt?"

"I'll say I do. Sell up your home, hock your wife, break

into Brandon's safe. As good as that. Two gets you six. The only thing that'll stop that horse is for someone to shoot it."

"Maybe someone will," Mifflin said, who was always over cautious. "Well if you say so."

"It's the safest bet you'll ever have. How about that number?"

"Sure, sure. Hang on. I'll have it for you in ten seconds."

While I was waiting I saw Jack Kerman busily dialing on the other phone.

"What do you think you're doing?" I asked.

"Getting my bookie. That Crab Apple sounds good."

"Forget it. I'm just telling him what someone told me. It's a safe enough tip for a copper, but not for a friend."

Kerman replaced the receiver as if it had bitten him.

"Suppose he sells up his home and hocks his wife? You know what a dope he is on these things."

"Have you seen his home and wife? Well I have. I'll be doing him a favor." As Mifflin's voice came on the line I said, "What have you got?"

"O.R.3345, did you say?"

"Yeah."

"Car's registered in the name of Jonathan Salzer, The Sanatorium, Foothill Boulevard. That what you want to know?"

I kept the excitement out of my voice.

"Maybe. Who's Salzer? Know anything about him?"

"Not much. He runs a crank's home. If you have a pain in your belly he fills you up with fruit juices and lets you ferment. He does all right."

"Nothing crooked on the side?"

"For crying out loud! He doesn't need to be crooked. He's making a hell of a lot of dough."

"Well thanks, Tim."

"You're sure about that horse?"

"Of course I'm sure," I said, and winked at Kerman. "Put your shirt on it."

"Well, I'll spring five bucks, but no more."

I hung up.

"Five bucks! The gambler!"

"Salzer's car, huh?" Kerman said.

I nodded.

"Maybe we did tip our hand." I looked at Paula. "Have you anything on Salzer?"

"I'll see." She put a card down before me. "That might interest you. It's all the information we have on Janet Crosby."

I read the details while she went into the card-index room that led off the outer office.

"Dancing, tennis and golf," I said, looking across the desk at Kerman. "Doesn't sound like someone with heart disease. Intimate friends, Joan Parmetta and Douglas Sherrill. A couple of years back she was engaged to Sherrill but broke it off. No reason given. Who's Sherrill anyway?"

"Never heard of him. Want me to find out?"

"It wouldn't be a bad idea if you went along and saw this Parmetta girl and Sherrill. Tell them you used to be an old friend of Janet in her San Francisco days. You'll have to get the background in case they try and trip you. Paula will get that for you. What I want, Jack, is their reaction to her having heart trouble. Maybe she did have a wacky heart, but if she didn't then we really have something to work on."

"Okay," Kerman said.

Paula came in.

"Nothing much," she said. "Salzer started his sanatorium in 1940. It's a luxury place. Two hundred dollars a week."

"Nice profit," I said enviously.

"Some people must be crazy. Imagine paying all that dough for a glass of fruit juice," Kerman said, horrified. "It sounds the kind of racket we should be in."

"Nothing else?"

"He's married. Speaks French and German fluently. Has a Doctor of Science degree. No hobbies. No children. Age fifty-three," Paula said, reading from the card. "That's all, Vic."

"Okay," I said, getting to my feet. "Give Jack a hand will you? He wants the dope on this Parmetta girl and Sherrill. I'm going downstairs to have a word with Mother Bendix. I want to check on the Crosby's staff. That butler struck me as a phony. Maybe she got him the job."

5

AT FIRST glance, and come to that even at second glance, Mrs. Martha Bendix, executive director of the Bendix Domestic Agency, could easily have been mistaken for a man. She was big and broad-shouldered and wore her hair cut short, a man's collar and tie, and a man's tweed coat. It was only when she stood up and moved away from her desk you were surprised to see the tweed skirt, silk stockings, and heavy oxford shoes. She was very hearty, and if you weren't careful to keep out of her reach, she had a habit of slapping you violently on the back, making you feel sick for the next two or three hours. She also had a laugh as loud as the bang of a twelve-gauge shotgun, and if you weren't watching for it, you jumped out of your skin when she let it off. A woman I wouldn't want to live with, but a goodhearted soul, generous with her money, and a lot more interested in nervous, frail little blondes than a big husky like me.

The timid bunny-faced girl who showed me into Mrs.

Bendix's cream and green office edged away from me as if I were full of bad intentions, and gave Mrs. Bendix a coy little smile that could have meant something or nothing depending on the state of your mind.

"Come on in Vic," Mrs. Bendix boomed from across a paper-littered desk. "Sit down. Haven't seen you in days. What have you been doing with yourself?"

I sat down and grinned at her.

"This and that," I told her. "Keeping the wolf from the door. I've looked in for a little help, Martha. Done any business with the Crosbys?"

"Not for a long time." She leaned down and hoisted up a bottle of scotch, two glasses, and half a dozen coffee beans. "Make it snappy," she went on. "I don't want to shock Mary. She doesn't approve of drinking during office hours."

"That Mary with the rabbit teeth?"

"Never mind about her teeth. She's not going to bite you with them." She handed me a glass half full of scotch and three of the coffee beans. "You mean the Crosbys on Foothill Boulevard?"

I said I meant the Crosbys on Foothill Boulevard.

"I did a job for them once, but not since. That was about six years ago. I fixed the whole of their staff then. Since Janet Crosby died, they cleared out the old crowd and put in a new lot. They didn't come to me for the new lot."

I sampled the scotch. It was smooth and silky and had plenty of authority.

"You mean they sacked everybody?"

"That's what I'm telling you."

"What happened to them?"

"I fixed them up elsewhere."

I chewed this over.

"Look Martha, between you and me and the coffee beans,

I'm trying to get the lowdown on Janet's death. I've had a tip, and it might or might not be worth working on. I'm not entirely sold on the idea she died of heart failure. I'd like to talk it over with some of the old staff. They may have seen something. The butler, for instance. Who was he?"

"John Stevens," Mrs. Bendix said after a moment's thought. She finished her drink, tossed three beans into her mouth, put her glass and the scotch out of sight and dug her thumb into a pushbutton on her desk.

The bunny-faced girl crept in.

"Where's John Stevens working now, honey?"

The bunny-faced girl said she would find out. After a couple of minutes she came back and said Stevens worked for Gregory Wainwright, Hillside, Jefferson Avenue.

"How about Janet's personal maid? Where's she now?" I asked.

Mrs. Bendix waved the bunny-faced girl away. When she had gone, she said, "That bitch? She's not working any more, and I wouldn't give her a job if she came to me on bended knees."

"What's the matter with her?" I asked, hopefully pushing my empty glass forward. "Let's be matey, Martha. One drink is no use to big, strong boys like you and me."

Mrs. Bendix sniggered, hoisted up the bottle again and poured.

"What's the matter with her?" I repeated when we had saluted each other.

"She's no good," Mrs. Bendix said, and scowled. "Just a goddamn lazy bum."

"We haven't got our lines crossed, have we? I'm talking about Janet Crosby's personal maid."

"So am I," Mrs. Bendix said, and fed three more coffee beans into her mouth. "Eudora Drew. That's her name. She's gone haywire. I wanted a good personal maid for Mrs. Randolph Playfair. I took the trouble to contact Drew to tell her I could fix her up. She told me to jump in a cesspit. That's a nice way to talk, isn't it? She said she wasn't ever going to do any more work, and if one cesspit wouldn't hold me anyone would dig me another if I told them what it was for." Mrs. Bendix brooded darkly at the insult. "At one time I thought she was a good, smart girl. Just shows you can't trust them further than you can throw them, doesn't it? It's my bet she's living on some man. She's got a bungalow in Coral Gables, and lives in style."

"Where in Coral Gables?"

"On Mount Verde Avenue. You interested?"

"I might be. What happened to the rest of the staff?"

"I fixed them all up. I can give you addresses if you want them."

I finished my drink.

"I may want them. I'll let you know. How soon after Janet's death did this Drew girl get the sack?"

"The next day. All the staff went before the funeral."

I ate a coffee bean.

"Any reason given?"

"Maureen Crosby went away for a couple of months. The house was shut up."

"Not usual to sack all the staff when you go away for a couple of months, is it?"

"Of course it isn't usual."

"Tell me more about this Drew girl."

"The things you want to know," Mrs. Bendix said, and sighed. "Give me that glass unless you want another."

I said I didn't want another and watched her hide the scotch and the two glasses. Then she dug her thumb into the pushbutton again.

The bunny-faced girl came in and gave her another coy smile.

"Dig out Eudora Drew's card honey," Mrs. Bendix said. "I want to have a look at it."

The bunny-faced girl came back after a while with a card. She gave it to Mrs. Bendix the way an adoring bobbysoxer might give Frank Sinatra a posy.

When she had gone Mrs. Bendix said, "I don t know if this is what you want. Age twenty-eight. Home address, 2243 Kelsie Street, Carmel. Three years with Mrs. Franklin Lambert. Excellent references. Janet Crosby's personal maid from July 1943. Any good to you?"

I shrugged.

"I don't know. Could be. I think I'd better go and talk to her. What makes you think she's living with a man?"

"How else does she get her money? She's not working. It's either a man or a lot of men."

"Janet Crosby might have left her a legacy."

Mrs. Bendix lifted her bushy eyebrows.

"I hadn't thought of that. She might, of course. Yes, come to think of it, it might be the answer."

"Well okay," I said, getting up. "Thanks for the drinks. Come and see us some time for a change. We have drinks too."

"Not me," Mrs. Bendix said firmly. "That Bensinger girl doesn't approve of me. I can see it in her eyes."

I grinned.

"She doesn't approve of me either. I don't let that worry me. It shouldn't worry you."

"It doesn't. And don't kid yourself, Vic. That girl's in love with you."

I considered this, then shook my head.

"You're wrong. She isn't in love with anyone. She isn't the

type to fall in love."

Mrs. Bendix pursed up her lips and made a loud, rude noise.

6

CORAL GABLES is the dead-end district of Orchid City, a shack town that has grown up around the harbor where an industry of sponge and fish docks, turtle crawls and markets, plus a number of shady characters flourish. The waterfront is dominated by Delmonico's bar, the toughest joint on the coast, where three or four fights a night is the normal routine, and where the women are more often tougher than the men.

Monte Verde Avenue lies at the back of Coral Gables—a broad, characterless road lined on either side by cabin-like houses, all more or less conforming to the same pattern. As a district it is perhaps one step above Coral Gables, but that isn't saying a great deal. Most of the cabin-like houses are occupied by professional gamblers, fast ladies, flashy-looking toughs who lounge on the waterfront during the day and mind their own business after dark, and the betting boys and their dolls. The only two-storied house in the road is owned by Joe Betillo, mortician and embalmer, coffin maker, abortionist and fixer of knife and bullet wounds.

I drove the Buick along the road until I came to Eudora Drew's cabin on the right and about three-quarters of the way down. It was a white and blue five-room wood cabin with a garden that consisted of a lawn big enough to play halma on and two tired-looking hydrangea plants in pots either side of the front door.

I stepped over the low wooden gate and rapped with the

little brass knocker that hadn't been cleaned in months.

There was about a ten-second delay, no more, and then the door jerked open. A solid young woman in grey-green slacks and a white silk blouse, her dark hair piled to the top of her head, looked me over with suspicious and slightly bloodshot eyes. She wasn't what you'd call a beauty, but there was an animal something about her that would make any man look at her twice, and some even three times.

She stopped me before I could open my mouth.

"Spare your breath if you're selling anything", she said in a voice a little more musical than a tin can being thrown downstairs, but not much. "I never buy at the door."

"You should have that put on the gate," I said cheerfully, "look at the time it would save. Are you Miss Drew?"

"What's it to you who I am?"

"I have business with Miss Drew," I said patiently. "Important business."

"Who are you?"

"The name's Vic Malloy. I'm an old friend of Janet Crosby."

A muscle in her upper lip suddenly twitched, but other-wise there was no reaction.

"So what?"

"Does that make you Miss Drew or doesn't it?"

"Yes. What is it?"

"I was hoping you might help me," I said, resting one hand on the wall and leaning on it. "The fact is I'm not entirely satisfied about Miss Crosby's death."

This time a wary expression came into her eyes.

"Excavating ancient history, aren't you? She's been dead long enough. Anyway, I don't know anything about it."

"Were you there when she died?"

She took hold of the front door and drew it against her

side.

"I tell you I don't know anything about it, and I haven't the time to waste on something that doesn't concern me."

I studied the hard, suspicious face.

"Miss Drew, do you know what makes scarcely any noise but can be heard a mile away?" I asked and smiled knowingly at her.

"You screwy or something?"

"Some people can hear it two miles away. Have a guess?"

She lifted her solid shoulders impatiently.

"Okay, I'll buy it—what?"

"A hundred-dollar bill, folded in two and rustled gently between finger and thumb."

The sullen look went from her face. Her eyes opened a trifle wider.

"Do I look as if a hundred-dollar bill would be of any use to me?" she said scornfully.

"Even J. P. Morgan could use a hundred dollars," I said. "Still, I might raise the ante if you have anything worth buying."

I could see her brain at work. At least now we were talking the same language. She stared past me, down the path into a world of dollar signs and secrets. She smiled suddenly, a half smirk, not directed at me, but at a thought that had come into her mind.

"What makes you think there's anything wrong about her death?" she asked abruptly, her eyes shifting back to me.

"I didn't say I thought there was something wrong. I said I wasn't entirely satisfied. I have an open mind about it until I have talked to people who were with her about the time she died. Did you notice if she suffered from heart trouble?"

"It's a long time ago mister," she said, and smirked. "I have a lousy memory for things like that. Maybe if you come back at nine tonight, I'll have had time to remember, and it's no use coming back with a hundred dollars. I'm a big girl now and I have big ideas."

"How big?" I asked politely.

"More like five. It would be worth my while to shake up my memory for five, but not for a nickel less."

I made believe to consider this.

"Nine o'clock tonight?" I said.

"About then."

"I wouldn't want to spend all that money unless I was sure the information was of value."

"If I can get my memory working," she said, "I wouldn't be surprised if the information was of value."

"See you at nine, then."

"Bring the money with you, mister. It has to be cash on the line."

"Sure. Let's hope this is the beginning of a beautiful friendship."

She gave me a long, thoughtful stare and then closed the door in my face. I walked slowly back up the path, climbed over the gate and got into the Buick.

Why nine o'clock? I wondered as I stepped on the starter. Why not now? Of course the money had something to do with it, but she wasn't to know I hadn't come heeled with five hundred dollars. She didn't ask. This was a smooth, bright baby, a baby who knew all the answers and could make four and four add up to nine. I sent the Buick down the road so the speedometer needle flickered up to seventy after the first hundred yards. At the bottom of the road I crammed on the brakes to make the turn into Beach Road, gave an elderly gentleman about to cross the street three different kinds of heart disease, straightened out of the skid and went on until I saw a drug store. I swung to the curb, ran across the sidewalk into the store and into a phone booth.

Paula answered the phone after the second ring.

"This is Universal Services," she said in her gentle, polite voice. "Good evening."

"And this is your old pal Vic Malloy calling from a drug store in Coral Gables. Grab your car bright eyes, and come a-running. You and me are going to hold hands and make love. How does it sound?"

There was a momentary pause. I'd have given a lot to have seen her expression.

"Where exactly are you?" she said, sounding as unexcited as if I had asked her the time.

"Beach Road. Come as fast as you can," I said, and hung up.

I left the Buick outside the drug store and walked to the corner of Beach Road. From there I could see Eudora Drew's cabin. I propped myself up against a lamp standard and kept my eyes on the gate of the cabin.

Nine o'clock. I had three hours to wait, and I wished I had asked Paula to bring some scotch and a sandwich to help while away the time.

For the next twenty minutes I lolled against the lamp standard and never took my eyes off the cabin. Nobody came out. Nobody went in. Several tough-looking hombres emerged from other cabins and either walked away or drove away. Three girls, all blondes, all with strident voices, came out of the cabin next to Eudora's and strolled down the road towards me, swinging their hips and ogling anything in trousers within sight. As they passed me they all looked my way, but I kept my eyes firmly on the cabin.

A nice neighborhood this, I thought. Not the kind of road Mrs. Bendix's bunny-faced pal would care to walk down.

Paula's smart little two-seater came bustling out of

Princess Street and headed towards me. It pulled up and the door swung open. Paula looked very trim and slightly glacial in her grey, pinstripe suit. She was hatless, and her brown eyes looked at me inquiringly.

"Where now?" she asked as I settled beside her.

"Drive up here nice and slow and stop at the bend. Eudora's place is that white and blue abomination on the right," I said, and as the car moved forward I rapidly told her what had happened. "I have an idea she might communicate with someone," I concluded. "I may be wrong, but I think it'll be worth while keeping an eye on her for the next couple of hours. The only way to watch the house without getting the neighbors in an uproar is for us to be a courting couple. That's something they all understand in this district."

"Pity you had to pick on me," Paula said coldly.

"Well I couldn't very well pick on Kerman," I said, a little peeved. "Let me tell you, some girls would jump at the opportunity."

"Can I help it if some girls have queer tastes?" she asked, pulling up at the bend. "Is this right?"

"Yeah. Now for the love of mike, relax. You're supposed to be enjoying this." I slid my arm round the back of her neck. She leaned against me and stared moodily down the road at the cabin. I might just as well have necked with a dressmaker's dummy. "Can't you work up a little enthusiasm?" And I tried to nibble her ear.

"That may go down big with your other girl friends," she said icily, jerking away, "but it doesn't with me. If you'll open the glove compartment you'll find some whisky and a couple of sandwiches in there. That might keep you more suitably employed."

I unwound my arm from her neck and dived into the glove compartment.

"You think of everything," I said, beginning to munch. "This is the only thing in the world that'd stop me kissing you."

"I knew that," she said tartly. "That's why I brought it."

I was working on the second sandwich when an olive-green Dodge limousine came tearing down the road. I didn't have to look twice to see it was the same olive-green Dodge and the same big tough driving it.

I wormed myself down in the seat to be out of sight.

"That's the guy who's been tailing me," I said to Paula. "Keep an eye on him and see where he goes."

"He's stopped outside Eudora's place and he's getting out," she told me.

Cautiously I lifted my head until my eyes were level with the windshield. The Dodge had stopped outside the blue and white cabin as Paula had said. The big tough got out, slammed the door with so much force he nearly knocked the car on its side, and went pounding down the path to the front door. He didn't knock but turned the handle and marched in—a man in a hurry.

"And that, bright eyes, is called a hunch," I said to Paula. "I thought she would either go out or telephone. Well, she telephoned. Big Boy has arrived for a consultation. It certainly looks as if I've tipped my hand. What happens from now on should be interesting."

"What will you do when he leaves?"

"I'll go in and tell her I couldn't raise five hundred. Then we'll see how she plays it."

I had finished the sandwich and was just starting on the whisky when the front door of the cabin opened and Big Boy came out. He had been inside eleven and a half minutes by the clock on the dashboard. He looked to right and left, scowled at Paula's parked car, but was too far away to see who was in it. He walked leisurely up the path, vaulted over the gate, climbed into the Dodge, and drove quietly away.

"Well that didn't take long," I said. "If everyone transacted business as fast as that there'd be an awful lot more work done. Come on honey, we may as well make the call. At least drive me over and wait outside. I wouldn't like her to get nervous."

Paula started the car and drove up to the gate of the blue and white cabin. I got out.

"You may or may not hear screams," I said. "If you do, think nothing of it. It'll only be Eudora impressed by my personality."

"I hope she hits you over the head with a flat iron."

"She may. She's one of those unpredictable types. I like them that way."

I climbed over the gate and walked down the path to the front door. I rapped and waited, whistling softly under my breath. Nothing happened. The house was as quiet as a mouse watching a cat.

I rapped again, remembering how Big Boy had looked up and down the road, and seeing in that memory a sudden sinister significance. I touched the door but it was locked. It was my turn now to look up and down the road. Apart from Paula and the car it was as empty as the face of an old man who is out of tobacco and has no money. I lifted the knocker and slammed it down three times, making quite a noise. Paula peered out of the car window and frowned at me.

I waited. Still nothing happened. The mouse was still watching the cat. Silence brooded over the house.

"Drive down to Beach Road," I said to Paula. "Wait for me there."

She started the engine and drove away without looking at me. That's one of the very good things about Paula. She knows an emergency when she sees one and obeys orders without question.

Again I looked up and down the road, wondering if anyone was peeping at me from behind the curtains of the many houses within sight. I had to take that risk. I wandered around to the back of the house. The service door stood open, and moving quietly I peered into a small kitchen. It was the kind of kitchen you would expect to find in a house owned by a girl like Eudora Drew. She probably washed the dishes monthly. Everywhere, in the sink, on the table, on the chairs and floor, were dirty saucepans, crockery and glasses. The trash can was crammed with empty bottles of gin and whisky. A frying-pan full of burned grease and bluebottle flies leered up at me from the sink. There was a nicely-blended smell of decay, dirt, and sour milk hanging in the air. Not the way I should like to live, but then tastes differ.

I crossed the kitchen, opened the door and peered into the small, untidy hall. The doors opened on to the hall—presumably the living room and the dining room. I gum-shoed to the right-hand door, peered into more untidiness, more dust, more slipshod living. Eudora wasn't in there, nor was she in the dining room. That left the upstairs rooms. I mounted the stairs quietly, wondering if she might be having a bath and that was the reason why she hadn't answered my ring, but decided it was unlikely. She wasn't the type to take sudden baths.

She was in the front bedroom. Big Boy had made a thorough job of it, and she had done her best to protect herself. She lay across the tumbled bed, her legs sprawled out, her blouse ripped off her back. Knotted around her throat was a blue and red silk scarf—probably hers. Her eyes glared out of her blue-black face, her tongue lay in a little bed of foamy froth. She wasn't a pretty sight, nor had death come to her easily.

I shifted my eyes away from her and looked around the room. Nothing had been disturbed. It was as untidy and as dusty as the other rooms and reeked of stale perfume.

I stepped quietly to the door, not looking at the bed again, and moved out of the room and into the passage. I was careful not to touch anything, and on my way downstairs I rubbed the banister rail with my handkerchief. I went into the smelly, silent little kitchen, pushed open the screen door that had swung closed in the hot breeze, on down the garden path to the gate, and walked without haste to where Paula was waiting.

Chapter Two

1

CAPTAIN of the Police Brandon sat behind his desk and glowered at me. He was a man around the wrong side of fifty, short, inclined to fat, with a lot of thick hair as white as a fresh fall of snow, and eyes that were as hard and as friendly and as expressionless as beer-stoppers.

We made an interesting quartet. There was Paula, looking cool and unruffled, seated in the background. There was Tim Mifflin, leaning against the wall, motionless, thoughtful, and as quiet as a centenarian taking a nap. There was me in the guest of honor's chair before the desk, and, of course, there was Captain of the Police Brandon.

The room was big and airy and well-furnished. There was a nice Turkish carpet on the floor, several easy chairs and one or two reproductions of Van Gogh's country scenes on the walls. The big desk stood in the corner of the room between two windows that overlooked the business section of the city.

I had been in this room before, and I still had memories of the little unpleasantness that had occurred then. Brandon liked me as much as Hiroshima liked the atomic bomb, and I was expecting unpleasantness again.

The interview hadn't begun well, and it wasn't improving. Already Brandon was fiddling with a cigar, a trick that denoted his displeasure.

"All right," he said in a thin, exasperated voice, "let's start from the beginning again. You had this letter . . ." He leaned forward to peer at Janet Crosby's letter as if it had been infected with tetanus. He was careful not to touch it. "Dated May 15th, 1948."

Well at least that showed he could read. I didn't say anything.

"With this letter were five one-hundred-dollar bills. Right?"

"Check," I said.

"You received the letter on May 16th, but put it unopened in a coat pocket and forgot about it. It was only when you gave the coat away the letter was found. Right?"

"Check."

He scowled down at the cigar, then rested his broad fat nose on it.

"A pretty smart way to run a business."

"These things happen," I said shortly. "I remember during the Tetzi trial, the police mislaid . . ."

"Never mind the Tetzi trial," Brandon said in a voice you could have sliced ham on. "We're talking about this letter. You went up to the Crosby's estate with the idea of seeing Miss Maureen Crosby. Right?"

"Yeah," I said, getting a little tired of this.

"But you didn't see her because she isn't well, so you had to stick your nose still further into this business by calling on Miss Janet Crosby's personal maid. Right?"

"If you like to put it like that I don't mind."

"Is it right or isn't it?"

"Oh, sure."

"This woman Drew said she wanted five hundred dollars before she talked. That's your story and I'm not sold on it. You watched the house, and after a while an olive-green

Dodge arrived and a big fella went in. He remained in there for about ten minutes, then came away. Then you went in and found her dead. Right?"

I nodded.

He removed the band from the cigar, groped for a match. All the while his beer-stopper eyes stared moodily at me.

"You claim the Dodge belongs to Dr. Salzer," he said, and scraped the match on the sole of his shoe.

"Mifflin says it does. I asked him to check the registration number."

Brandon looked over at Mifflin who stared with empty eyes at the opposite wall.

"A half an hour after Malloy telephoned you asking you who owned this car, you received a report from Dr. Salzer that the car had been stolen. That's right, isn't it?"

"Yes, sir," Mifflin said stonily.

Brandon's eyes swiveled in my direction.

"Did you hear that?"

"Sure."

"All right." Brandon applied the burning match to his cigar and sucked in smoke. "Just so long as you understand, and just so long as you don't get any fancy ideas into your head about Dr. Salzer. You may not know it but Dr. Salzer is a very respectable and eminent citizen of this city, and I'm not going to have him bothered by you or anyone like you. Do you understand that?"

I pulled thoughtfully at my nose. This was unexpected.

"Sure," I said.

He blew smoke across the desk into my face.

"I don't like you Malloy, and I don't like your itsy-bitsy organization. Maybe it has its uses, but I doubt it. I'm damned sure you are a troublemaker. You stirred up enough trouble with that Cerf case some months ago, and if you hadn't been so damned smooth you would have been in a lot of trouble yourself. Miss Janet Crosby's dead." He leaned forward to peer at the letter again. "The Crosbys were and still are a very wealthy and influential family, and I'm not standing for you stirring up trouble for them. You have no legal right to the five hundred dollars Miss Crosby sent you. That is to be paid back to her estate—immediately. You are to leave Miss Maureen Crosby alone. If she is in trouble with a blackmailer—which I doubt—she will come to me if she needs help. This business has nothing to do with you, and if I find you are making a nuisance of yourself I'll take steps to put you where you won't trouble anyone for a very long time. Do you understand?"

I grinned at him.

"I'm beginning to," I said, and leaned forward to ask, "How much does Salzer pay into your sports fund, Brandon?"

The fat pink and white face turned a dusky-mauve color. The beer-stopper eyes sparked like chipped flint.

"I'm warning you Malloy," he said, a snarl in his voice. "My boys know how to take care of a punk like you. One of these nights you'll get taken up a dark alley for a beating. Lay off the Crosbys and lay off Salzer. Now get out!"

I stood up.

"And how much does the Crosby estate pay into your welfare fund, Brandon?" I asked. "How much did old man Crosby slip you for hushing up that auto-killing Maureen performed two years ago? Respectable and eminent? Don't make me laugh. Salzer's as respectable and eminent as Delmonico's bouncer. How come he signed Macdonald Crosby's death certificate when he isn't even qualified?"

"Get out!" Brandon said very quietly.

We stared at each other for perhaps the best part of four seconds, then I shrugged, turned my back on him and made for the door.

"Come on Paula, let's get out of here before we suffocate," I said, and jerked open the door. "Remember that little crack about taking me up a dark alley. It's just as much fun suing the Captain of Police for assault as it is anyone else."

I stamped down the long passage behind Paula. Mifflin came after us walking like a man in hobnailed boots treading on eggs.

He caught up with us at the end of the passage.

"Wait a minute," he said. "Come in here," and he opened his office door.

We went in because both Paula and I liked Mifflin, and besides, he was too useful to fall out with. He shut the door and leaned against it. His red rubbery face was worried.

"That was a sweet way to talk to Brandon," he said bitterly. "You're crazy, Vic. You know as well as I do that kind of stuff won't get you anywhere."

"I know," I said, "but the rat got me mad."

"I would have tipped you off, only I hadn't time. But you ought to know Brandon hates your guts."

"I know that too. But what could I do? I had to tell him the story. What's Salzer to him?"

Mifflin shrugged.

"Salzer's a good friend to the police. Sure, I know he runs a racket up at that sanatorium. But there's nothing illegal in it." He lowered his voice, went on, "Where the hell do you think Brandon got his Cadillac from? A Captain of Police's money doesn't run to a job like that. And another thing: Maureen Crosby put Brandon's kid through college and she takes care of Mrs. Brandon's doctor's bills. You picked on two of Brandon's best patrons."

"I guessed there must be something like that to throw Brandon into such an uproar," I said. "Look Tim, did Salzer really report his car stolen?"

"Yeah, I took the call myself."

"What are you going to do about this killer? Anything or nothing?"

"Why sure. We're going to find him. I know what you're thinking Vic, but you're wrong. Salzer's too smooth to get mixed up in a killing. You can count him out."

"Well, okay."

"And watch out. That stuff about a beating wasn't fiction. You won't be the first or the last guy who's had his ears smacked down because Brandon doesn't like him. I'm telling you. Watch out."

"Thanks Tim. I'll watch out, but I can take care of myself."

Mifflin rubbed his shapeless nose with the back of his hand.

"It's not that simple. You start fighting back and you get caught with a police assault rap. They'll fake a charge against you and take you in, and then the crew boys will really go to town on you."

I patted his arm.

"Don't let it worry you. It's not going to worry me. Anything else?"

Mifflin shook his head.

"Just watch out," he said, then opened his office door, peeped up and down the passage to make sure the coast was clear and then waved us out.

We went down the stone stairs into the lobby. Two big plain clothes men lounged by the double doors. One of them had fiery red hair and a white flabby face. The other was thin and as hard looking as a lump of rusty pig iron. They both eyed us over slowly and thoughtfully, and the red-headed one spat accurately at the brass spittoon six yards from him.

We went past them, down the steps into the street.

2

AT the back of the Orchid Buildings complex there is a
narrow alley, used primarily as a parking lot for cars
belonging to the executives and their staffs working in the
building, and at the far end of the alley you will find
Finnegan's bar.

Mike Finnegan was an old friend of mine, a useful man to
know as he had contacts with most of the hoods and con men
who arrived in Orchid City, and any shady activity that
happened to be cooking he knew about. Some years ago I
had taken a hand in a little argument between Finnegan and
three toughs whose ambition at that time was to poke
Finnegan's eyes out with a broken whisky bottle. Finnegan
seemed to think if it hadn't been for me he would have lost
his sight, and he was embarrassingly grateful.

Besides a source of useful information, Finnegan's bar
was also a convenient after-office-hours meeting-place, and
guessing Kerman would be there, I parked the Buick outside
and went in with Paula.

It was a little after eleven o'clock and only a few stragglers
remained up at the counter. Jack Kerman lolled at a corner
table, a newspaper spread out before him, a bottle of scotch
within easy reach. He looked up and waved.

As we crossed the room I flapped a hand at Finnegan,
who gave me a broad smile. Finnegan would never win a
beauty prize. Built like a gorilla, his battered, scarred face as
ugly as it was humorous, he looked like a cross between King
Kong and a ten-ton truck.

Kerman rose to his feet and gave Paula an elaborate bow.

"Imagine you coming to a joint like this," he said. "Don't

tell me you've left your vinegar and repressions locked up in the office safe."

"Skip it Jack," I said, sitting down. "Things are popping. Before I tell the tale, have you anything for me?"

Before he could answer Finnegan arrived.

"'Evening, Mr. Malloy. 'Evening, lady."

Paula smiled at him.

"Another glass, Mike," I said. "I'll help Kerman finish the scotch." I looked at Paula. "Coffee?"

She nodded.

"And coffee for Miss Bensinger."

When Finnegan had brought the glass and the coffee and had gone back to the bar, I said, "Let's have it."

"I saw Joan Parmetta," Kerman said, and rolled his eyes. "Very nice, very lush." He made curves in the air with his hands. "If it hadn't been for the butler who kept popping in and out, a beautiful friendship might have developed." He sighed. "I wonder what it is about me women find so attractive?"

"Your lack of intelligence," Paula said promptly. "It's a change for women to talk down to men."

"All right, break it up!" I said sharply, as Kerman began to rise slowly from his chair, his hand reaching for the whisky bottle. "Never mind what she looks like. What did she say about Janet?"

Kerman resumed his seat, glaring at Paula.

"She said she was the most surprised person on earth to hear Janet had died of heart failure. Two days before she died she played tennis with the Parmetta girl, and wiped the floor with her. Does that sound like heart trouble?"

"Anything else?"

"I asked her about this guy Sherrill. He's out of town, by the way. I didn't see him. Joan Parmetta said Janet was madly in love with Sherrill. They saw a lot of each other. Then a week before Macdonald Crosby's death Sherrill stopped going to the house, and the engagement was broken off. There was no reason given and even Joan, who was intimate with Janet, didn't get the lowdown although she fished for it. Janet said they had a disagreement and she didn't want to talk about it."

"Did she say what kind of a guy this Sherrill was?" Kerman shrugged.

"She only met him a few times. She said he was handsome, but she has no idea what his job is, whether he his money or not. He has a house on Rossmore Avenue. Small, but nice. A Chinese girl looks after the place." He blew a kiss to the ceiling. "She's nice too. I didn't get much out of her though. She had no idea when Sherrill would be back. The guy lives well and must be making money. There was a Cadillac the size of a battleship in the garage, and the garden looked as if plenty of dough had been spent on it. There was a swimming pool too, and the usual lush trappings; all on the small side but very, very nice."

"That the lot?"

Kerman nodded.

Briefly I told him of my call on Eudora Drew, how Big Boy had arrived, of the murder, and my interview with Brandon. He sat listening, his eyes growing rounder and rounder, his drink forgotten.

"For the love of Pete!" he exploded when I had finished. "Some evening! So what happens? Do we quit?"

"I don't know," I said, pouring myself another drink. "We'll have to return the money. To do that we'll have to find out who takes care of the estate. It's a certain bet Maureen doesn't. She must have lawyers or some representative who takes care of her affairs. Maybe we can find that out from

Crosby's will. I want to have a look at Janet's will too. I want to find out if she left Eudora any money. If she didn't, where was Eudora's money coming from? I'm not saying we're not going on with this, I'm not saying we are. We'll get a few more facts and then decide. We'll have to be very careful how we step. Brandon could make things difficult."

"If we return the money the case should be closed," Paula said. "There's no point in working for nothing."

"I know," I said. "All the same this setup interests me. And besides, I don't like taking orders from Brandon." I finished my drink and pushed back my chair. "Well I guess we'd better break this up. I could do with some sleep."

Kerman stretched, yawned and stood up.

"I've just remembered I have to take the Hofflin kids to Hollywood tomorrow morning," he said, grimacing. "A personally-conducted tour of Paramount Studios. If it wasn't for the chance of seeing Dorothy Lamour I'd be fit to climb a tree. Those three brats terrify me."

"Okay," he said. "You'll be back the day after tomorrow?"

"Yeah. If I'm still in one piece."

"I'll have made up my mind by then what we're going to do. If we do go ahead we'll have to put in some fast, smooth work. Hang on a moment. I want a word with Mike."

I went over to the bar where Finnegan was lazily polishing glasses. An old letch and his blonde were just leaving. The blonde looked at me from under spiked eyelashes and winked. I winked back.

When they were out of earshot I said, "There's a guy who's been tailing me, Mike. Big, built like a boxer; squashed ear and nose, wears a fawn-colored hat with a cord around it. Smokes a cheroot and looks tough enough to eat rusty nails. Ever seen him?"

Mike rubbed the tumbler he was holding, raised it to the

light and squinted at it. Then he placed it carefully on the shelf.

"Sounds like Benny Dwan. It's a cinch it's Benny if his breath smells of garlic."

"I never got that close. Who's Benny Dwan"

Mike picked up another glass, rinsed it under the tap and began to polish it. He could be annoyingly deliberate when answering questions. He didn't mean anything by it, it was just his way.

"He's a tough torpedo," he said, squinted at the glass and polished some more. "Got a job up at Salzer's sanatorium. He was a small-time gambler before he joined up with Salzer. Served a five-year stretch for robbery with violence back in 1938. He's supposed to have settled down now, but I doubt that."

"What's he doing at Salzer's sanatorium?"

Mike shrugged.

"Odd jobs: cleans cars, does a bit of gardening, stuff like that."

"This is important, Mike. If it is Dwan he's up against a murder rap."

Mike pursed his thick lips in a soundless whistle.

"Well, it sounds like him. I've seen him in that hat."

I went over the description again, in detail and carefully.

"Yeah," Mike said. "That sounds like him all right. He's never without a cheroot and his nose and right ear are flattened. Must be the guy."

I felt vaguely excited.

"Well, thanks Mike."

I went back to the other two who had been watching me from across the room.

"Mike's identified Big Boy," I told them. "He's a guy named Benny Dwan and guess what, he works for Salzer."

"Isn't it marvelous how you find things out?" Kerman said, grinning. "So what are you going to do?"

"Tip Mifflin," I said. "Wait a second will you? I'll call him now."

They told me at police headquarters that Mifflin had gone home. I turned up his home telephone number in the book and put the call through. After a delay, Mifflin's voice came over the line. He sounded sleepy and exasperated.

"This is Malloy," I told him. "Sorry to wake you up Tim, but I'm pretty sure I can identify the guy who rubbed out Eudora Drew."

"You can?" Mifflin's voice brightened. "Say, that's fine. Who is he?"

"Benny Dwan. And get this, Tim. He works for Salzer. If you go out to the sanatorium right now you might lay your hooks into him."

There was a long, heavy silence. I waited, grinning, imagining Mifflin's expression.

"Salzer?" he said at last. His voice sounded as if he had a mouth full of hot potatoes.

"That's right. Brandon's little pal."

"Are you sure about this?"

"Yeah. Anyway, I'll identify him for you and so will Paula. We'd be glad to."

"You will?" Indecision and agony crept into his voice.

"Sure. Of course Salzer may be annoyed, but apart from Brandon, who cares about Salzer?"

"Aw, hell!" Mifflin said in disgust. "I'll have to have a word with Brandon. I'm not stirring up that kind of trouble."

"Go ahead and have a word with him. Be sure to tell him I'm phoning the night editor of the *Herald* with this story. I wouldn't like Dwan to slip through your fingers because Brandon doesn't want to upset his little pal."

"Don't do that!" Mifflin yelled. "Listen Vic, for God's sake don't go monkeying with the press. That's something Brandon won't stand for."

"Pity, because that's what I'm going to do. Tell him and get after Dwan unless you want the press to get after you. So long Tim," and while he was still yelling I hung up.

Paula and Kerman had come over to the phone booth and were listening.

"Got him in an uproar?" Kerman asked, rubbing his hands.

"Just a little hysterical. They don't seem anxious to annoy Salzer." I dialed, waited, then when a man's voice announced, "*Herald* offices", I asked to be put through to the night editor.

It took me about two minutes to give him the story. He accepted it the way a starving man accepts a five-course lunch.

"Salzer sort of pampers Brandon," I explained. "I wouldn't be surprised if he tries to hush this up."

"It won't be my fault if he succeeds," the night editor said with a ghoulish laugh. "Thanks, Malloy. I've been looking for a club to beat that rat with. Leave it to me. I'll fix him."

I hung up and moved out of the booth.

"Something tells me I've started a little trouble," I said. "If my bet's right, Brandon won't have pleasant dreams tonight."

"What a shame," Kerman said.

3

DRIVE North along Orchid Boulevard, past the Santa Rosa Estate, and eventually you will come to a narrow road which leads to the sand dunes and my cabin.

As a place to live in it's nothing to get excited about, but at least it's out of earshot of anyone's radio, and if I want to yodel in my bath no one cares. It is a four-room bungalow made of Canadian knotty pine with a garden the size of a pocket handkerchief, kept reasonably tidy by Toni, my Filipino boy. A hundred yards from my front door is the blue Pacific Ocean, and at the back and to the right and left are scrub bushes, sand, and a half-circle of blue palmetto trees. It is as lonely and as quiet as a pauper's grave, but I like it. I have lived and slept there for more than five years, and I wouldn't care to live or sleep anywhere else.

After I had left Finnegan's bar I drove along the sandy road, heading for home. The time was twenty minutes to midnight. There was a big watermelon moon in the sky, and its fierce white rays lit up the scrub and sand like a searchlight. The sea looked like a black mirror. The air was hot and still. If there had been a blonde within reach it would have been a romantic night.

Tomorrow, I told myself as I drove along, would be a busy day. Paula had promised to check both Macdonald and Janet Crosby's wills as soon as county buildings opened. I wanted to see Nurse Gurney again. I wanted to find out who Maureen Crosby's lawyer was and have a talk to him. If I could, I wanted more information about Douglas Sherrill. If the wills didn't produce anything of interest, if Maureen's lawyer was satisfied with the setup, and if there appeared to be nothing sinister about Douglas Sherrill then I decided I'd hand back the five hundred dollars and consider the case closed. But I was pretty sure at the back of my mind that I wouldn't close the case; although I was open to be convinced, I was wasting my time.

I pulled up before the pinewood hut that serves me as a garage, trudged through hot loose sand to open the doors. I got back into the Buick, drove in, switched off the engine and paused to light a cigarette. As I did so I happened to look into the rearview mirror. A movement in the moonlit bushes caught my eye.

I flicked out the match and sat very still, watching the clump of bushes in the mirror. It was, at a guess, about fifty yards away, and in direct line with the back of the car. It moved again, the branches bending and shivering, and then became motionless once more.

There was no wind, no reason why those bushes should move. No bird could be big enough to cause a movement like that, and it seemed to me someone—a man or possibly a woman—was hiding behind them and had either pushed back the branches to see more clearly, or else had lost balance and had grabbed at the branches to save himself from falling.

I didn't like this. People don't lurk in bushes unless they're up to no good. In the past Paula had repeatedly told me the cabin was dangerously lonely. In my job I made enemies, and there had been quite a few who had threatened at one time or the other to rub me out. I reached forward and stubbed out my cigarette. This spot was temptingly isolated for anyone with evil intentions. You could have started a miniature war right here without anyone hearing it, and I thought regretfully of the .38 police special in my wardrobe drawer.

After I had cut the car engine, I had dowsed the head-lights, and it was pitch dark in the garage. If whoever was lurking in those bushes planned to start something, the time to do it would be when I stepped out of the garage into the moonlight to shut the doors. As a target in that light and from that distance I couldn't be missed.

If I was to surprise the lurker, I would have to do something fast. The longer I sat in the car, the more alert and suspicious he would become—if it was a he. And if I wasn't ready for it he might even start blazing away at the back of the car in the hope a stray slug might find me, always supposing he had a gat, and I fervently hoped he hadn't.

I opened the car door and slid out into the darkness. From where I stood I could see the stretch of beach, the thick shrubs, and the trees startlingly sharp in the moonlight. It would be a crazy thing to walk out there into that blaze of white light, and I wasn't going to do it. I stepped back and ran my hands over the rough planks of the rear wall. Some time ago, after I had had a night out with Jack Kerman, I had driven a little too fast into the garage and had very nearly succeeded in driving right through it. I knew some of the planks had never recovered, and the idea now was to force an opening and slide out that way.

I found a wacky plank and began to work it loose. All the time I was doing this I didn't take my eyes off that clump of bushes. Nothing moved out there. Whoever was lurking behind the bushes was lying very, very doggo. The plank gave under my pressure. I pushed a little more and then turning sideways, edged through the opening.

At the back of the garage there was an expanse of sand and then bushes. I legged it across the sand and got under cover without making any noise, but losing a considerable amount of breath. It was a little too hot for that kind of exercise, and panting, I sat down on the sand to figure things out.

The sensible thing to do would be to creep around to the back of the cabin keeping out of sight, get inside, and collect the .38 from my wardrobe drawer. Once I had that I felt I'd be able to cope with anyone looking for trouble. A shot fired from my bedroom window a couple of feet above that clump of bushes would very likely take the starch out of whoever was lurking there.

The only snag to this idea was that as I hadn't appeared from the garage the intruder might guess I had spotted him, and he might be moving in this direction to cut me off. On the other hand he might think I was still in the garage, too scared to come out, and was prepared to wait until I did come out.

I rose slowly to my feet and keeping my head down began a quiet creep towards the cabin, sheltering behind the bushes and treading carefully. That was all right so long as the bushes lasted, but ten yards ahead they petered out and started again after a gap of twenty feet or so. That gap looked distressingly bare, and the light of the moon seemed to be pointing directly at it. By now I had left the protecting screen of the garage. The lurker in the clump of bushes couldn't fail to see me if I crossed that open space. I kept on until I was within a few feet of the gap, then paused and peered through the scrub. The only consoling thing about this new setup was I had greatly increased the distance between the clump of bushes and myself. Instead of being fifty yards away I was now something like a hundred and twenty, and to hit a moving target even as big as me at that distance called for some pretty fancy shooting. I decided to take a chance.

I took off my hat and, holding it by its brim, sent it sailing into the air towards the clump of bushes in the hope it would distract attention. Then before the hat settled on the sand, I jumped forward and ran.

It is one thing to get up speed on firm ground but quite something else when your feet sink up to your ankles in loose sand. My body went hurtling forward but my feet remained more or less where they were. If it hadn't been for the diversion of the hat as it sailed into the moonlight, I would have been a dead duck.

I sprawled on hands and knees, scrambled up somehow, and dove for cover. The still, quiet night was shattered by the bang of a gun. The slug fanned the top of my head as it zipped past like a vicious hornet. That shooting was much too good. I threw myself flat, rolled my legs under me, turned a somersault and was under cover again. The gun banged once more and the slug flung up sand into my face.

I was now as calm as an old lady with burglars in the house. Sweating and swearing I plunged on, diving towards thicker cover, shaking the bushes and stamping the sand like a runaway rhinoceros. Again the gun banged, and this time the slug slid along the back of my hand, breaking the skin and burning me as if I had been touched with a red-hot poker. I dropped flat and lay panting, holding my hand, unable to see anything beyond roots and branches and prickly sand-grass.

If Buffalo Bill out there took it into his head to close in for the kill I would be in a pretty lousy position. I had to keep moving. The cabin still seemed to be a long way away but there was cover, and providing I could move without making any noise, I still felt confident I'd get there. I wasn't going to take any more chances. Whoever it was out there could shoot. At that distance he had nearly bagged me, and that is shooting of a very high order. I wasn't in a panic, but I was sweating ice, and my heart was banging like a steam-hammer. I began to crawl on hands and knees through the sand, moving as quickly as I could, making no noise. I had gone about fifty feet when I heard a rustle of grass and a sudden snapping of a dry twig. I froze, listening, holding my breath, my nerves creeping like a spider's legs up and down my spine. More grass rustled, followed by a soft, *whooshing* sound of disturbed sand—close, too damned close. I lowered myself flat and lay hugging the sand, the hair on the back of my neck bristling.

A few yards away a bush moved, another twig snapped, then silence. He was right on top of me, and listening, I imagined I heard him breathing.

There was nothing for me to do but wait, so I waited. Minutes ticked by. He probably guessed I was right by him and he waited too, hoping I would make a sound so he could locate me. I was willing to wait like that all night, and after what seemed to me hours he again shifted his position, but this time away from me. I still didn't move. I listened to his footfalls as he moved from bush to bush, searching for me. Very slowly, very cautiously, I came up on hands and knees. Inch by inch I raised my head until I could see through the thinning branches of the scrub bush. Then I saw him. Big Boy! There he was in his fawn hat, his shoulders like a barn door, his flattened nose and ear ugly in the moonlight. He stood about thirty yards from me, a Colt .45 in his fist. He was half-turned away from me, his eyes searching the bushes to my right. If I had had a gun, I could have picked him off with no more trouble than shooting a rabbit at the same distance with a shotgun. But I hadn't got a gun, and all I could do was to watch him and hope he would go away.

He remained motionless, tense, his gun arm advanced. Then he turned and faced me and began to move towards me, a little aimlessly as if he wasn't sure if he was coming in the right direction but determined to find me.

I began to sweat again. Ten good paces would bring him right on top of me. I crouched down, listening to his cautious approach, my heart hammering, my breath held behind clenched teeth.

He stopped within three feet of me. I could see his thick trousered legs through the bush. If I could get his gun . . .

He turned so his back was towards me. I jumped him. My hands, my brain, my spring were all directed on his gun. Both my hands closed on his thick wrist and my shoulder thudded into his chest, sending him staggering. He gave a startled yelp, a blend of fury and alarm. I bent his wrist, crushed his fingers, clawed at the gun. For a split second I had it all my own way. He was paralyzed by the surprise of my spring, by the pain as I squeezed his fingers against the butt of the gun. Then as I had the gun he came into action. His fist slammed into the side of my neck—a chopping blow, hard enough to drive a six-inch nail into oak. I dove into the bushes, still clinging to the gun, trying to get my finger around the trigger, but not making it before his boot kicked the gun out of my hand. It went sailing away into the scrub. Well that was all right. If I hadn't got it, he hadn't either.

He came at me with a shambling rush, tearing his way through the bushes to get at me. But those sand bushes require respect. They don't like being rushed at, and he hadn't taken more than a couple of leaping steps before his toe stubbed against a root and he went sprawling. That gave me time to get to my feet and leg it towards the open. If we had to fight I wasn't going to be hampered by a lot of grass turfs, scrub, and bush roots. This guy was a lot heavier than I and had a punch like the kick of a mule, and I was still dazed from that chop on the neck. I didn't want another. The only satisfactory way to fight him was to have plenty of space to get away and come in again.

He was up on his feet and after me in split seconds, and he could move. He caught up with me as I broke through the last screen of bushes. I dodged his first rush, socked him on the nose as he came in again, and collected a bang on the side of my head that made my teeth rattle.

The moonlight fell fully on his face as he came in again: a

cold, brutal, murderous mask; the face of a man who intends to kill, and nobody or nothing is going to stop him. I jumped away, wheeled back and slugged him on his squashed ear sending him reeling, and that gave me confidence. He might be big, but he could be hit and he could be hurt. He grunted, crouched, shook his head, his hands moving forward with hooked fingers. I didn't wait for his rush but went in hitting with both fists. But this time his face wasn't there and his hands fastened on the front of my coat, pulling me against him.

I jerked up my knee but he knew all about that kind of fighting, and had already turned sideways on, taking the hard jab of my knee against his thigh. One of his hands shifted and grabbed at my throat as I slugged him in the ribs. He grunted again but his fingers, like steel hooks, dug into my windpipe.

Then I really went for him. I knew once he weakened me I was done for, and that paralyzing grip on my throat could sap my strength in seconds if I didn't break his hold. I hammered at his ribs, then as he still clung on, I dug my fingers into his eyes.

He gave a sharp screech, let go of my throat and staggered back. I went after him, belting him about the body. He held his eyes and took what I handed out. There was nothing much he could do about it and I hammered him to his knees. There was no point in breaking my fists on him, so I stepped back and waited for him to uncover. His breath came in short sobbing gasps. He tried to get to his feet but couldn't make it. Groaning, he dropped his hands to hoist himself up, and that was what I was waiting for. I measured him, swung a punch at him that came up from the sand and connected on the point of his jaw. He went over backwards, flopped about, scrabbling in the sand like a wounded squirrel, started climbing to his feet, fell over and straightened out.

I went over to him. He was out all right, and looking down at the blood running out of the corners of his eyes, I felt sorry for him. I didn't mean to hurt him as badly as that, but it was his life or mine, and at least I hadn't killed him.

I leaned forward and pulled the thick leather belt from around his waist, rolled him over and strapped his hands behind him. I took off my belt and lashed it around his ankles.

He was too heavy to carry, and I wanted to get to my phone and my gun. I thought he would be all right until I got back, and I turned and pelted towards the cabin.

It took me a couple of minutes to wake up Mifflin again. This time he sounded as mad as a hornet you've slapped with a flyswatter.

"All right, all right," I said. "I've got Dwan here."

"Dwan?" Anger went out of his voice. "With you?"

"Yeah. Come on. Get the boys and the wagon. I want some sleep tonight."

"Dwan! But Brandon said . . ."

"To hell with what Brandon said!" I bawled. "Come on out and get him."

"Keep your shirt on," Mifflin said dismally. "I'm coming."

As I slammed down the receiver a gun went off with a choked bang somewhere out on the dunes. I made two quick jumps to my wardrobe, flung open the door and grabbed the .38. I was back at the front door almost before the echo of the shot had died away. I didn't rush out into the moonlight. I stood looking around, in the shadow of the verandah, seeing nothing, hearing nothing and feeling spooked.

Then somewhere behind the palmetto trees a car started up and drove away with a rapid change of gears.

I sneaked down the verandah steps, holding my gun waist

high, down the garden path and across the moonlit stretch of sand. The sound of the departing car became fainter and fainter and finally died away.

I reached Benny Dwan and stood over him. Someone had shot him in the head, firing very close. The bullet had smashed in the side of his skull and burned his squashed ear with the gun flash.

He looked very harmless and lonely. He also looked very dead.

4

THE little blonde who looked after the PBX in the outer office gave me a coy little smile as I pushed open the frosted panel door on which was inscribed in gold letters: UNIVERSAL SERVICES, and on the right-hand bottom corner, in smaller letters: *Executive Director*: VICTOR MALLOY.

"Good morning, Mr. Malloy," she said, showing her nice white little teeth. She had a snub nose and puppy-dog manners. You felt you had only to pat her for her to wag her tail. A nice kid. Eighteen if she was a day, and only two heart throbs: me and Bing Crosby.

The two kids sitting behind typewriters, also blondes and also puppies, smiled the way bobbysoxers smile and also said, "Good morning, Mr. Malloy."

Mr. Malloy looked his harem over and said it was a swell morning.

"Miss Bensinger is over at the county buildings. She may be a little late," the PBX blonde told me.

"Thanks Trixy. I'll be right in the office. When she comes in tell her I want her."

She ducked her head and flashed me a look that might

have meant something to me if she had been a couple of years older and didn't work for me, and swung around on her stool to take an incoming call.

I went into my office and shut the door. My desk clock told me it was five past ten, early for a drink although I wanted one. After a little hesitation, I decided the bottle wouldn't know it was too early, hoisted it out of the desk drawer and gave myself a small, rather shamefaced nip. Then I sat down, lit a cigarette and pawed over the morning's mail without finding anything to hold my interest. I dropped the mail in the out tray for Paula's attention, put my feet on the desk and closed my eyes. After the night's excitement I felt a little frayed at the edges.

A bluebottle fly buzzed sleepily around my head. The two typewriters clacked in the outer office. Trixy played with her plugs. I dozed.

At twenty minutes to eleven I woke with a start at the sound of Paula's voice in the outer office. I had time to get my feet off the desk and drag my out tray towards me before she opened the door and came in.

"There you are," I said as brightly as I could. "Come on in."

"If you must sleep in the office, will you try not to snore?" she said, pulling up a chair and sitting down. "It's demoralizing the staff."

"They've been demoralized for years," I said, grinning. "I had about two hours sleep last night. I'm a tired old man this morning and I must be treated kindly."

Her cool brown eyes rested on the bruise on my cheekbone and her eyebrows climbed a half-inch.

"Trouble?"

"Well, excitement," and I told her about Benny Dwan's visit.

"He's dead?" she said, startled. "Who shot him?"

"I don't know for certain, but I have an idea," I said, hoisting my feet on to the desk. "Ten minutes after my call to Mifflin the cops arrived, but Mifflin wasn't with them. You remember those two coppers we ran into at Headquarters: the guy with the red hair and the tough-looking one? Well they turned up. Sergeant MacGraw; that's the redhead, and Sergeant Hartsell. A couple of nice, well-behaved, quiet-mannered heels you could wish to avoid any day of the week. They made no bones about how pleased they were to find Dwan dead. Of course, that was understandable. His death lets Salzer completely out. All he has to do now is to claim Dwan was no longer working for him. Why Dwan stole Salzer's car, knocked off Eudora and tried to knock off me is something for the police to find out. It's my bet they never will find out."

"You said you had an idea who killed him."

"Yeah. When those two boys took Dwan away I wandered around and looked for clues. They came in a police car fitted with diamond tread tires. I found the same pattern in the sand at the back of my cabin. It's my guess they came out early in the evening to keep an eye on me and had a front-row seat for the little show Dwan put on for my benefit, and when I knocked him out and left him tied up the temptation was too much for them. While I was phoning Mifflin they strolled over to Dwan and silenced him."

"You mean two police officers . . . ?" Paula began, her eyes growing wide.

"Look at the trouble it saves," I said. "Put yourself in their place. Here is a guy wanted for murder, who will most certainly talk if he is ever brought to trial. He probably has a lot of things to say about Dr. Salzer that would make interesting reading in the papers. Brandon is a pal of Salzer.

What could be more convenient than to put a slug into Dwan's head and save the cost of a trial and inconvenience to Brandon's little pal? Simple, isn't it? I may be wrong of course, but I doubt it. Anyway, there's not much we can do about it so let's skip it and get down to something we can do something about. Have you looked up the Crosbys' wills?"

Paula nodded.

"Janet didn't make a will. Crosby left three-quarters of his fortune to her and a quarter to Maureen. Obviously, Janet was his favorite. If Janet died Maureen was to have the lot, providing she behaved herself. But if she ever gets mixed up in a scandal and gets herself in the newspapers, the whole fortune is to go to the Orchid City Research Center, and she is to be paid only one thousand dollars a year. Crosby's trustees are Glynn & Coppley, on the third floor of this building. Half the capital is tied up, the other half Maureen has the free run of, providing of course, she behaves herself."

"That's a nice setup for a blackmailer," I said. "If she has put a foot wrong, and some crook has heard about it, he could shake her down for as much as she's got. It wouldn't be a lot of fun for her to live on a thousand a year, would it?"

Paula lifted her shoulders.

"Lots of girls live on less."

"Sure, but not millionaire's daughters." I picked up the letter opener and began to dig holes in the blotter. "So Janet didn't leave a will. That means Eudora didn't come into a legacy. Then from where was she getting her money?" I looked up and stared thoughtfully at Paula. "Suppose she knew about Maureen's drug cure? Suppose Maureen was paying her to keep her mouth shut? It's an idea. Then I come along, and Eudora thinks she can screw a little money out of Maureen. She tells me to call back at nine and puts through a telephone call either to Maureen or her representative who might be Dr. Salzer. In fact, could be Dr. Salzer. 'Let's have some more dough or I'll talk,' she might have said. Salzer sends Dwan down to reason with her. Instead, or even acting on orders, Dwan knocks her off. How do you like that?"

"It sounds all right," Paula said dubiously. "But it's guess-work."

"That's right, it's guesswork. Still, I don't dislike it myself." I made three more little holes in the blotter before saying, "I think I'd better have another word with Nurse Gurney. Look, Paula, she's off duty during the day. Will you phone the Nurses' Association and see if you can get her private address? Spin them a yarn. They'll probably let you have it."

While she was out of the office, I had another nip out of the bottle and lit another cigarette. First Nurse Gurney, I told myself, and then Glynn & Coppley.

Paula came back after a few minutes and placed a slip of paper on my disfigured blotter.

"Apartment 246, 3882 Hollywood Avenue," she told me. "Did you know she's one of Dr. Salzer's nurses?"

"She is?" I pushed back my chair. "Well what do you know? It keeps coming back to Salzer, doesn't it?" I edged my out tray towards her. "There's not much here. Nothing you can't cope with."

"That's nice to know." She picked up the tray. "Are you going ahead with this case?"

"I'm not sure. I'll tell you this afternoon." I reached for my hat. "I'll be seeing you."

It took me half an hour to reach Hollywood Avenue. The mid-morning traffic on Centre Avenue made the going slow, but I was in no hurry.

3882 Hollywood Avenue turned out to be a six-story

apartment block that had been thrown together with an eye to quick profits and little if any comfort for the customers. The lobby was dim and shabby. The elevator was big enough to hold three people if they didn't mind packing in like sardines. A chipped metal sign with a hand pointing to the basement stairs had *Janitor* printed on it in faded blue letters and hung lopsided on the wall.

I entered the elevator, pushed the grill shut and pressed the button marked *2nd Floor*. The elevator rose creakily as if it was in a mood not to rise at all, came to a sighing standstill two floors up. I tramped down an endless corridor flanked on either side by shabby, paint-chipped doors. After what seemed to me to be a half-mile walk, I arrived at Apartment 246 which was up a cul-de-sac, one of two apartments facing each other. I screwed my thumb into the doorbell, then propped up the wall and selected a cigarette. I wondered if Nurse Gurney was in bed. I wondered if she would be glad to see me again and hoped she would.

I had to wait about a couple of minutes before I heard sounds, then the door opened. Nurse Gurney looked a lot more interesting out of her nurse's uniform. She was wearing a housecoat thing that reached to her ankles but fell apart from her knees down. Her feet and legs were bare.

"Why hello," she said. "Do you want to come in?"

"I wouldn't mind."

She stood aside.

"How did you find my address?" she asked, leading me into a small living room. "This is a surprise."

"Yeah, isn't it?" I said, dropping my hat on a chair. "You look knocked for a loop."

She giggled.

"I happened to look out of the window and saw you coming. So I've had time to recover. How did you know I lived here?"

"Phoned the Nurses' Association. Were you going to bed?"

"Uh-huh, but don't let that drive you away."

"You get into bed and I'll sit beside you and hold your hand."

She shook her head.

"That sounds dull. Let's have a drink. Was there anything special or is this just a social call?"

I lowered myself into an armchair.

"Fifty-fifty, although the accent's on the social side. Don't ask me to fix the drinks. I'm feeling a little under the weather. I didn't sleep too good last night."

"Who were you out with?"

"Nothing like that." I reached gratefully for the highball and saluted her with it.

She came over and flopped on the divan. Her housecoat fell back. My eyes had time to pop before she adjusted it.

"You know I never expected to see you again," she said, holding the tumbler of whisky and ice so her chin could rest on the rim. "I thought you were one of those hit-and-run artists."

"Me? Hit-and-run? Oh no, you've got me dead wrong. I'm one of those steady, faithful, clinging types."

"I bet—wait until the novelty wears off," she said a little bitterly. "Is that drink all right?"

"It's fine." I stretched out my legs and yawned. I certainly felt low enough to creep in a gopher's hole and pull the hole in after me. "How long do you expect to go on nursing the Crosby girl?"

I said it casually, but she immediately gave me a sharp, surprised look.

"Nurses never talk about their cases," she said primly, and drank a little of the highball.

"Unless they have a good reason to," I said. Seriously, would you like a change of jobs? I might fix you up."

"Wouldn't I! I'm bored stiff with my present work—it's cock-eyed to call it work, seeing I don't have a thing to do."

"Well, surely there must be something to do."

She shook her head, began to say something, then changed her mind.

I waited.

"What's this job of yours?" she asked. "Do you want nursing?"

"Nothing would please me more. No, it's not me. A friend of mine. He's an iron-lung case and wants a pretty nurse to cheer him up. He has plenty of money. I could put in a word for you if you like."

She considered this, frowning, then shook her head.

"I can't do it. I'd like to, but there are difficulties."

"I shouldn't have thought there would be any difficulty. The Nurses' Association will fix it."

"I'm not employed by the Nurses' Association."

"That makes it easier still, right? If you're a freelance . . ."

"I'm under contract to Dr. Salzer. He runs the Salzer Sanatorium up on Foothill Boulevard. Maybe you've heard of it."

I nodded.

"Is Salzer Maureen's doctor?"

"Yes. At least I suppose he is. He never comes near her."

"What's he got then—an assistant?"

"No one comes near her."

"That's odd, isn't it?"

"You're asking a lot of questions, aren't you?"

I grinned at her.

"I'm a curious guy. Isn't she bad enough to have a doctor?"

She looked at me.

"Between you and me, I don't know. I've never seen her."

I sat up, spilling some of my whisky.

"You've never seen her? What do you mean? You nurse her, don't you?"

"I shouldn't be telling you this but it worries me, and I have to tell someone. Promise you won't pass it on?"

"Who would I pass it on to? Do you mean you've never even seen Maureen Crosby?"

"That's right. Nurse Flemming won't let me into the sick-room. My job is to fend off visitors, and now no one ever visits, I haven't a thing to do."

"What do you do then, at night?"

"Nothing. I sleep at the house. If the telephone rings I'm supposed to answer it. But it never rings."

"You've looked in Maureen's room when Nurse Flemming isn't around, surely?"

"I haven't, because they keep the door locked. It's my bet she isn't even in the house."

"Where else would she be?" I asked, sitting forward and not bothering to conceal my excitement.

"If what Flemming says is right, she could be in the sanatorium."

"And what does Nurse Flemming say?"

"I told you, she's sweating out a drug jag."

"If she's in the sanatorium, then why the deception? Why not say right out she's there? Why put in a couple of nurses and fake a sickroom?"

"Brother, if I knew I'd tell you," Nurse Gurney said, and finished her drink. "It's a damned funny thing, but whenever you and I get together we have to talk about Maureen Crosby."

"Not all the time," I said, getting up and crossing to the divan. I sat by her side. "Is there any reason why you can't leave Salzer?"

"I'm under contract to him for another two years. I can't leave him."

I let my fingers stroke her knee.

"What kind of guy is Salzer? I've heard he's a quack."

She slapped my hand.

"He's all right. Maybe he is a quack, but the people he treats are just overfed. He starves them and collects. You don't have to be a qualified man to do that."

My hand strayed back to her knee again.

"Do you think you could be a clever, smart girl and find out if Maureen is in the sanatorium?" I asked and began a complicated maneuver.

She slapped my hand, hard this time.

"There you go again—Maureen."

I rubbed the back of my hand.

"You have quite a slap there."

She giggled.

"When you have my looks you learn to slap hard."

Then the front doorbell rang: one long, shrill peal.

"Don't answer it," I said. "I'm now ready not to talk about Maureen."

"Don't be silly." She swung her long legs off the divan. "It's the groceryman."

"What's he got I haven't?"

"I'll show you when I come back. I can't starve just to please you."

She went out of the room and closed the door. I took the opportunity to freshen my drink, and then lay down on the divan. What she had told me had been very interesting. The uncared-for garden, the crap-shooting Chinese, the whittling chauffeur, the smoking butler all added up to the obvious truth that Maureen wasn't living at Crestways. Then where was she? Was she at the sanatorium? Was she sweating out a drug jag? Nurse Flemming would know. Dr. Jonathan Salzer would know, too. Probably Benny Dwan and Eudora had known. Perhaps Glynn & Coppley knew, or if they didn't, they might wish to know. I began to see a way to put this business on a financial footing. My mind shifted to Brandon. If I had Glynn & Coppley behind me I didn't think Brandon would dare start anything. Glynn & Coppley were the best, the most expensive, the top-drawer lawyers in California. They had branch offices in San Francisco, Hollywood, New York, and London. They were not the kind of people who'd allow themselves to be nudged by a shyster copper like Brandon. If they wanted to they had enough influence to dust him right out of office.

I closed my eyes and thought how nice it would be to be rid of Brandon and have a good, honest Captain of Police like Mifflin in charge at headquarters. How much easier it would be for me to get cooperation instead of threats of dark alley beatings.

Then it occurred to me that Nurse Gurney had been away longer than it was necessary to collect a few groceries, and I sat up, frowning. I couldn't hear her talking. I couldn't hear anything. I sat my drink down and stood up. Crossing the room, I opened the door and looked into the foyer. The front door was ajar, but there was no one to see. I peeped into the hallway. The door of the opposite apartment looked blankly at me and I returned to the foyer. Maybe she was in the john, I thought, and went back into the living room. I sat and waited, getting more and more fidgety, then after five minutes I finished my drink and went to the door again.

Somewhere in the apartment a refrigerator gave a whirring grunt and made me jump halfway out of my skin. I raised my voice and called, "Hey!" but no one answered.

Moving quietly, I opened the door opposite the living room and looked around what was obviously her bedroom. She wasn't there. I even looked under the bed. I went into the bathroom and the kitchen and a tiny room that was probably the guestroom. She wasn't in any of these rooms. I went back to the living room but she wasn't there either. It was beginning to dawn on me she wasn't in the apartment, so I went to the front door, then along the hallway until I arrived at the main corridor. I looked to right and left. Stony-faced doors looked back at me. Nothing moved, nothing happened; just two lines of doors, a mile of shabby carpet, two or three grimy windows to let in the light, but no Nurse Gurney.

5

I STARED blankly out of the window of the small living room at the roof of the Buick parked below.

Without shoes or stockings she couldn't have gone far, I told myself, unless . . . and my mind skipped to Eudora Drew, seeing a picture of her as she lay across the bed with the scarf biting into her throat.

For some moments I stood undecided. There seemed nothing much I could do. I had nothing to work on. The front doorbell rings. She says it's the groceryman. She goes into the foyer. She vanishes. No cry, no bloodstains, no nothing.

But I had to do something, so I went to the front door and opened it and looked at the door of the opposite apartment. It didn't tell me anything. I stepped into the hallway and dug my thumb into the doorbell. Almost immediately the door opened as if the woman who faced me had been waiting for my ring.

She was short and plump, with white hair, a round, soft-skinned face, remarkable for the bright, vague, forget-me-not blue eyes and nothing else. At a guess, she was about fifty, and when she smiled she showed big, dead-looking white teeth that couldn't have been her own. She was wearing a fawn-colored coat and skirt that must have cost a lot of money but fitted her nowhere. In her small, fat, white hand she held a paper sack.

"Good morning," she said, and flashed the big teeth at me.

She startled me. I wasn't expecting to see this plump, matronly woman who looked as if she had just come in from a shopping expedition and was now about to cook the lunch.

"I'm sorry to trouble you," I said, lifting my hat. "I'm looking for Nurse Gurney." I waved to the half-open front door behind me. "She lives there, doesn't she?"

The plump woman dipped into the paper sack and took out a plum. She examined it closely, the eyes in her vacant, fat face suspicious. Satisfied, she popped it into her mouth. I watched her, fascinated.

"Why, yes," she said in a muffled voice. "Yes, she does." She raised her cupped hand, turned the pit out of her mouth into her hand in a refined way and dropped the stone back into the sack. "Have a plum?"

I said I didn't care for plums and thanked her.

"They're good for you," she said, dipped into the sack and fished out another. But this time it didn't pass her scrutiny and she put it back and found another more to her liking.

"You haven't seen her, have you?" I asked, watching the plum disappear between the big teeth.

"Seen who?"

"Nurse Gurney. I've just arrived, and I find the front door open. I can't get any answer to my ring."

She chewed the plum while her unintelligent face remained blank. After she had got rid of the plum pit, she said, "You should eat plums. You haven't got a very healthy color. I eat two pounds every day."

From the shape of her that wasn't all she ate.

"Well maybe I'll get around to them one day," I said patiently. "Nurse Gurney doesn't happen to be in your apartment?"

Her mind had wandered into the paper sack again, and she looked up, startled. "What was that?"

Whenever I run into a woman like this I am very, very glad I am a bachelor.

"Nurse Gurney." I felt I wanted to make signs the way I do when I talk to a foreigner. "The one who lives in that apartment. I said she doesn't happen to be in your apartment."

The blue eyes went vague.

"Nurse Gurney?

"That's right."

"In my apartment?"

I drew a deep breath.

"Yeah. She doesn't happen to be in your apartment, does she?"

"Why should she be?"

I felt blood begin to sing in my ears.

"Well, you see, her front door was open. She doesn't appear to be in her apartment. I wondered if she had popped over to have a word with you."

Another plum came into view. I averted my eyes. Seeing those big teeth bite into so much fruit was beginning to undermine my mental stability.

"Oh, no, she hasn't done that."

Well, at least we were making progress.

"You wouldn't know where she is?"

The plum pit appeared and dropped into the sack. A look

of pain came over the fat, blank face. She thought. You could see her thinking the way you can see a snail move if you watch hard enough.

"She might be in the—the bathroom," she said at last. "I should wait and ring again."

Quite brilliant in a dumb kind of way.

"She's not in there. I've looked."

She was about to put the bite on another plum. Instead she lowered it to look reproachfully at me.

"That wasn't a very nice thing to do."

I took off my hat and ran my fingers through my hair. Much more of this and I would be walking up the wall.

"I knocked first," I said, through clenched teeth. "Well, if she's not with you I'll go back and try again."

She was still thinking. The look of pain was still on her face.

"I know what I would do if I were you," she said.

I could guess, but I didn't tell her. I had a feeling she would insult at the drop of a hat.

"Tell me," I said.

"I'd go downstairs and see the janitor. He's a very helpful man." Then she spoiled it by adding, "Are you sure you won't have a plum?"

"Yeah, I'm quite sure. Well thanks, I'll see the janitor like you said. Sorry to have taken up so much of your time."

"Oh, you're welcome," she said, and smiled.

I backed away, and as she closed the door she put another plum into the maw she called her mouth.

I rode down the elevator to the lobby and walked down a flight of dark, dusty stairs to the basement. At the bottom of the stairs a door faced me. It bore a solitary legend: *Janitor*.

I raised my hand and rapped. A lean old man with a long, stringy neck, dressed in faded dungarees, appeared. He was old and bored and smelt faintly of creosote and whisky.

He squinted at me without interest, said one word out of a phlegmy old throat, "Yes?"

I had a feeling I wasn't going to get much help out of him unless I shook him out of his lethargy. From the look of him he seldom came up out of the darkness and his contacts with human beings were rare. He and Rip Van Winkle would have made a fine business team, providing Winkle took charge of things—not otherwise, decidedly not otherwise.

I leaned forward and hooked a finger in his top pocket.

"Listen pally," I said, as tough as an Orchid City cop. "Shake the hay out of your hair. I want a little cooperation from you." While I talked, I rocked him to and fro. "Apartment 246—what gives?"

He swallowed his Adam's apple twice. The second time I didn't think it would come to the surface again, but eventually it did—but only barely.

"What's up?" he said, blinking. "What's the matter with Apartment 246?"

"I'm asking you. Front door's open, no one's there. That's where you come in, pally. You should know when a front door's been left open."

"She's up there," he said owlishly. "She's always up there at this time."

"Only this time she's not. Come on pally, you and me are going up there to take a look around."

He went with me as meek as a lamb. As we rode in the elevator he said feebly, "She's always been a nice girl. What do the police want with her?"

"Did I say the police want anything with her?" I asked, and scowled at him. "All I want to know is why the front door's open when she isn't there."

"Maybe she went out and forgot to shut it," he said after

turning the matter over in his mind. I could see he was pleased with this idea.

"Now you're getting cute," I said as the elevator came to a creaking standstill. I was glad to get out of it. It didn't seem strong enough to haul one, let alone two people. "Did you see her go out?"

He said he hadn't seen her go out.

"Would you have seen her if she went?"

"Yes." He blinked, and his Adam's apple jumped a couple of notches. "My room overlooks the front entrance."

"Are you sure she didn't come out during the past ten minutes?"

No, he couldn't be sure about that. He had been cooking his lunch.

We went down the long corridor into the cul-de-sac and into Nurse Gurney's apartment. We went into each room, but she still wasn't in any of them.

"Not there," I said. "How else could she have left the building without using the front entrance?"

After staring blankly at the wall, he said there was no other way out.

I poked a finger towards the opposite apartment.

"Who's the fat woman who eats plums?"

This time his Adam's apple went for good.

"Plums?" he repeated and backed away. I guess he thought I was crazy.

"Yeah. Who is she?"

He looked at the door of Apartment 244, blinked, turned scared old eyes on me.

"In there, mister?"

"Yeah."

He shook his head.

"No one's in there. That apartment's for rent."

I felt a sudden chill run up my spine. I shoved past him and sank my thumb into the doorbell. I could hear the bell ringing but nothing happened; nobody came to the door.

"Got a pass key?"

He fumbled in his pocket, dragged out a key and handed it over.

"Ain't nobody in there, mister," he said. "Been empty for weeks."

I turned the lock, pushed open the door and went into a foyer just like Nurse Gurney's foyer. I went quickly from room to room. The place was as empty and as bare as Mrs. Hubbard's cupboard.

The bathroom window looked out onto a fire escape. I pushed up the window and leaned out. Below was an alley that led into Skyline Avenue. It would have been easy for a strong man to have carried a girl down the escape to a waiting car below.

Leaning far out I saw a plum pit on one of the iron steps. Pity she hadn't swallowed it. It might have choked her.

Chapter Three

1

THERE was a time when I proudly imagined I had a well-furnished, impressive, non-gaudy, super-deluxe office to work in. Between us, Paula and I had spent a lot of hard-earned money on the desk, the carpet, the drapes, and the bookcases. We had even run to a couple of original water-colors by a local artist who, to judge by his prices, considered himself in the Old Master class; probably he was, although it was a pretty close-kept secret. But all this was before I had a chance of seeing the other offices in the Orchid Buildings. Some of them were smarter than mine, some were not, but those I had seen didn't make me wish to change mine until I walked into the office of Manfred Willet, the President of Glynn & Coppley, Attorneys at Law. Then I saw at a glance I would have to save many more dollars before I could hope to get anywhere near the super-deluxe class. His office made mine look like an Eastside slum.

It was a big room, high ceilinged and oak-paneled. A desk big enough to play billiards on stood at the far end of the room before three immense windows stretching up to the ceiling. There were four or five lounging chairs and a big chesterfield sofa grouped around a fireplace that could have been used as a hidey-hole for a small-sized elephant. The fitted carpet was thick enough to be cut with a lawn mower. On the mantel and scattered around the room on tricky little tables were choice pieces of jade carvings. The desk furniture was of solid silver that glittered with loving care and constant polishing. Off-white Venetian blinds kept out the sun. A silent air conditioning plant controlled the temperature. Double windows, soundproof walls and a rubber-lined door insisted on complete silence. A stomach rumble in this office would sound like a ton of gravel going down a shoot.

Manfred Willet sat in a padded swivel chair behind the immense desk, smoking a fat oval cigarette fitted with a gold-tipped mouthpiece. He was tall and solid, around forty-five. His dark hair was flecked with gray, his clean-shaven, strikingly-handsome face matched the color of his mahogany desk. His London-cut suit would have made any movie star green with envy, and his linen was as immaculate and as white as the first snowdrop of spring.

He let me talk. His gray-green eyes didn't shift from the elaborate silver pen set on his desk. His big frame didn't move. His mahogany-colored face was as expressionless and as empty as a hole in a wall.

I began by showing him Janet Crosby's letter, then told him about my visit to Crestways, the state of the place, that Maureen was supposed to be ill, that Janet had been playing tennis two days before she died of endocarditis. I mentioned Dr. Bewley and that Benny Dwan, who worked for Dr. Salzer, had tailed me. I told him briefly of my visit to Eudora Drew, how Dwan had arrived and had strangled her. I dwelt on my interview with Captain of Police Brandon, and how he had warned me to lay off Salzer and Maureen Crosby. I mentioned casually that Brandon was prejudiced in their favor and why. I went on to describe how Dwan had tried to shoot me, and how he had been knocked off by someone who drove a car with diamond-tread tires. I mentioned that Sergeants MacGraw and Hartsell had driven a car fitted with such tires. I concluded by telling him of my visit to Nurse Gurney's apartment, of the fat woman who ate plums, and how Nurse Gurney had vanished. It was a long story and it took time to tell, but he didn't hurry me or interrupt me or suggest I should cut out the details. He sat staring at his pen set, as still as a graven image, and I had an idea he wasn't missing anything, that every little detail registered, and behind that blank, empty mahogany face his brain was very, very much awake.

"Well, that's the story," I concluded, and reached forward to knock my cigarette ash into the ashtray on his desk. "I thought that you, as the Trustee of the estate, should know about it. I have been told by Brandon to return the five hundred dollars." I took out my wallet and laid the money on the desk, put my finger on it and without any show of reluctance, pushed it towards him. "Strictly speaking that lets me out. On the other hand, you may think there should be an investigation, and if that's what you think I would be glad to carry on. Frankly Mr. Willet, the setup interests me."

He turned his eyes on me and stared. Seconds ticked by. I had the idea he wasn't seeing me. He was certainly thinking.

"This is an extraordinary story," he said suddenly. "I don't think I would have believed it if I didn't know your organization by reputation. You have handled several tricky jobs for clients of mine, and they have spoken very highly of you. From what you have told me I think we have grounds to begin an investigation, and I should be glad if you would handle it." He pushed back his chair and stood up. "But it must be understood that such an investigation must be secret, and my firm must not be associated with it in any way. We will be prepared to pay your fee, but you must keep us covered. Our position is a difficult one. We have no business to pry into Miss Crosby's affairs unless we are certain there is something wrong, and we are not certain of that, although it looks like it. If you uncover any tangible evidence that definitely connects Miss Crosby with these extraordinary happenings, then of course we can come out into the open. But not before."

"That makes it awkward for me," I pointed out. "I was relying on you to keep Brandon from bothering me."

There was a twinkle in his eyes as he said, "I'm sure you will be able to handle Brandon without my help. But if the going happens to become difficult you can always quote me as your lawyer. If there was an assault, I should be happy to represent you in court without charge."

"That's swell," I said sarcastically. "But in the meantime, I have been assaulted."

He didn't seem to think that was anything to worry about.

"No doubt you will adjust your fee to cover personal risks," he said lightly. "After all, I suppose a job like yours does involve risks."

I shrugged. The fee, I told myself, would certainly be jacked up to the ceiling.

"All right," I said. "Then I can go ahead?"

He began to pace about the room, his hands behind him, his head bent, frowning at the carpet.

"Oh, yes. I want you to go ahead."

"There are some questions I'd like to ask," I said, lighting another cigarette. "When did you last see Maureen Crosby?"

"At Janet's funeral. I haven't seen her since. Her affairs are quite straightforward. Any papers that need her signature are sent to her through the mail. I have had no occasion to see her."

"You haven't heard she is ill?"

He shook his head. No, he had no idea she was ill.

"Are you satisfied Macdonald Crosby's death was an

accident?" I shot at him.

He wasn't expecting this and looked up sharply.

"What do you mean? Of course it was an accident."

"Couldn't it have been suicide?"

"There was no reason why Crosby should have committed suicide."

"As far as you know."

"A man doesn't usually kill himself with a shotgun if he owns a revolver, and Crosby owned a revolver. A shotgun is liable to be messy."

"If he had committed suicide would it have affected his estate?"

"Why, yes." A startled look came into his eyes. "His life was insured for a million and a half dollars. The policy carried a non-payment suicide clause."

"Who received the insurance money?"

"I don't quite see where all this is leading to," he said, returning to his desk and sitting down. "Perhaps you will explain."

"It seems odd to me that Salzer, who is not a qualified doctor, should have signed the death certificate. The coroner and Brandon must have agreed to this. I'm trying to convince myself there was nothing sinister in Crosby's death. Suppose he did commit suicide. According to you the estate would have lost a million and a half dollars. But if a nice, willing quack and a grafting coroner and Captain of Police got together it could be arranged to look like an accident, couldn't it?"

"That's a pretty dangerous thing to say. Isn't Salzer qualified?"

"No. Who received the insurance money?"

"It was left to Janet, and at her death to Maureen."

"So Maureen now has a million and a half in cash, is that

right?"

"Yes. I tried to persuade Janet to invest the money, but she preferred to leave it in the bank. It passed in cash to Maureen."

"What's happened to it? Is it still in the bank?"

"As far as I know. I have no access to her account."

"Couldn't you have?"

He regarded me steadily for a moment or so.

"I might. I don't know whether I'd care to."

"It would be helpful to find out just how much is left." I nodded towards Janet's letter lying on the desk. "There's this business of blackmail. And if Franklin Lessways, the coroner, and Brandon had to be squared it is possible not a great deal of it remains. I'd be glad if you could find out."

"All right. I'll see what can be done." He rubbed his jaw thoughtfully. "I suppose I could take action against Salzer if what you say is true. He had no right to sign the certificate, but I'm not anxious to come out into the open just yet. There seems to be no doubt the shooting was accidental. The insurance company was satisfied."

"They would be if Brandon and the coroner passed the certificate. It looks to me as if Salzer is financing Lessways as well as Brandon. What do you know about Lessways?"

Willet grimaced.

"Oh, he could be bought. He has a pretty rotten reputation."

"Did you know Janet Crosby well?"

He shook his head.

"I met her two or three times. No more."

"Did she strike you as having a bad heart?"

"No, but that doesn't mean anything. Lots of people have bad hearts. It doesn't always show."

"But they don't play tennis two days before they die as

Janet did."

I could see he was beginning to get worried.

"What are you hinting at?"

"Nothing. I'm just stating a fact. I'm not sold on the idea she died of heart failure."

While he stared at me the silence in the room was heavy enough to sink a battleship.

"You're not suggesting . . ." he began and broke off.

"Not yet," I said. "But it's something we should keep in mind."

I could see he didn't like this at all.

"Suppose we leave that for the moment?" I went on. "Let's concentrate on Maureen Crosby. From the look of the house and from what Nurse Gurney tells me it is possible Maureen isn't living at Crestways. If she isn't there—where is she?"

"Yes," he said. "There's that."

"Is she in Salzer's sanatorium? Has it occurred to you she may be a prisoner there?"

That brought him bolt upright in his chair.

"Aren't you letting your imagination run away with you? I had a letter from her only last week."

"That doesn't mean much. Why did she write?"

"I asked her to sign some papers. She returned them signed, with a covering note thanking me for sending them."

"From Crestways?"

"The address on the notepaper was Crestways."

"That still doesn't prove she isn't a prisoner, does it? I'm not saying she is, but that's another thing we shall have to keep in mind."

"We can find out about that right away," he said briskly. "I'll write to her and ask her to call on me. I can find some business excuse for an interview."

"Yeah. That's an idea. Will you let me know what happens? It might be an idea to follow her when she leaves you and find out where she goes."

"I'll let you know."

I stood up.

"I think that's about all. You'll remember to check on her bank statement?"

"I'll see what I can do. Go slow on this, Malloy. I don't want any blow-back. You understand?"

"I'll watch it."

"What's your next move?"

"I've got to do something about Nurse Gurney. I liked that girl. If she's alive, I'm going to find her."

When I left him he wasn't looking like a graven image anymore. He was looking like a very worried, much-harassed, middle-aged lawyer. At least it showed the guy was human.

2

THE desk sergeant said Mifflin was free and for me to go on up. He looked at me with hopeful eyes, and I knew he was expecting me to name the winner of Tomorrow's races, but I had other things on my mind.

I went up the stone stairs. On the landing I ran into red-headed Sergeant MacGraw.

"Well, well, the Boy Wonder again," he said sneeringly. "What's biting you this time?"

I looked into the hard little eyes and didn't like what I saw in them. This was a guy who would enjoy inflicting pain; one of those tough coppers who would volunteer when there was a softening job to be done, and how he would love it.

"Nothing's biting me," I said. "But if I stick around you

long enough something may."

"Smart—huh?" He grinned, showing small yellow teeth. "Keep your nose clean, Wonder Boy. We're watching you."

"Just so long as you don't shoot me through the head,"

I returned, pushed past him and went on down the corridor to Mifflin's office.

I paused before I rapped and looked over my shoulder. MacGraw was still standing at the head of the stairs, staring at me. There was a startled expression on his face, and his loose-lipped mouth hung open. As our eyes met, he turned away and went down the stairs.

Mifflin looked up as I entered his office and frowned.

"You again. For Pete's sake don't keep coming to see me. Brandon doesn't like it."

I pulled up a straight-back chair and sat down.

"Remind me to cry when I have time. I'm on official business. If Brandon doesn't like it, he can go jump in the ocean."

"What business?" Mifflin asked, pushing back his desk chair and resting his big hairy hands on the desk.

"One of the nurses attending Miss Crosby has vanished," I said. "Brandon should be interested because this nurse is employed by Salzer."

"Vanished?" Mifflin repeated, his voice off-key. "What do you mean—vanished?"

I told him how I had called on Nurse Gurney, how the front doorbell had rung, how she had gone to answer it and hadn't returned. I gave him the details about the fat woman in the empty apartment opposite, the plum pit on the escape and how simple it would have been for a strong man to have carried Nurse Gurney down the escape to a waiting car.

"Well that's a damned funny thing," Mifflin said, and ran his fingers through his shock of black hair. "About a couple of years ago another of Salzer's nurses disappeared. She was never found."

"Did you ever look for her?"

"All right Vic, you needn't be that way," he said angrily. "Of course we looked for her, but we didn't find her. Salzer said he thought she had run away to get married. Her father wasn't struck on her boyfriend or something like that."

"Salzer hasn't reported Nurse Gurney is missing?"

He shook his head.

"He'd scarcely have had time, would he? Besides, she might have remembered something and gone out to get it. There must be any number of reasons why she left the apartment."

"Without shoes and stockings and in the middle of a conversation? Don't kid yourself. This is kidnapping, and you know it."

"I'll go over there and talk to the janitor. You better keep out of this. I'll tell Brandon the janitor reported it."

I shrugged.

"Just so long as something's done. This other case interests me. Who was the nurse?"

Mifflin hesitated, then got up and went over to one of his many filing cabinets.

"Her name was Anona Freedlander," he said, pawed through a number of files, selected one and brought it to his desk. "We haven't a lot of information. Her father's George Freedlander. He lives at 257 California Street, San Francisco. She disappeared on 15th May of last year, Salzer reported to Brandon. Freedlander came to see us, and it was his idea she had run off with this boyfriend, a guy named Jack Brett. Brett was in the Navy. A couple of weeks before Anona disappeared he deserted. Brandon said we needn't look too hard; we didn't."

"Did you ever find Brett?"

"No."

"I wonder how hard you are going to look for Nurse Gurney."

"Well, we'll have to be convinced she has been kidnapped. Brandon won't act on your say-so. It'll depend on Salzer."

"This damned city seems to be run by Salzer."

"Aw now, Vic, you don't mean that."

I got to my feet.

"Find her Tim, or I'll start something. I liked that girl."

"Just take it easy. If she has disappeared, we'll find her. You're sure that horse Crab Apple's okay? I don't want to lose five bucks."

"Never mind Crab Apple. You concentrate on Nurse Gurney," I said and stamped out of the room.

I drove back to the Orchid Buildings. Paula was waiting for me in my office.

"We go ahead," I said, and sat down behind my desk. "I've seen Willet, he'll finance an investigation, but he wants to keep his firm well in the background."

"Plucky of him," Paula said scornfully. "You take all the risks I suppose?"

"He seemed to expect to pay a little extra," I said, and grinned. I told her about my visit to headquarters. "This guy Salzer seems in the habit of making his nurses vanish. You note the date? May 15th: the day Janet died. No one's going to convince me her disappearance doesn't somehow tie in with Janet's death."

Paula studied me.

"You think Janet was murdered, don't you?"

I lit a cigarette and put the match carefully in the ashtray before replying.

"I think it's possible. The motive's there, all that money.

She certainly didn't die of heart failure. Arsenic poisoning, among other poisons, produces heart failure. An old goat like Bewley might easily have been deceived."

"But you don't know!" Paula said. "Surely you don't think Maureen murdered her sister?"

"The incentive is pretty strong. Besides collecting a fortune of two million dollars there's also the little insurance item. I don't say she did it but that kind of money is a big temptation, especially if you are in the hands of a blackmailer. And another thing, I'm not entirely satisfied that Crosby himself wasn't murdered. If there had been nothing wrong about the shooting, why didn't Salzer call in someone like Bewley to sign the death certificate? Why sign it himself? He had to square Lessways, the coroner, and probably Brandon. It was either suicide or murder. I'm willing to bet it wasn't an accident. And as Willet pointed out, if a man owns a revolver he isn't likely to shoot himself with a shotgun. So that leaves murder."

"You're jumping to conclusions," Paula said sharply. "That's your big failing, Vic. You're always making wild guesses."

I winked at her.

"But how I do enjoy myself."

3

AS a form of relaxation I do jigsaw puzzles. Paula gets them for me from a legless hero she visits on her afternoon off. This guy spends all his time cutting jigsaws from railway posters Paula gets for him. They make terrific puzzles and one takes me about a month to do. Then I pass it on to a hospital and get another off Paula's pal.

From long experience in doing these puzzles I have found the apparently small and unimportant-looking piece is very often the key to the whole picture, and I'm always on the lookout for such a piece. In the same way, when I'm on a job I'm always on the lookout for some insignificant trifle that appears to have no bearing on the case, but very often has.

I had been sitting in my office for the past hour, brooding. The time was a few minutes past seven. The office was closed for the night. Only the whisky bottle remained.

I had jotted down a number of notes that looked impressive but didn't add up to much. And on reading through the list of likely clues I paused at Douglas Sherrill's name. Why, I asked myself, had Janet suddenly broken off the engagement a week before Macdonald Crosby's death? This fact didn't appear to have any bearing on the case, but it might have. I couldn't be sure until I found out just why the engagement had been broken off. Who could tell me? Douglas Sherrill obviously, but I couldn't go to him without tipping my hand, and I wasn't ready to do that at the moment. Then who else was there? I consulted my notes. John Stevens, Crosby's butler, was a possibility. I decided it wouldn't be a bad idea to see what kind of a guy Stevens was. If he looked as if he could be trusted it might pay me to take him into my confidence. Martha Bendix had said he now worked for Gregory Wainwright.

No time like the present I thought and looked Wainwright up in the book. I put through the call, and after the second or third ring a stately voice said, "This is Mr. Wainwright's residence."

"Is that Mr. John Stevens?" I asked.

There was a pause, the voice said cautiously, "Stevens speaking. Who is that, please?"

"My name is Malloy. Mr. Stevens, I would like to talk to

you about an important and private matter. It has to do with the Crosbys. Can you meet me sometime tonight?"

Again that pause.

"I don't understand." It was an old man's voice, gentle, and perhaps a little dull-witted. "I'm afraid I don't know you."

"Maybe you have heard of Universal Services."

Yes, he had heard of Universal Services.

"I run it," I said. "It is important for me to talk to you about the Crosbys."

"I don't think I have any right to discuss my last employer with you," he said distantly. "I'm sorry."

"It won't hurt you to hear what I have to say. After I have explained the position you may feel inclined to tell me what I want to know. If you don't there are no bones broken."

The pause was longer this time.

"Well I might meet you, but I can't promise . . ."

"That's all right Mr. Stevens. At the corner of Jefferson and Felman there's a cafe. We might meet there. What time would suit you?"

He said he would be there at nine.

"I'll be the guy wearing a hat and reading the *Evening Herald,*" I told him.

He said he would look out for me and hung up.

I had nearly two hours to wait before I met him, and so decided to pass the time at Finnegan's. It took me a few minutes to lock up the office. While I was turning keys, closing the safe, and shutting the windows, I thought about Nurse Gurney. Who had kidnapped her? Why had she been kidnapped? Was she still alive? Thoughts that got me nowhere but worried me. Still thinking, I went into the outer office, looked around to make sure the place was bedded down for the night, crossed the room, stepped into the hallway and locked the outer door behind me.

At the end of the corridor I noticed a short, stockily-built man lolling against the wall by the elevator doors and reading a newspaper. He didn't look up as I paused near him to thumb the button calling the elevator attendant. I gave him a casual glance. He was dark-skinned and his blunt-featured face was pock-marked. He looked like an Italian; could have been Spanish. His navy-blue serge suit was shiny at the elbows and his white shirt dirty at the cuffs.

The elevator attendant threw open the doors, and the Wop and I entered. On the third floor the elevator paused to pick up Manfred Willet who stared through me with blank eyes and then interested himself in the headlines of the evening paper. He had said he wanted secrecy, but I thought it was carrying it a little far not to know me in the elevator. Still, he was paying my fee so he could call the tune.

I bought an *Evening Herald* at the bookstall, giving Willet a chance to leave the building without falling over me. I watched him drive away in an Oldsmobile the size of a battleship. The Wop with the dirty shirt cuffs bad collapsed into one of the armchairs in the lobby and was reading his newspaper. I walked down the corridor to the back exit and across the alley to Finnegan's bar.

The saloon was full of smoke, hard characters, and loud voices. I had only taken a couple of steps towards my favorite table when Olaf Kruger, who runs a boxing academy on Princess Street, clutched hold of me.

Olaf was not much bigger than a jockey, bald as an egg, and as smart as they come.

"Hello Vic," he said, shaking hands. "Come on over and get drunk. Haven't seen you for weeks. What have I done?"

I pushed my way towards the bar and winked at Mike Finnegan as he toiled under the double row of neon lights, jerking beer.

"I've been to the fights pretty regular," I said as Olaf climbed up on a stool, elbowing a little space for himself with threatening gestures that no one took seriously. "Just didn't happen to see you. That boy O'Hara shapes well."

Olaf waved tiny hands at Finnegan.

"Whiskies, Mike," he bawled, in his shrill, piping voice. "O'Hara? Yeah, he shapes all right but he's a sucker for a cross counter. I keep telling him but he don't listen. One of these days he's going to meet a guy with the wind behind him, and then it's curtains."

We talked boxing for the next half-hour. There was nothing much else Olaf could talk about. While we talked, we ate our way through two club sandwiches apiece and drank three double whiskies.

Hughson, the *Herald's* sportswriter, joined us and insisted on buying another round of drinks. He was a tall, lean, cynical-looking bird, going bald, with liverish bags under his eyes and tobacco ash spread over his coat front. He was never without a cigar that smelled as if he had found it a couple of years ago in a garbage can. Probably he had.

After we had listened to three or four of his longwinded dirty stories, Olaf said, "What was that yarn about the Dixie Kid getting into a shindig last night? Anything to it?"

Hughson pulled a face.

"I don't know. The Kid won't talk. He had a shiner, if that means anything. One of the taxi-drivers on the pier said he swam ashore."

"If he was thrown off the *Dream Ship*, that's quite a swim," Olaf said, and grinned.

"You two guys talk to yourselves," I said, lighting a cigarette. "Don't mind me."

Hughson hooked nicotine-stained fingers into my breast

pocket.

"The Dixie Kid went out to the *Dream Ship* last night and got into an argument with Sherrill. Four bouncers are supposed to have tossed him overboard, but not before he's supposed to have socked Sherrill. There's a rumor Sherrill's going to bring an assault charge. If he does, the Kid's washed up. He's over his ears in debt now."

"It's my guess Sherrill will bring a suit," Olaf said, shaking his bald head. "He has a mean reputation for that kind of thing."

"He won't," Hughson said. "He can't afford the publicity. I told the Kid he was safe enough, but even at that the little rat won't talk."

"Who's Sherrill, anyway?" I asked as calmly as I could and crooked a finger at Finnegan to refill the glasses.

"You're not the only one who's asking that," Hughson told me. "No one knows. He's a mystery man. Came to Orchid City about a couple of years ago. He took a job selling real estate on commission for Selby & Lowenstein's. I believe he made a little money—not much, but enough to buy himself a small house on Rossmore Avenue. Then somehow or other he got himself engaged to Janet Crosby, the millionairess, but that didn't last long. He dropped out of sight for about six months and then suddenly reappeared as owner of the *Dream Ship*, a three hundred-ton schooner he's converted into a gambling den which he keeps anchored just outside the three-mile limit. He has a fleet of water taxis going to and fro, and the members of the club are as exclusive as the Governor's Ball."

"And gambling's not the only vice that goes on in that ship," Olaf said, and winked. "He's got half a dozen hand-picked girls on board. It's a sweet racket. Being three miles outside the city limits he can thumb his nose at Brandon. I bet he makes a pile of jack."

"What foxes me," Hughson said, reaching for the whisky I had bought him, "is how a heel like Sherrill ever found enough money to buy a goddamn great schooner like the *Dream Ship*."

"They say he floated a company," Olaf said. "If he had come to me and offered to sell me a piece of that ship, I'd have jumped at it. I bet whoever owns shares in her makes a packet, too."

I listened, thinking what a marvelous thing it was to meet two guys in a bar and hear the very thing I wanted to hear without even asking.

"That ship sounds fun," I said casually. "I wouldn't mind being a member."

Hughson sneered.

"And you're not the only one. You haven't a hope. Only guys in *Who's Who* stand a chance. Every member is handpicked. If you haven't got dough, Sherrill doesn't want you. The entrance fee is two hundred and fifty dollars, and the sub works out at five hundred a year. He caters for the big boys, not the proletariat."

"What kind of a guy is Sherrill?" I asked.

"One of those smooth Alecs," Hughson said. "Handsome, slick, tough, and bright. The kind of heel women fall for. Curly hair, blue eyes, big muscles, and dresses like a movie star. My idea of a genuine, top-drawer, son-of-a-bitch."

"Any idea why Janet Crosby broke the engagement?"

"That girl had sense. I don't know what happened, but it's my guess she saw the red light. All he was after was her money, and I guess she realized that before it was too late. Any girl who marries a runt like Sherrill is heading for trouble."

Olaf, who was getting bored with this conversation, said,

"Do you fellas think the Dixie Kid would make a show against O'Hara? I gotta chance to match him, but I'm not sure it would be much of a fight."

For the next fifteen minutes we argued back and forth about the Dixie Kid's merits, then looking at the clock above the bar I saw it was time I got moving.

"I'll have to leave you guys," I said, and slid off the stool. "I'll be around at the gym one of these days. See you then."

Olaf said he would be glad to see me any time, and would I give his best respects to Paula. Hughson said to tell Paula he dreamed of her most nights. I left them buying more whisky.

As I crossed the room to the exit I spotted the Wop with the dirty shirt cuffs sitting at a table near the door, still engrossed in his newspaper, and as I pushed open the double swing doors he casually folded the paper, shoved it into his pocket and got to his feet.

I walked swiftly to where I had parked the Buick, got in, started the engine and drove down the dark alley. From somewhere in the rear another car engine roared into life and a set of parking lights swam into my driving-mirror.

I drove along Princess Street, keeping my eye on the mirror. The car following me was a Lincoln. The blue, tinted windshield prevented me from seeing the driver but I guessed who it was.

At the bottom of Princess Street I turned right into Felman Street. The traffic was thinning out and I drove fast, but the Lincoln had no trouble sitting on my tail. Ahead of me I could see the red neon sign of the cafe where I had arranged to meet John Stevens. Just before I reached the cafe I pulled sharply into the curb and braked hard. The Lincoln was following me too closely to do anything but drive straight on. It went past, slowing down.

I nipped out of the Buick and dodged into a dark shop doorway. The Lincoln had pulled into the curb fifty yards ahead. The Wop got out and looked down the street without attempting to conceal his actions. He was quick enough to spot I had left the Buick, and he walked towards my parked car, his hands buried deep in his coat pockets.

I stepped back into the shadows and watched him glance into the empty car, look right and left, then walk on. He didn't seem disconcerted when he couldn't see me but continued on down the street just like any Spick out for an airing.

I watched him out of sight, then crossed the street by way of the underpass and nipped into the cafe.

The wall clock facing me as I entered showed five minutes to nine o'clock. There were only about half a dozen people at the tables: a blonde bobbysoxer and her boy, two elderly men playing chess, two women with shopping bags, and a girl with a thin, pinched face at a corner table, drinking milk.

I picked a table away from the door and sat down, opened the *Evening Herald* and spread it on the table. Then I lit a cigarette and wondered about the Wop. Was he another of Salzer's playmates or was he a new angle in this business? He was tailing me all right, and doing a very bad job of it. Either that or he didn't care if I knew he was after me. I had taken a note of his car license number. Another little job for Mifflin, I thought, and that reminded me. I turned to the sports pages and checked the races. Crab Apple had won her race. Well that was all right. Mifflin wouldn't mind checking the car number now he had made a little money.

On the stroke of nine the double glass doors pushed open and a tall old man came in. I knew he was Stevens the moment I saw him. He looked like an archbishop on vacation. He came towards me with that stately walk butlers have when they come in to announce dinner is served. The expression on his face was slightly forbidding, and there was a cautious, distant look in his eyes.

I stood up.

"Mr. Stevens?"

He nodded.

"I'm Malloy. Sit down, will you? Have a coffee?"

He put his bowler hat on one of the chairs and sat down. Yes, he would have a coffee.

To save time I went to the counter, ordered two coffees and carried them over. The bobbysoxer was staring at Stevens and giggling with the bad manners of the very young. She said something to her boy, a fresh-faced youth in a striped jersey and a college cap at the back of his head. He looked over at Stevens and grinned. Maybe they thought it was funny for an archbishop to come to a help-yourself cafe or maybe the bowler hat amused them.

I put the two cups on the table.

"Nice of you to come, Mr. Stevens," I said, and offered him a cigarette. While he was lighting it I studied him. He was all right. The faithful family retainer who could keep his mouth shut. He could be trusted but the trouble would be to get him to talk. "What I have to say is in strict confidence," I went on, sitting down. "I've been hired to investigate Miss Janet Crosby's death. A certain party isn't entirely satisfied she died of heart failure."

He stiffened and sat bolt upright.

"Who is the certain party?" he asked. "Surely it's little late for an investigation?"

"I'd rather not say at the moment," I told him. "I agree it is late, but only within the past few days have certain facts come to light that make an investigation necessary. Do you think Janet Crosby died of heart failure?"

He hesitated.

"It's not my business," he said reluctantly. "Since you ask me, I admit it was a great shock to me. She seemed such an active young person. But Dr. Salzer assured me that in her case a sudden stoppage of an artery would cause heart failure without previous symptoms. All the same I found it hard to believe."

"I wonder if you have any idea why Miss Crosby broke off her engagement with Douglas Sherrill?"

"I'm afraid I couldn't tell you that without knowing who is making this investigation," he said primly. "I have heard of your organization and I believe it is well spoken of, but I am not prepared to gossip about my late employer unless I know who I am dealing with."

That was as far as we ever got.

There was a sudden frozen stillness in the cafe that made me look up sharply.

The double glass doors swung open, and four men walked in. Two of them carried Thompson submachineguns, the other two had Colt automatics in their hands Four dark-skinned Wops: one of them was my pal with the dirty shirt cuffs. The two with the Thompsons fanned out and stood either side of the room where they had a clear field of fire. The Wop with the dirty cuffs and a little dago with red-rimmed eyes marched across the room towards my table.

Stevens gave a kind of strangled grunt and started to his feet, but I grabbed him and shoved him back on his chair.

"Take it easy," I hissed at him.

"All right, hold it!" one of the Wops with the Thompson said. His voice cut through the silent room like a bullet through a ton of ice cream. "Sit still, and keep your yaps shut or we'll put the blast on the lot of you!"

Everyone sat or stood as still as death. The scene looked

like a stage set in a waxworks show. There was a bartender with his hand frozen on the soda pump, his eyes goggling. One of the elderly men's fingers rested on his Queen as he was moving it to checkmate his friend. His face was tight with horror. The thin, pinched-looking girl sat with her eyes tight closed and her hands across her mouth. The bobby-soxer leaned forward, her pretty, painted mouth hanging open and a shrill scream in her eyes.

As the Wop passed her, the scream popped out of her mouth. It made a shrill, jarring sound in the silent room, and cursing, the Wop hit her savagely with his gun barrel across her cute, silly little hat. He hit very hard and the barrel made an ugly sound as it thudded on the straw of the hat, crushing it into her skull. She fell out of the chair, and blood began to run from her ears, making a puddle on the floor. The kid with her turned the color of a fish's belly and began to retch.

"Quiet everybody!" the guy with the Thompson said, raising his voice.

I could see by the look of these Wops that if anyone made a move they would start shooting. They were ruthless, murderous and trigger-happy. All they wanted was an excuse. There was nothing I could do about it. Even if I had a gun I wouldn't have started anything. A gun against two Thompsons is as useless as a toothpick against a meat cleaver, and I wouldn't have been the only one to have got shot up.

The two Wops arrived at my table.

I sat like a stone man, my hands on the table, looking up at them. I could hear Stevens breathing painfully at my side: the breath snored through his nostrils as if he were going to have a stroke.

The Wop with the dirty cuffs grinned evilly at me.

"Make a move, you son-of-a-bitch, and I'll drop your guts

on the floor," he said.

Both of them were careful to keep out of the line of fire of the Thompsons.

The Wop reached out and grabbed Stevens by his arm.

"Come on, you. You're going for a little ride."

"Leave him alone," I said through tight lips.

The Wop smacked me across the face with the gun barrel. Not too hard, but hard enough to hurt.

"Shut your yap!" he said.

The other Wop had rammed his gun into Stevens' side and was dragging him out of his chair.

"Don't touch me," Stevens gasped, and feebly tried to break the Wop's hold. Snarling, the Wop clubbed him with his fist, caught him by his collar and hauled him away from the table.

My pal with the dirty cuffs stepped away from me and the guy with the Thompson came a little closer, the gun sight centered on my chest. I sat still, holding the side of my face, feeling blood against my fingers, hot and sticky.

Stevens fell down.

"Come on, hurry," the Wop with the dirty cuffs said furiously. "Get this dumb old punk out of here." He bent and grabbed hold of one of Stevens' ankles. The other Wop caught hold of the other ankle, and they ran across the room dragging Stevens along on his back with them, upsetting tables and chairs in their progress to the door.

They kicked open the double doors and dragged the old man across the sidewalk to a waiting car. Two other Wops were standing outside with machineguns, threatening a gaping crowd lined up on either side of the cafe entrance.

It was the coolest, nerviest, most cold-blooded thing I have ever seen.

The two Wops with the Thompsons backed out of the cafe

and scrambled into the car. One of the Wops in the street swung around and started firing through the plate-glass window at me. I was expecting that, and even as he swung around I threw myself out of my chair and lay flat under the table, squeezing myself into the floor. Slugs chewed up the wall just above me and brought plaster down on my head and neck. One slug took the heel of my shoe off. Then the firing stopped and I peered around the table in time to see the Wop spring on to the running-board of the car as it shot away from the curb and went tearing down the street.

I scrambled to my feet and made a dive for the telephone.

4

THE VOICE sounded like an echo in a tunnel. It crept into the corners of my room—the subdued whisper of a turned-down radio. For the past half-hour I had been waiting for that voice. The jigsaw puzzle spread out on the table before me interested me as much as the dead mouse I had found in the trap this morning . . . probably a little less. The shaded reading lamp made a pool of lonely light on the carpet. A bottle and glass stood on the floor within easy reach. Already I had had a drink or perhaps even two or three. After an evening like this a drink one way or other doesn't make a great deal of difference.

I was still a little jumpy. No one likes to have a whole magazine of a submachinegun fired at him, and I was no exception. The way those two Wops had dragged that old man out of the cafe haunted me. I felt I should have done something about it. After all it was my fault he was there.

"At nine o'clock this evening," the announcer said, breaking into my thoughts, "six men, believed to be Italians, armed with machineguns and automatics, entered the Blue Bird Cafe at the corner of Jefferson and Felman. While two of the gunmen guarded the entrance, and two more terrorized the people in the cafe, the remaining two seized John Stevens and dragged him from the cafe to a waiting car.

"Stevens, who will be remembered by the city's socialites as butler to Mr. Gregory Wainwright, the steel millionaire, was later found dead by the side of the Los Angeles and San Francisco Highway. It is believed he died of a stroke, brought on by the rough handling he received from the kidnappers, and when he was found to be dead, the kidnappers brutally threw his body from the speeding car."

The announcer's voice was as unemotional and as cold as if he were reading the pork belly prices. I should have liked to have been behind him with a machinegun and livened him up with a burst above his head.

"The police are anxious for any information that will lead to the arrest of the criminals," the announcer went on. "These six men have been described as short, stocky, dark-skinned, and all wearing blue suits and black hats.

"The police are also anxious to question an unknown man who was with John Stevens when the kidnappers arrived. After telephoning police headquarters, giving a description of the criminals and the number of their car, he disappeared. Eyewitnesses have described him as tall, powerfully-built, dark hair, sallow complexion and sharp-featured. He has a wound on the right side of his face from a blow from one of the kidnappers. Anyone recognizing this man should communicate immediately to Captain of Police Brandon, Police Headquarters, Graham 3444 . . ."

I leaned forward and snapped down the switch.

"Sallow and sharp-featured, but not handsome. No one said he was handsome."

I turned slowly in my chair.

Sergeant MacGraw stood in the open French windows, and behind him lurked Sergeant Hartsell.

I didn't jump more than a foot. It was one of those reflex actions over which I had no control.

"Who told you to blow in?" I asked, getting to my feet.

"He wants to know who told us to blow in," MacGraw said, speaking out of the side of his mouth. "Shall we tell him?"

Hartsell came into the room. There was a cold, bleak look on his thin face, his deep-set eyes were stony.

"Yeah, tell him."

MacGraw closed the French windows without taking his eyes off me.

"A little bird told us," he said, and winked. "There's always a little bird to tell us the things we want to know. And the little bird also told us you were with Stevens tonight."

I sweated gently. Maybe it was because it was a hot night. Maybe I didn't like the look of these two. Maybe I was remembering what Brandon had said about a beating up in a dark alley.

"That's right," I said. "I was with him."

"Now that's what I call being smart," MacGraw said, and beamed. "Wonder Boy tells the truth for a change." He poked a thick finger in my direction. "Why didn't you stick around? The prowl boys would have liked to have talked to you."

"There was nothing I could tell them," I said. "I gave the desk sergeant a description of the car and the men. That let me out, and besides, I had enough for one night so I blew."

MacGraw sat down in one of the armchairs, felt in his inside pocket and hooked out a cigar. He bit off the end, spat the shred pf tobacco messily against my wall and lit up.

"I like that," he said, rolling thick smoke around in his

mouth before releasing it. "You had enough for one night. Yeah, that's very nice. But pally, how wrong you are. The night hasn't even started for you yet."

I didn't say anything.

"Let's get going," Hartsell said in a hard voice. "I'm on duty in another hour."

MacGraw frowned at him.

"Take it easy, can't you? What's it matter if you are a little late? We're on duty right now, aren't we?" He glanced at me. "What were you talking to Stevens about?"

"I wanted to know if he was satisfied Janet Crosby died of heart failure. He wasn't."

MacGraw chuckled and rubbed his big white hands together. He seemed genuinely pleased to hear this.

"You know the Captain's no fool," he said to Hartsell. "I'm not saying he's everyone's bedfellow, but he's no fool. Those were his very words. 'I'll bet that son-of-a-bitch was talking to Stevens about the Crosbys.' That's what he said to me as soon as we got the description. And he was right."

Hartsell gave me a long, mean look.

"Yeah," he said.

"Was that all you wanted to know, Wonder Boy?" MacGraw asked. "Or were there other questions you asked Stevens?"

"That's all I wanted to know."

"Didn't the Captain tell you to lay off the Crosbys?"

Now it was coming.

"He mentioned it."

"Maybe you think the Captain talks just to hear his own voice?"

I looked from MacGraw to Hartsell and back to MacGraw again.

"I don't know. Why not ask him?"

"Don't get tricky, Wonder Boy. We don't like 'em tricky, do we, Joe?"

Hartsell made an impatient movement.

"For Pete's sake, let's get on with it," he said.

"Get on with—what?" I asked.

MacGraw leaned forward to spit at the wall again. Then he scattered ash on the carpet.

"The Captain didn't seem happy about you, pally," he said, and grinned. "And when the Captain's unhappy he gets sore, and when he gets sore he takes it out of the boys, so we thought we'd better make him happy again. We figured the way to get his smile back would be to come and see you and give you a little workout. We thought it would be a good idea to sort of smack your ears down; maybe tear them off. Then we thought it would be another good idea to sort of wreck your place; kick the furniture around and hack bits out of the wall. That's the way we figured it, didn't we, Joe?"

Hartsell licked his thin lips and allowed a leer to come into his stony eyes. He took out a short length of rubber hose from his hip pocket and balanced it lovingly in his hand.

"Yeah," he said.

"And did you think what would happen if you carried out these good ideas?" I asked. "Did it ever occur to you I might sue for assault, and that someone like Manfred Willet might take you apart in court and get the badge off your coats? Did that come into your sweet little minds or was that something you overlooked?"

MacGraw leaned forward and screwed his burning cigar down on the polished surface of the table. He glanced up, grinning.

"You're not the first punk we've called on, Wonder Boy," he told me. "And you won't be the last. We know how to take care of lawyers. A lush like Willet doesn't scare us, and besides you won't take us to court. We came here to get a statement from you about Stevens. For some reason or other—maybe you don't like our faces, maybe you're a little drunk, maybe you have a boil where it hurt—anything will do, you get tough. In fact, Wonder Boy, you get very tough indeed; so tough me and Joe have to sort of restrain you, and while we're restraining you as gently as we possibly can, you get a little roughed up and the room sort of gets wrecked. But it's not our fault. We don't like it that way—not much, anyway, and if you hadn't disliked our faces or hadn't been a little drunk or hadn't had a boil where it hurts, it wouldn't have happened. That's what they call in court your word against two respectable, hard-working police officers', and even a lush like Willet couldn't make much out of it, and besides that we could take you to headquarters and keep you in a nice quiet cell where the boys could drop in from time to time and wipe their boots on your face. It's a funny thing, but a lot of our boys like dropping in on certain of our prisoners and wiping their boots on their faces. I don't know why it is; probably they're high-spirited. So don't let's have any more talk about assault charges and badges off coats and smart lawyers; not unless you don't know what's good for you."

I had a sudden cold feeling in my stomach. It would be my word against theirs. There was nothing to stop them arresting me and slinging me into a cell. By the time Willet got moving a lot of things could have happened. This didn't seem to be my evening for fun and games.

"Got it all worked out, haven't you?" I said as calmly as the circumstances allowed.

"We've got to, pally," MacGraw said, grinning. "There are too many punks making trouble, and our jail isn't that large. So we just hand out a little discipline every now and then and save the city some dough."

I should have kept my eyes on Hartsell who was standing a few feet to my left and rear. Not that I could have done a great deal about it. They had me and I knew it, and what was worse, they knew it too. But all the same I was dumb not to have watched him. I heard a sudden swish and began to duck, but I was much, much too late. The rubber hose caught me on the top of the head, and I fell forward on hands and knees.

MacGraw was waiting for that, and his foot shot out; the square steel-tipped toe of his shoe caught me in the throat. I fell over on my side, trying to get breath through a constricted, contracting windpipe. Something hit me on the forearm sending pain crawling up into my skull. Something thudded on the back of my neck; a sharp something crashed into my ribs.

I rolled away, got on my hands and knees, saw Hartsell coming at me and tried to duck. The hose seemed to bounce against my brain; just as if the top of my head had been trepanned and my brain was there to be hit. I sprawled on to the carpet, clenching my fists, holding back the yell that tried to burst its way out of me.

Hands grabbed me and hauled me to my feet. Through a misty-red curtain MacGraw seemed over-large, over-broad and over-ugly. I began to fall forward as he released me. I fell on his fist that was travelling towards me in a punch that sent me reeling across the room, knocking over the table. I landed on my back amid a shower of jigsaw puzzle pieces.

I lay still. The light in the ceiling came rushing towards me, stopped, and then rushed away again. It did that several times, so I dosed my eyes. At the back of my mind I was thinking this could go on and on until they were tired, and it would take a lot to tire a couple of thugs like MacGraw and Hartsell. By the time they were through with me there wouldn't be a great deal left. I wondered dreamily why they didn't move in; why they left me laying on the floor. So long as I didn't move the pain that rode me was bearable. I didn't like to think what would happen to my head if I did move. It felt as if it were hanging on a thread. One little movement would be enough to send it rolling across the floor.

Out of the pain and the mist I heard a woman say, "Is this your idea of fun?"

A woman!

That last punch must have made me slug-happy, I thought, or maybe it was the beating I had taken on top of my head.

"This guy's dangerous, ma'am," MacGraw said in a gentle, little-boy-caught-in-the-pantry voice. "He was resisting arrest."

"Don't you dare lie to me!" It was a woman's voice all right. "I saw what happened through the window."

I wasn't going to miss this, even if it killed me. Very carefully I raised my head. All the veins, arteries and nerves in it yelled murder, pulsed, expanded and became generally hysterical, but I managed to sit up. The light dug arrows into my eyes, and for a moment or so I held my head in my hands. Then I peeped through my fingers.

MacGraw and Hartsell were standing by the door looking as if their feet were resting on a red-hot stove. MacGraw had a cringing this-has-really-nothing-to-do-with-me smile on his face. Hartsell looked as if a mouse had run up his trousers leg.

I turned, keeping my head still, and looked towards the French windows.

A girl stood between the half-drawn curtains; a girl in a white strapless evening-gown that showed off her deeply-tanned shoulders and the snug little hollow between her breasts. Her raven-black hair lay about her shoulders in a pageboy bob. I had a little trouble in focusing, and her beauty came to me slowly, like a picture thrown on the screen by an amateur projectionist. The blurred outlines of her face slowly became sharp-etched. The misty hollows that were her eyes filled in and came alive. An oval, small-featured, very lovely face with a small, perfectly-molded nose, red sensual lips and wide, big eyes as dark and as hard as nuggets of coal.

Even with the blood pounding in my head and my throat aching and my body feeling as if it had been fed through a wringer, I felt the impact of this girl's allurement the way I had felt the impact of MacGraw's fist. She not only had the looks, but she also had that thing—you could see it there in her eyes, in the way she stood, in the curves of her body, in the tanned column of her throat—shouting at you like the twenty-foot letters on an advertising hoarding.

"How dare you beat this man!" she said in a voice which carried across the room with the heat and the force of a flamethrower. "Is this Brandon's idea?"

"Now look, Miss Crosby," MacGraw said pleadingly. "This guy's been sticking his snout into your affairs. The Captain thought maybe we should discourage him. Honest, that's all there is to it."

For the first time as far as I knew she turned her head to stare at me. I couldn't have looked a particularly pretty object. I knew I had collected a number of bumps and bruises and the cut on my right cheek where the Wop had hit me was bleeding again. Somehow I managed to grin at her . . . a little crooked, not much heart in it, but still, a grin.

She looked at me the way you look at a frog that's jumped into your morning cup of coffee.

"Get up!" she snapped. "You can't be as badly hurt as all

that."

But then she hadn't been slapped over the skull three or four times or kicked in the throat and ribs or punched in the jaw, so it wasn't fair to expect her to know if I was badly hurt or not.

Maybe it was because she was such a lovely that I made the effort and somehow got to my feet. We Malloys have our pride and we don't like our women to think we are soft. I had to grab hold of the back of a chair as soon as I was on my feet, and I very nearly spread out on the floor again, but by clinging on and riding the pain that went shooting down into my heels and back again to my skull like a rollercoaster gone haywire, I began to come out of it and get what is termed my second wind.

MacGraw and Hartsell were looking at me the way tigers look at a lump of meat that's been sneaked out of their cage.

She began speaking to them again in that scornful, blistering voice:

"I don't like your sort. And I'm going to do something about it. If this is the way Brandon runs his police force the sooner he gets the hell out of it the better!"

While MacGraw was mumbling excuses, I set my compass and steered a zigzag course towards the overturned whisky bottle. The cork was well home so no damage had been done. It was quite a feat to bend and pick it up, but I managed it. I anchored myself to the mouthpiece and drank.

"And before you go you're having a taste of your own medicine," she was saying, and as I lowered the bottle, she thrust the rubber sap she had picked up towards me. "Go on, hit them!" she said viciously. "Get your own back!"

I took the cosh because otherwise she would probably have pushed it down my throat, and I looked at Hartsell and MacGraw, who stared back at me like two pigs waiting to have their throats slit.

"Hit them!" she repeated, her voice rising. "It's time someone did. They'll take it. I'll see to that."

It was an extraordinary thing, but I was pretty sure they would have stood there and let me beat their heads off.

I tossed the cosh on to the settee.

"Not me Lady, that's not the way I get my fun," I said, my voice sounding like a record being played with a blunt gramophone needle.

"Hit them!" she commanded furiously. "What are you frightened of? They won't dare touch you again. Beat them up!"

"Sorry," I said. "It wouldn't amuse me. Let's turn them out. They're lousing up the room."

She turned, snatched up the cosh and walked up to Mac-Graw. His white face turned yellow, but he didn't move. Her arm flashed up and she hit him across his face. An ugly red weal sprang up on his flabby cheek. He gave a whimpering grunt, but he still didn't move.

As her arm flashed up again I grabbed her wrist and snatched the cosh out of her hand. The effort cost me a stab of pain through the head and a hard-stinging slap across the face from Miss Spitfire. She tried to get the sap from me but I held on to her wrists and yelled, "Beat it, you two lugs! Beat it before she knocks the hell out of you!"

Holding her was like holding an angry tigress. She was surprisingly strong. As I wrestled with her MacGraw and Hartsell charged out of the room as if the devil was after them. They fell down the steps in their hurry to get away. When I heard their car start up, I released her wrists and stepped away.

"Take it easy," I said, panting with my exertions. "They've gone now."

For a moment she stood gasping, her face set and her eyes blazing; a lovely thing of fury, and then the anger went and her eyes lost their explosive quality and she suddenly threw back her head and laughed.

"Well, we certainly scared the daylights out of those two rats, didn't we?" she said, and flopped limply on the settee. "Give me a drink and have one yourself. You certainly look as if you need one."

As I reached for the bottle I said, looking at her intently, "The name, of course, is Maureen Crosby?"

"You've guessed it." She rubbed her wrists, making a comical grimace. "You've hurt me, you brute!"

"Sorry," I said, and meant it.

"Lucky I looked in. If I hadn't, they would have had your hide by now."

"So they would," I said, pouring four fingers of scotch into a glass. My hand was very unsteady and some of the whisky splashed onto the carpet. I handed her the glass and began to fix myself a drink. "Whiterock or water?"

"In its bare skin," she returned, holding the glass up to the light. "I don't believe in mixing business with pleasure or water with scotch. Do you?"

"It depends on the business and the scotch," I said, and sat down. My legs felt as if the shin bones bad been removed. "So, you are Maureen Crosby. Well, well, quite the last person I expected to call on me."

"I thought you would be surprised." There was a mocking expression in the dark eyes and the smile was calculated.

"How's the drug cure going?" I asked, watching her. "I've always heard a dopey should lay off liquor."

She continued to smile, but her eyes were not amused.

"You shouldn't believe all you hear."

I drank some of the whisky. It was very strong. I shuddered and put the glass on the table.

"I don't. I hope you don't either."

We sat for a long moment, looking at each other. She had the knack of making her face expressionless without losing her loveliness which was quite an achievement.

"Don't let's get complicated. I'm here to talk to you. You're making a lot of trouble. Isn't it time you took your little spade and dug in someone else's graveyard?"

I made believe to think this over.

"Are you just asking or is this a proposition?" I said finally.

Her mouth tightened and the smile went away.

"Can you be bought? I was told you were one of those clean, simple, non-grafting characters. I was particularly advised not to offer you money."

I reached for a cigarette.

"I thought we had agreed we didn't believe all we heard," I said, leaning forward to offer the cigarette. She took it, so I had to reach for another. Lighting hers caused me another stab of pain in the head and didn't improve my temper.

"It could be a proposition," she said, leaning back and blowing smoke at the ceiling. "How much?"

"What are you trying to buy?"

She studied the cigarette as if she hadn't seen one before, said, without looking at me, "I don't want trouble. You're making trouble. I might pay you to stop."

"What's it worth?"

She looked at me then.

"You know you're a big disappointment to me. You're just like any of the other slimy little blackmailers."

"You'd know about them, of course."

"Yes, I know all about them. And when I tell you what I think it's worth I suppose you will laugh the way they always laugh and raise the ante. So, you will tell me what it's worth to you and give me the chance to laugh."

I suddenly didn't want to go on with this. Maybe my head was aching too badly; maybe, even, I found her so attractive I didn't want her to think me a heel.

"All right, let's skip it," I said. "I was kidding. I can't be bought. Maybe I could be persuaded. What makes you think I'm stirring up trouble? State your case. If it's any good I might take my spade and go dig elsewhere."

She regarded me for perhaps ten seconds, thoughtfully, silently, and a little doubtfully.

"You shouldn't kid about those things," she said seriously. "You might get yourself disliked. I wouldn't like to dislike you unless I had a reason."

I leaned back in the chair and closed my eyes.

"That's fine. Are you just talking to gain time or do you mean that?"

"I was told you had the manners of a hog and a way with women. The hog part is right."

I opened my eyes to leer at her.

"The woman part is on the level too, but don't rush me."

Then the telephone rang, startling us both. It was right by me, and as I reached for it she dipped swiftly into her handbag and brought out a .25 automatic. She pushed the gun against the side of my head, the little barrel rested on my skin.

"Sit where you are," she said, and there was a look in her eyes that froze me. "Leave the telephone alone!"

We sat like that while the bell rang and rang. The shrill sound gnawed at my nerves, bounced on the silent walls of the room, crept through the closed French windows and lost itself in the sea.

"What's the idea?" I asked, drawing back slowly. I didn't

like the feel of the gun against my face.

"Shut up!" There was a rasp in her voice. "Sit still!"

Finally, the bell got tired of ringing and stopped. She stood up.

"Come on, we're getting out of here," and again the automatic threatened me.

"Where are we going?" I asked, not moving.

"Away from telephones. Come on if you don't want to get shot in the leg."

But it wasn't the thought of being shot in the leg that made me go with her, it was my curiosity. I was very, very curious because all of a sudden she was frightened. I could see the fear in her eyes as plainly as I could see the little hollow between her breasts.

As we walked down the steps to a car parked just outside my front gate, the telephone began to ring again.

5

THE CAR was a streamlined black Rolls, and its power and pace was tremendous. There was nothing about the car to convey a feeling of speed: no sway, no roll, no sound from the engine. Only the thunder of the wind ripping along the streamlined roof and the black, blurred smudge of a madly-rushing night told me the needle of the speedometer, flickering on ninety, wasn't fooling.

I sat beside Maureen Crosby in what felt like a low-slung armchair and stared at the dazzling pool of light that lay on the road ahead of us and that fled before us like a scared ghost.

She had whipped the car along Orchid Boulevard, blasting a path for herself through the theatre traffic by the strident, arrogant use of the horn. She overtook cars in the teeth of oncoming traffic, slipping between diminishing gaps and a certain head-on crash by the thickness of her fender paint-work. She stormed up the broad, dark Monte Verde Avenue and onto San Diego Highway. It was when she got on to the six-traffic-lane highway she really began to drive, overtaking everything that moved on the road with a silent rush that must have made the drivers start right out of their skins.

I had no idea where we were going, and when I began to say something, she cut me off with a curt, "Don't talk! I want to think." So, I gave myself up to the mad rush into the darkness, admiring the way she handled the car, sinking back into the luxury of the seat and hoping we wouldn't hit anything.

San Diego Highway makes its way through a flat desert of sand dunes and scrub and comes out suddenly right by the ocean, and then cuts in again to the desert. Instead of keeping to the highway when we reached the sea, she slowed down to a loitering sixty, and swung off the road onto a narrow track that kept us by the sea. The track began to climb steeply and the sea dropped below us until we breasted the hill and came out onto a cliff head. We were slowing down all the time and were now crawling along at a bare thirty. After the speed we had been travelling at, we scarcely seemed to be moving. The glaring headlights picked out a notice: *Private. Positively No Admittance*, at the head of another narrow track lined on either side by tall scrub bushes. She swung the car into it, and the car fitted the track like a hand fits in a glove. We drove around bends and hairpin corners, getting nowhere as far as I could see. After some minutes she slowed down and stopped before a twelve-foot gate smothered in barbed wire. She tapped her horn button three times: short, sharp blasts that echoed in the still air and was still coming back at us when the gate swung open apparently of its own accord.

"Very, very tricky," I said.

She didn't say anything nor look at me but drove on, and, looking back I saw the gate swing shut. I wondered suddenly if I was being kidnapped the way Nurse Gurney had been kidnapped. Maybe the whisky I had swallowed was taking a hold, for I really didn't care. I felt it would be nice to have a little sleep. The clock on the dashboard showed two minutes to midnight—my bedtime.

Then suddenly the track began to broaden out into a driveway, and we slipped through another twelve-foot gate standing open, and again looking back, I saw it swing shut behind us as if closed by an invisible hand.

Into the glare of the headlights appeared a chalet-styled wooden house, screened by flowering shrubs and blossoming tung trees. Lights showed through the windows of the ground floor. An electric lantern shed a bright light on the steps leading to the front door. She pulled up, opened the car door and slid out. I got out more slowly. A terraced garden built into the cliff spread out before me in the moonlight. At the bottom, and it looked a long way down, I could see a big swimming pool. The sea provided a soft background of sound and glittered in the far distance. The scent of flowers hung in the hot night air in overpowering profusion.

"Is all this yours?" I asked.

She was standing by my side. The top of her sleek dark hair was in line with my shoulder.

"Yes." After a pause she said, "I'm sorry about the gun but I had to get you here quickly."

"I would have come without the gun."

"But not before you had answered the telephone. It was very important for you not to answer it."

"Look, I have a headache and I'm tired. I've been kicked in the throat, and although I'm tough, I have still been kicked in the throat. All I ask is for you not to be mysterious. Will you tell me why you have brought me here? Why it was important I shouldn't answer the telephone and what you want with me?"

"Of course. Shall we go in?" I'll get you a drink."

We went up the steps. The front door stood open, and we walked into a lobby, then through an archway into a big lounge that ran the width of the house. It was everything you would expect a millionairess to have. No money had been spared. The color scheme was cream and magenta, and the room was showy without being vulgar. Not my idea of a room, but then I run to very simple tastes.

"Let's sit on the verandah," she said. "Will you go through? I'll bring the drinks."

"Are you alone here?"

"Except for a servant. She won't worry us."

I walked out onto the verandah. There was one of those big swing lounging seats about ten feet long arranged so you could sit and admire the view; as a view it was well worth admiring. I dropped on to a soft leather cushion and stared at the distant sea. All the time I had been in the car I had been wondering what she wanted with me. I still wondered.

She came out after a few minutes, pushing a trolley on which were bottles, glasses and an ice-pail. She sat down at one end of the seat. There was about eight feet of leather and space between us.

"Whisky?"

"Thank you."

I watched her pour the whisky. Dark blue lights in the verandah roof made enough light for me to see her, but not enough to try the eyes. I thought she was about the loveliest lovely I had ever seen. Even her movements were a pleasure to watch.

We were both careful not to say anything while she poured the drinks. She offered me a cigarette and I took it. I lit hers, then mine.

We were now ready to begin but she still seemed reluctant to say anything, and I wasn't chancing a wrong remark that might put her off. We stared at the garden, the sea, and the moon while the hands of my wristwatch moved on.

She said suddenly, "I'm sorry about the way I—I acted. I mean offering you money to leave me alone. I know it was the wrong approach, but I didn't want to give anything away until I had had a chance to find out what kind of man you are. The fact is I want your help. I'm in a mess, and I don't know how to get out of it. I've been an awful fool, and I'm scared. I'm scared out of my wits."

She didn't look scared, but I didn't tell her so.

"I wish I knew for certain if he knows of this place," she went on, as if talking to herself. "If he does, he's certain to come here."

"Suppose we take this nice and slow?" I said mildly. "We have all the time in the world. Why was it important I shouldn't answer the telephone? Let's start with that one."

"Because he would know where you were, and he's looking for you," she said, as if she were talking to a dim-witted child.

"You haven't told me who he is. Is it Sherrill?"

"Of course," she said shortly.

"Why is he looking for me?"

"He doesn't want trouble, and you're making trouble. He's determined to get rid of you. I heard him tell Francini to do it."

"Is Francini a little Wop with pockmarks on his face?"

"Yes."

"And he works for Sherrill?"

"Yes."

"So it was Sherrill who engineered Stevens' kidnapping?"

"Yes. That settled it for me. When I heard the poor old man had died, I came straight to you."

"Does Sherrill know you have this place?"

She shook her head.

"I don't think so. I've never talked about it and he hasn't ever been here. But he might know. There's very little he doesn't know."

"All right, now we have got that ironed out, suppose we begin at the beginning?"

"I want to ask you something first," she said. "Why did you come to Crestways, asking for me? Why did you go and talk to Dr. Bewley? Has anyone hired you to find out what I have been doing?"

"Yes," I said.

"Who?"

"Your sister, Janet," I told her.

If I had hit her across the face she wouldn't have reacted more violently. She reared back in the seat as if she had trodden on a snake, making the swing rock violently.

"Janet?" The word came out in a horrified whisper. "But Janet's dead. What do you mean? How can you say such a thing!"

I took out my wallet, found Janet's letter and held it out to her.

"Read this."

"What is it?" she asked and seemed afraid to look at it.

"Read it and look at the date. It was mislaid for fourteen months. I only read it myself for the first time a day or so ago."

She took the letter. Her face stiffened and the pupils of her eyes contracted at the sight of the handwriting. After she had read it she sat still for several minutes, staring at it. I didn't hurry her. Fear, real and undisguised, was plain to see on her face.

"And this—this started you making inquiries?" she asked at last.

"Your sister sent me five hundred dollars. I felt bound to earn it. I came out to Crestways to see you and talk it over. If you had been there and had explained the letter, I should have returned the money and dropped the inquiry. But you weren't there. Then all kinds of things started to happen, so I continued the investigation."

"I see."

I waited for her to say something else, but she didn't. She sat still, staring at the letter, her face white and her eyes hard.

"Were you being blackmailed?" I asked.

"No. I don't know why she wrote to you. I suppose she was trying to make trouble. She was always trying to make trouble for me. She hated me."

"Why did she hate you?"

She stared down at the garden for a long time without saying anything. I drank some of the whisky and smoked. If she was going to tell me she would in her own time. She wasn't the type to be rushed.

"I don't know what to do," she said. "If I tell you why she hated me I'll be putting myself entirely at your mercy. You could ruin me."

I didn't have anything to say to that.

"But if I don't tell you," she went on, clenching her fists, "I don't know how I'm going to get out of this mess. I must have someone I can trust."

"Haven't you a lawyer?" I said, for something to say.

"He would be worse than useless. He's my trustee. By the terms of my father's will if I get involved in a scandal, I lose everything. And I'm up to my ears in what would be a horrific scandal if it got out."

"You mean with Sherrill?" I said. "Did you finance the *Dream Ship*?"

She stiffened, turned, stared at me.

"You know that?"

"I don't know it. I'm making a guess. If it got out you were behind the *Dream Ship* it would make a scandal."

"Yes." She suddenly moved along the seat so she was close to me. "Janet was in love with Douglas. I was crazy about him too. I stole him from her. She tried to shoot me, but father saved me. He was shot instead of me," she blurted out and hid her face in her hands.

I sat as still as a stone man, waiting. I wasn't expecting this, and I was startled.

"It was hushed up," she went on after a long pause. "Never mind how. But it preyed on Janet's mind. She—she poisoned herself. That was hushed up, too. We were afraid it would come out why she killed herself. It was easy enough to hush up. The doctor was old. He thought it was heart failure. Then, when I came into the money, and there was a lot of it, Douglas showed himself for what he is. He said unless I gave him the money to buy *Dream Ship* he would circulate the story that I had stolen him from Janet and she had tried to kill me, but killed father, and had poisoned herself—all because of me. You can imagine what the papers would have made of that, and I would have lost everything. So, I gave him the money for his beastly ship, but that didn't satisfy him. He keeps coming to me for more money, and he watches every move I make. He found out you had started to make inquiries. He was afraid you would uncover the story, and, of course, if you did he would lose his hold on me. He did everything he could to stop you. When he heard Stevens was meeting you, he kidnapped him. And now he's going to wipe you out. I don't know what to do! I've got to go somewhere and hide. I want you to help me. Will you help me? Will you?" She was clutching my hands now. "Will you promise you won't give me away? I'll do anything for you in return. I mean it! Will you help me?"

There was a slight sound behind us, and we both turned. A tall, powerfully-built man with dark curly hair, dressed in a scarlet sleeveless sweatshirt and dark blue slacks, stood just behind us. He held a .38 automatic in his hand and it pointed directly at me. There was a cheerful, patronizing smile on his tanned face as if he was enjoying a private joke that was a little too deep for the average intelligence.

"She tells a pretty tale, doesn't she?" he said in one of those ultra-masculine voices. "So, she wants to run away and hide? Well, so she shall. She'll be hidden all right, where no one will ever find her, and that goes for you too, my inquisitive friend."

I was calculating the distance between us, wondering if I could get up and reach him before he fired, when I heard the all too familiar swish of a descending cosh and the inside of my head seemed to explode.

The last sound I heard was Maureen's wild, terrified scream.

Chapter Four

1

THE ROOM was big and airy, and the walls and ceiling were a dead Chinese white. Cold, white plastic curtains were drawn across the windows, and a shaded lamp made a pool of light over the opposite bed.

There was a man sitting up in the bed. He was reading. His small-boned face with its high, wide forehead gave the impression of a young student reading for an examination.

I watched him through half-closed eyes for some minutes, wondering in a vague, detached sort of way who he was and what he was doing in this room with me. There was something odd about the book he was reading. It was a big volume, and the print was close set and small. It was only when he turned a page and I saw a chapter heading that I realized he was holding the book upside down.

I wasn't surprised to find myself in this room. I had a vague idea I had been in it for some time: perhaps days, perhaps weeks. The feel of the narrow high bed I was lying in was familiar; almost as familiar as the feel of my own bed in my beach cabin which now seemed as remote as last year's snow.

I knew in an instinctive kind of way—I was quite sure I hadn't been told—that I was in hospital, and I tried to remember if I had been knocked down by a car, but my mind was working badly. It refused to concentrate and kept jumping across the room to the man in the opposite bed. Its only interest was to find out why he was holding his book the wrong way up, for it seemed to me the book looked dry and complicated enough without adding to the difficulty of reading it.

The man in the bed was young, not more than twenty-four or so, and his thick fair hair was over-long and silky-looking. He had very deep-set eyes, and the lamp cast shadows in them so they seemed to be two dark holes in his face.

I suddenly became aware that he was also watching me, although he pretended to be reading; watching furtively from under his eyelids; watching as he turned a page slowly with a concentrated frown on his face.

"You'll find it easier if you turn the book the right way up," I said, and was surprised how far away my voice sounded, as if I were speaking in another room.

He glanced up and smiled. He was a nice-looking young-ster—a typical collegian, more at home with a baseball bat than a book.

"I always read books this way up," he said; his voice was unexpectedly high-pitched. "It's more fun, and it's just as easy once you get the knack of it, but it does take a lot of practice." He laid the book down. "Well, how do you feel, Mr. Seabright? I'm afraid you have had a pretty rotten time. How's the head?"

It was a funny thing, but now he mentioned it I dis-covered my head ached and an artery was pounding in my temple.

"It aches," I said. "Is this a hospital?"

"Well not exactly a hospital. I think they call it a sani-tarium."

"You mean a sanatorium, don't you? A sanitarium is a nut

foundry."

He smiled and nodded his blond head.

"That's it exactly: a nut foundry."

I closed my eyes. Thinking was difficult, but I made the effort. It took me several minutes to remember the swish of a descending sap, the man in the scarlet sweatshirt, and Maureen's wild, terrified scream. A sanitarium. I felt a little prickle of apprehension run up my spine like spider's legs. A sanitarium!

I sat up abruptly. Something held my left wrist, pinning it to the bed. I turned to see what it was. A bright nickel-plated, rubber-lined handcuff gripped my wrist. The other cuff was fastened to the rail of the bed.

The blond man was watching me with mild interest.

"They think it's safer for us to be chained up like that," he said. "Ridiculous, really, but I have no doubt they mean well."

"Yes," I said and lay back. More spider's legs ran up my spine. "Who runs this place?"

"Why Dr. Salzer of course. Haven't you met him? He's quite charming. You'll like him. Everyone does."

Then I remembered the man in the scarlet sweatshirt had said he would hide me away where no one would ever find me. An asylum, of course, was a pretty foolproof hiding-place. But Salzer didn't run an asylum. His place was a retreat for the overfed, Nurse Gurney had said so.

"But I thought Salzer ran a kind of nature cure racket," I said carefully. "Not a nut foundry."

"So he does, but there's a wing set aside for the mentally sick," the blond man explained. He walked two fingers along the edge of the night table. "It is not usually talked about." He walked his fingers back again. "It's so much more plea-sant for relatives to say you are having a health cure than that you're locked up in a padded cell."

"Is that where we are?" I asked.

"Oh yes. The walls are padded. They don't look like it but try punching them. It's quite fun." He leaned out of bed and hit the wall. His fist made no sound. "It's rubber, I think. By the way, my name's Duncan Hopper. You may have heard of my father, Dwight Hopper."

As far as I could remember Dwight Hopper was something big in the paint and distemper trade. I didn't know he had a son.

"I'm Malloy," I said. "Victor Malloy."

He cocked his head on one side and regarded me fixedly.

"Who?"

"Malloy."

"Are you sure?" He smiled slyly now. "They tell me your name is Edmund Seabright."

"No—Malloy," I said, again feeling spider's legs run up my spine.

"I see." He began once more to walk his fingers along the edge of the night table. He seemed to like doing that. "I wonder if you would mind if I called you Seabright? Bland calls you Seabright. Dr. Salzer calls you Seabright. Seabright is the name on your papers. I know, because I persuaded Bland to let me look at them. You are described as a manic depressive. Did you know?"

My mouth suddenly went dry.

"A—what?"

"Manic depressive. I suppose it's nonsense."

"Yes, it's nonsense." I found it increasingly difficult to speak and think calmly.

"I'm so glad. Depressives can be so tiresome. I didn't think you were and I told Bland so. But Bland is very stupid —a very uneducated person. He never listens to what I say.

I'm afraid you won't like him. He says I am a paranoiac, but that's complete nonsense. We had a terrific argument about it this morning, and he lent me this book. It tells you about paranoia. Really quite interesting. But I haven't one single symptom. There's quite an interesting chapter on manic depressives." He walked his fingers along the table edge before saying, "Do you have hallucinations?"

I said I didn't have hallucinations.

"I'm so glad." He seemed genuinely pleased. "But it is odd you think your name is Malloy, isn't it? Or perhaps you don't think so?"

I said very distinctly and slowly, "It isn't odd because Malloy happens to be my name."

"I see." He reached for the book and began to flip over the pages. "Then if you are not Edmund Seabright why are you here?"

"It's a long story," I said, and it seemed to me to be suddenly tremendously important to make this blond man believe me. If he didn't, who else would? "I'm a sort of private investigator and I am engaged on a case. I have found out Dr. Salzer is responsible for the murder of Eudora Drew. It's too involved to go into now, but because of what I have found out I have been kidnapped." I don't know how I got those last words out. It sounded terrible, but to save my life I couldn't have put it any better. A little spark of panic began to well up inside me as I saw the look of polite incredulity on Hopper's face.

"Dr. Salzer?" he said and gave his charming smile. "A murder? That's interesting. And you are some sort of detective? Is that right?"

"Now look," I said, struggling up in bed. "I know what you are thinking. You think I'm crazy, don't you?"

"Of course not, Mr. Seabright," he said gently. "I don't

think anything of the kind. I know you aren't very well, but not crazy . . . definitely and certainly not."

"You're sure about that?"

"Of course."

But I saw by the amused sly expression in the deep-set eyes that he was lying.

2

HOPPER told me that around nine o'clock Bland would come in to turn out the light.

"In about five minutes," he said, consulting his wrist-watch. "Bland lets me have this watch because I give him a hundred cigarettes a week. My father sends them in to me, and, of course, I am not allowed to smoke. They seem to think I would set fire to the bed." He laughed, showing small, even, white teeth. "Ridiculous, of course, but I suppose they mean well."

Under cover of the sheet I had been trying to work my hand out of the handcuff. If I could once get free, I told myself, nothing, not even a machinegun would stop me getting out of this place. But the cuff was shaped to my wrist, and short of cutting off my hand or having the key there was no way out of it.

"What day is it?" I asked suddenly.

Hopper opened a drawer in the night table and consulted a diary.

"It's the 29th of July. Don't you keep a diary? I do. Tomorrow is an anniversary. I have been here three years."

But I wasn't listening. I had to think long and carefully before I remembered that it had been the 24th of July when Maureen had taken me to her retreat. Five days! Paula and

Kerman would be searching for me. Would they think to look
here? Even if they thought I was here, how could they get at
me? Salzer had Brandon's protection, and Brandon wouldn't
pay attention to anything Kerman said. If Sherrill—and I was
sure the man in the scarlet sweat-shirt had been Sherrill—
hadn't been absolutely sure that no one could get at me here,
wouldn't he have put a slug through my head and chucked
me into the sea? Why hadn't he done that anyway? Perhaps
he stopped at murder. Stevens hadn't been murdered. His
death had been an accident. But Salzer didn't stop at murder,
unless Dwan had exceeded his orders. It might even be
better, I thought, to be murdered than left locked up in a
padded cell for the rest of my days.

Pull yourself together Malloy, I said to myself. Snap out of
it! All right, you have been bashed on the head and by the
woolly feeling behind your eyes and in your mouth you have
had a cartload of drug pushed into you, but that's no excuse
to go off at half-cock now. Paula and Kerman will get you out
of this. Hang on and take it easy until they do.

The door opened suddenly and silently and a short, dark
man came in. He had a pair of shoulders you would expect to
find on a gorilla, and his round red face was freckled and
creased in a fixed, humorless grin. He was dressed in a white
lab coat, white trousers and white, rubber-soled shoes. He
carried a tray covered with a towel, and he moved as silently
and as lightly as a feather settling on the floor.

"Hello Hoppie," he said, putting the tray on a table by the
door. "Beddy-byes now. How are you? Did you get any dope
out of that book?"

Hopper waved his hand towards my bed.

"Mr. Seabright is with us now," he said.

Bland—for this must be Bland—came to the foot of my
bed and stared at me. The smile was still there; a little wider

if anything. The greenish eyes were as hard and as cold and as sharp as ice-chips.

"Hello, baby," he said. He had a curious whispering voice; hoarse and secretive, as if something was wrong with his larynx. "I'm Bland. I'm going to look after you."

I found myself starting to clutch hold of the sheet, but I stopped that. Take it easy, I told myself. Relax. Don't rush things.

"Hello," I said, and my voice sounded as tight as a piano wire. "You don't have to look after me. Where's Salzer? I want to talk to him."

"*Doctor* Salzer, baby," Bland said reprovingly. "Don't be disrespectful." He gave Hopper a long, slow wink. "You'll see him tomorrow."

"I want to see him now," I said steadily.

"Tomorrow, baby. The Doc has to have a little time off. If there's anything you want, you tell me. I'm boss of this floor. What I say goes."

"I want Salzer," I said, trying to keep my voice under control.

"Tomorrow, baby. Now, settle down. I gotta little shot for you, and then you'll sleep."

"He thinks he's a detective," Hopper said, suddenly scowling. "He says Dr. Salzer has murdered someone."

"Very disrespectful, but what does it matter? "Bland said, taking a hypodermic syringe from its case.

"But it does matter. That's hallucinations," Hopper said crossly. "It says so in this book. I don't see why I should have him in with me. I don't like it. He may be dangerous."

Bland gave a short barking laugh.

"That's funny, coming from you. Button up baby, I gotta lot to do." He screwed in the needle and filled the syringe with colorless liquid.

"I shall complain to Dr. Salzer," Hopper said. "My father wouldn't like it."

"Nuts to your father, and double nuts to you," Bland said impatiently. He came over to me. "All right, let's have your arm: the right one."

I sat up abruptly.

"You don't stick that in me," I said.

"Don't be that way, baby. It won't get you anywhere," Bland said, his fixed grin widening. "Lie down and take it easy."

"Not in me you don't," I said.

He caught hold of my wrist in his right hand. His short thick fingers clamped into my flesh like a vice.

"If you want it the hard way," he said, his red, freckled face close to mine, "it's okay with me."

I exerted my muscles in a quick twist, hoping to break his hold, but instead I nearly broke my arm. I heaved forward, trying to hit him in the chest with my shoulder, but that didn't work either.

He retained his grip, grinning at me, waiting to see what else I would do. I didn't keep him waiting long and tried to kick my legs free of the sheet, but that wasn't possible. The sheet was as tough as canvas and had been tucked in so tightly there was no shifting it.

"Finished, baby?" he asked, almost cheerfully. "I'm going to stick the needle in now, and if you struggle it'll break off in you, so watch your step."

I gritted my teeth and heaved away from him, pulling him off-balance so he stumbled. He recovered immediately, and his grin vanished.

"So you think you're strong, do you?" he whispered. "Okay, baby, let's see how strong you are."

He began to bend my arm. I resisted, but it was like pushing against a steamroller. He was much, much too strong—unbelievably strong, and my arm slowly twisted behind me, creaking in every muscle. Cold sweat ran down my back, and my breath whistled out of me as I fought him.

I braced myself and regained a couple of inches. Bland was beginning to breathe heavily himself. Maybe if I could have added my weight to the struggle I might have held him. But sitting up in a bed with one arm pinned and my legs hampered I hadn't a chance against his strength and weight.

He bent me forward inch by inch, and I fought him inch by inch. Slowly my arm went up behind me, was wedged into my shoulder blades. I wasn't aware of any pain. I could have killed him. Then I felt the sharp prick of the needle, and he stepped back, releasing my arm.

There was sweat on his face, too, and his breath was labored. He hadn't had it all his own way.

"There you are, baby," he gasped. "You asked for it and you got it. If I wasn't such a soft chicken, I'd have busted your arm."

I tried to take a swing at him, but my arm didn't respond. I don't know what he had pushed into me, but it worked fast. The red, freckled, hateful face began to recede. The walls of the room fell apart. Beyond the face and the walls was a long, black tunnel.

3

I opened my eyes.

Pale sunshine came through the barred windows, carrying the shadows of the bars to the opposite white wall: six sharp-etched lines to remind me I was a prisoner.

Bland was moving silently about the room, a duster in his

broad thick hand, a look of concentration on his freckled face. He dusted everywhere, nothing escaped his attention.

Hopper was sitting up in bed, reading his book. There was a peevish scowl on his face, and he paid no attention to Bland, even when he dusted his night table.

Bland came over to me and dusted my night table. Our eyes met and the fixed grin on his face widened.

"Hello baby," he said. "How are you feeling?"

"All right," I said, and shifted higher in the bed. My right arm and shoulder ached, and I still had the imprint of his thick fingers on my wrist.

"That's good. I'll be along with a shaving kit in a few minutes. Then you can have a bath."

That would mean taking off the handcuff, I thought.

Bland seemed to guess what was going through my mind.

"And look baby, don't let's have any trouble," he said. "Don't get the idea you can get away. You can't. There are a couple more guys like me around. The door at the head of the stairs is locked, and there are bars at the windows. You ask Hoppie. He'll tell you. When Hoppie first came here there was trouble. He tried to get away but it didn't work."

I stared at him woodenly and didn't say anything.

"You ask Hoppie what we do to a baby who makes trouble. He'll tell you." He looked at Hopper, grinning. "You'll tell him, won't you Hoppie?"

Hopper looked up and scowled at him.

"Don't talk to me, you lowborn rat. I hate the sight of you."

Bland chuckled.

"That's all right, baby. I don't mind. I'm used to it."

Hopper called him an obscene name.

"Take it easy, baby," Bland said, still smiling. "Don't bear down on it. He went to the door. "Shave, then a bath and then breakfast. I'll see if I can get you an extra egg."

Hopper told him what he could do with the egg.

Bland went away, chuckling.

"Don't try it, Seabright," Hopper said. "It's not worth it. They'll put you in a strait jacket and keep you in a bath of cold water for days. He's not lying about the door. You can't get out without a key."

I decided to wait and see.

After a while Bland came back with two electric razors. He plugged them in and gave Hopper one and me the other.

"Make it snappy, babies," he said. "I gotta lot to do today."

"You're always grumbling," Hopper said angrily. "I wish you'd go. I'm sick of seeing your ugly face."

"It's mutual baby," Bland said cheerfully. "Hurry up and make a job of it. Dr. Salzer likes to see his patients looking smart."

So I was going to see Salzer. Not that I could hope for anything from him, but maybe I could scare him. If Sherrill had put me in here, maybe Salzer could be persuaded it was a dangerous game to kidnap anyone. I thought it was unlikely but it might be worth trying.

When I had finished shaving, Bland came in with a white cotton bathrobe.

"No funny business, baby," he said in his whispering voice, and came around the bed to unlock the handcuff.

"Just take it easy."

I lay still while he took off the handcuff. Hopper was watching me with concentrated interest. Bland moved back a few feet and also watched me.

"Up you get, baby."

I wriggled my legs from under the sheet, swung them to the floor and stood up. The moment I put my weight on my legs I knew it would be hopeless to start anything. My legs were too shaky and too weak. I couldn't have run away from a charging bull.

I took a staggering step forward and promptly sat on the floor. I didn't have to sit on the floor but it occurred to me it wouldn't be a bad idea to let Bland think I was a lot weaker in the legs than I actually was.

I crawled up on hands and knees and regained my feet. Bland hadn't moved. He was suspicious and wasn't going to be caught in any trap.

"Give me a hand, can't you?" I snarled at him. "Or let me get back to bed."

"Look baby, I'm warning you," he said softly. "If you start anything it'll be the last thing you start for a very long time."

"Cut out the yap. What's the matter with you? Scared of me?"

That seemed the kind of language he understood, for he grabbed hold of my arm.

"Not of you, baby, or of anyone else."

He helped me on with the bathrobe, opened the door and together we stepped out into a long broad corridor. I took a couple more steps and paused as if I still wasn't feeling too sure of myself. The pause gave me time to look to right and left. One end of the corridor terminated in a massive-looking door, the other end was sealed off by a high window covered with a close-mesh grill.

"Okay baby," Bland said, grinning. "Now you have had a look, let's get moving. I told you how it was. Well now you've seen for yourself."

Yes, I had seen for myself.

I went along the corridor with Bland, my mind busy. Somehow I had to get the key for that door and the key for the handcuff. Either that or stay here until they got tired of keeping me or until I rotted.

A sudden commotion brought us to a halt . . . a startled

cry, a heavy thud as if someone or something heavy had fallen.

Bland caught hold of my arm.

A nearby door suddenly jerked open and a girl shot into the corridor. The first and obvious thing about her was her complete nakedness. She seemed to have jumped right out of a bath, for water glistened on her white skin and a fine film of soap made patterns on her slender arms. She was fair, and her hair grew in a curly halo around her head. She wasn't pretty, nor was she plain. She was interesting, definitely and emphatically interesting, and I had a suspicion she wouldn't be quite so interesting with her clothes on as she was without them. At a guess she was about twenty-five. She had a beautiful body, long-legged, high-breasted, and her skin was the color of whipped cream.

I heard Bland suck in his breath sharply.

"Hot damn!" he said under his breath, and jumped forward, his thick fingers reaching out for the girl, his eyes alight with brutish excitement. He grabbed hold of the girl's arm. Her scream hit the ceiling and bounced along the walls. His hand slid off her soapy arm and she spun round and raced down the corridor. She ran with unexpected grace, and as swiftly as the wind.

Bland took a step forward and then changed his mind. She couldn't get away. Already she had reached the massive door and was beating on it with clenched fists.

All this happened in so many seconds, then a nurse appeared from the bathroom—a tall, powerfully-built woman whose hatchet face was white with alarm and fury. She looked down the corridor at the girl's naked back. She looked at Bland.

"Get your patient away," she said. "And get out yourself, you—you ape!"

"Take it easy," Bland said, his eyes still on the girl. "You
let her out, you silly old hag."

"Get your patient away or I'll report you," the nurse said
furiously.

"And you would, too," Bland returned, sneering.

He grabbed hold of my arm.

"Come on baby, the fun's over. You can't say this ain't the
place to live in. The best of attention and the *Follies Bergère*
thrown in for free. What more do you want?"

He hustled me into a bathroom opposite the one the girl
had escaped from as the nurse went down the corridor. The
girl saw her coming and turned to face her, her screams went
through my head and set my nerves jangling. I was glad
when the bathroom door closed on the sound, shutting it
out.

Bland was excited. His hard, little eyes gleamed, and he
kept running his tongue along his lips.

"Some dish!" he said, half to himself. "I wouldn't have
missed that for a week's pay. Here you, get your things off
and get into the bath. My luck having to sit around and look
at you when that dish out there's on show."

"Stop acting like a kid," I said, stripping off the bathrobe
and pajamas. "Who is she, anyway?"

"The cupcake? No one you'd know. She used to be a nurse
here, suddenly went crackers when her boy walked out on
her. That's the story, anyway. She was here before I came.
Why she should go nuts because she lost her boy, beats me. I
would have given her a twirl any time she wanted one."

I lay still in the bath, my face expressionless. A nurse!
Was this the missing nurse Mifflin had told me about? It
sounded like her.

"Her name's Anona Freedlander—right?" I shot out.

Bland showed his surprise.

"How did you know?"

"I'm a detective," I said solemnly.

Bland grinned. He sat on a stool near the bath and lit a cigarette.

"Get going, baby. Never mind the detection now. I gotta lot to do." Absent-mindedly he dropped the match into the water.

"What's wrong with Hopper?" I asked, changing the subject. "Why's he here?"

"Hoppie's quite a case," Bland said, and shook his head. "There are certain times in the month when even I don't go near him. You wouldn't think that to look at him, would you? A very deceptive guy. If it wasn't for his old man's money he would be in a criminal asylum. He killed a girl—tore her throat out with his teeth. He'll be here for the rest of his days. You never know with him. When he's in the wrong mood he's a killer. One day he's okay, the next he's as dangerous as a tiger on hunger strike."

I began wondering about Bland, asking myself if he could be bought.

"How about a cigarette?" I asked, lying back in the water. "I could do with one."

"Sure baby. So long as you behave yourself, I'll treat you like my brother." He produced a package of Lucky Strikes, gave me one and lit it for me. "When you first come here all you guys try to be smart and start trouble. Take my tip and don't. We've got an answer for most things. Just remember that."

I dragged down smoke. It didn't taste quite as good as I was expecting.

"How long do you think you're going to keep me here?"

He took an old envelope out of his pocket and tapped ash into it, put it on the side of the bath for my use.

"From the look of your record, baby, you're in here for good."

I decided I would try it.

"How would you like to earn a hundred dollars?"

"Doing what?" The small eyes alerted.

"Simple enough. Telephone a friend of mine."

"And what would I say?"

But it was a little too quick and a little too glib. I studied him. It wasn't going to work. The mocking smile gave him away. He was playing with me.

"Never mind," I said, drowned the cigarette and put the soggy butt into the envelope. "Forget it. Let's have a towel."

He handed me a towel.

"Don't get that way, baby. I might play. I could use a hundred bucks, what's the telephone number?"

"Forget it," I said.

He sat watching me, a grin on his face, the butt of his cigarette resting on his lower lip.

"Maybe you'd like to raise the ante," he suggested. "Now, for five hundred . . ."

"Just get it out of the thing you call your mind," I said, and put on my pajamas. "One of these days we'll meet on more equal terms. It's something I'm looking forward to."

"That's okay, baby. Have your pipe dreams. They don't hurt me," he said, opened the door and looked out. "Come on. I've got to get Hoppie up."

There was no commotion from the opposite bathroom as I walked down the corridor. The bath had done me good. If there had been a chance to get past that door, I would have taken it. But I was already making up my mind I would have to be very patient. I purposely walked slowly, leaning on Bland's arm. The weaker he thought me, the more I would surprise him when it came to a showdown.

I got into bed and meekly allowed him to lock the hand-cuff.

Hopper said he didn't want a bath.

"Now baby, that's no way to act," Bland said reprovingly. "You gotta look smart this morning. There's an official visit at eleven o'clock. Coroner Lessways is coming to talk to you." He glanced at me and grinned. "And he'll talk to you, too. Every month the city councilmen come around to see the nuts. Not that they pay a lot of attention to what the nuts tell them, but they come, and sometimes they even listen. But don't give them that stuff about murder, baby. They've heard it all. To them you're just another nut along with a lotta nuts, and it won't do you any good."

He persuaded Hopper to get out of bed and they went off together to the bathroom. That left me alone. I lay in the bed, staring at the six sharp-etched lines on the opposite walls and used my head. So, Coroner Lessways was coming. Well, that was something. As Bland had said there wasn't much point in my telling Lessways that Salzer was responsible for Eudora Drew's killing. It was too far-fetched; too unbelievable, but if I had the chance, I might give him something to chew on. For the first time since I had been in this trap I felt a little more hopeful.

I looked up suddenly to see the door slowly open. There was no one in sight. The door swung right open and remained open. I leaned forward to look into the empty corridor, thinking at first the wind had opened the door, but remembered the latch had clicked shut when Bland and Hopper had left the room.

I waited, staring at the open door, and listened. Nothing happened. I heard nothing, and because I knew someone had opened the door I felt suddenly spooked.

After what seemed ages, I heard a rustle of paper. In the

acute silence it sounded like a thunderclap. Then I saw a movement, and a woman came into sight.

She stood in the doorway, a paper sack in one hand, a vacant, unintelligent expression in her washed-out eyes. She regarded me steadily with no more interest than if I was a piece of furniture, and her hand groped blindly in the sack. Yes, it was her all right—the plum-eating woman, and what was more, she was still eating plums.

We looked at each other for a long moment of time. Her jaw moved slowly and rhythmically as her teeth chewed up a plum. She looked as bright and happy as a cow chewing the cud.

"Hello," I said, and it irritated me that my voice had gone husky.

Her fat fingers chased after a plum, found one and hoisted it into sight.

"It's Mr. Malloy, isn't it?" she said, as polite as a minister's wife meeting a new member of the congregation.

"That's right," I said. "The last time we met we didn't have the time to get chummy. Who are you?"

She chewed for a moment, turned the pit out into her cupped hand and transferred it to the paper sack.

"Why, I'm Mrs. Salzer," she said.

I should have guessed that. She really couldn't have been anyone else.

"I don't want to seem personal," I said, "but do you like your husband, Mrs. Salzer?"

The vague look was chased away by surprise which in turn gave way to a look of weak pride.

"Dr. Salzer is a very fine man. There is no one in the world like him," she said, and pointed her soft, round chin at me.

"That's a pity. You'll miss him. Even in our enlightened jails they still separate husbands and wives."

The vague look came back again.

"I don't know what you mean."

"Well you should. If they don't sit your husband in the gas chamber, they'll give him twenty years. Kidnapping and murder earn a sentence like that."

"What murder?"

"A woman named Eudora Drew was murdered on your husband's instructions. I have been kidnapped, and there's a girl across the way who I think has been kidnapped, too: Anona Freedlander. And then there's Nurse Gurney."

A sly little smile lit up the woman's fat face.

"He has nothing to do with any of that. He thinks Miss Freedlander is a friend of mine who has lost her memory."

"And I suppose he thinks I'm a friend of yours, too?" I said sarcastically.

"Not exactly a friend, but a friend of a friend of mine."

"And how about Eudora Drew?"

Mrs. Salzer shrugged her shoulders.

"That was unfortunate. She wanted money. I sent Benny to reason with her. He got too rough."

I scratched my jaw with my thumbnail and stared at her. I sensed more than believed she was telling the truth.

"Where's Nurse Gurney? I asked.

"Oh, she met with an accident," Mrs. Salzer said, and peered into the sack again. She brought out a plum, offered it to me. "Will you have one? They are good for you when you are in bed."

"No. Never mind the plums. What happened to her?" The face went vague again.

"Oh, she was going down the fire escape when she slipped. I put her in the car but I think she must have broken her neck. I don't know why but she seemed very frightened of me."

I said in a tight voice: "What did you do with her?"

"I left her in some bushes out in the sand." She bit into the plum, waved vaguely towards the window. "Out there in the desert. There wasn't anything else I could do with her."

I ran my fingers through my hair. Maybe she was crazy, I thought, or else I was.

"Was it you who arranged for me to come here?"

"Oh yes," she said, leaning against the doorway. "You see, Dr. Salzer has no knowledge of medicine or of mental illness. But I have. I used to have a very big practice, but something happened. I don't remember what it was. Dr. Salzer bought this place for me. He pretends to run it, but I do all the work really. He is just a figure head."

"No, he's not," I said. "He signed Macdonald Crosby's death certificate. He had no right to. He's not qualified."

"You are quite wrong," she said calmly. "I signed it. We happen to have the same initials."

"But he was treating Janet Crosby for malignant endo-carditis," I said. "Dr. Bewley told me so."

"Dr. Bewley was mistaken. Dr. Salzer happened to be at the Crosby house on business for me when the girl died. He told Dr. Brewley I had been treating her. Dr. Bewley is an old man and a little deaf. He misunderstood."

"Why was he called in at all?" I demanded. "Why didn't you sign the certificate if you were treating her?"

"I was away at the time. My husband did the correct thing to call Dr. Bewley. He always does the correct thing."

"That's fine," I said. "Then he better let me out of here."

"He thinks you are dangerous," Mrs. Salzer said, and peered into the sack again. "And you are, Mr. Malloy. You know too much. I'm sorry for you, but you really shouldn't have interfered." She looked up to smile in a goofy sort of way. "I'm afraid you will have to stay here, and before very

long your mind will begin to deteriorate. You see, people who
are continually drugged often become feeble-minded. Have
you noticed that?"

"Is that what's going to happen to me?"

She nodded.

"I'm afraid so, but I didn't want you to think unkindly of
Dr. Salzer. He is such a fine man. That's why I have told you
so much. More than I should really, but it won't matter. You
won't get away."

She began to drift away as quietly as she had come.

"Hey! Don't go away," I said, sitting forward. "How much
is Maureen Crosby paying you to keep me here?" Her vague
eyes popped a little.

"But she doesn't know," she said. "It's nothing to do with
her. I thought you knew," and she went away rather like a
tired ghost after a long and exhausting spell of haunting.

4

HOPPER was better-tempered after his bath, and while we
were having breakfast I asked him if he had ever tried to
escape.

"I haven't anywhere to go," he said, shrugging. "Besides, I
have a handcuff on my ankle and it's locked to the bed. If the
bed wasn't fastened to the floor I might have tried it."

"What's the bed got to do with it?" I asked, spreading
marmalade on thin toast. It wasn't easy with one hand.

"The spare key of the handcuff is kept in that top drawer,"
he explained, pointing to a chest of drawers against the
opposite wall. "They keep it there in case of fire. If I could
move the bed, I could get to it."

I nearly hit the ceiling.

"What! In that drawer there?"

"That's right. No one's supposed to know, but I saw Bland take it out once when he lost his key."

I judged the distance between the foot of my bed and the chest of drawers. It was closer to me than to Hopper. If I was held by the ankle, I imagined I could reach it. It would be a stretch, but I reckoned I could just do it. But handcuffed by the wrist as I was made it impossible.

"How is it you're fastened by the leg and I by the wrist?" I asked.

"They fastened me by the wrist at first," Hopper said indifferently, and pushed his tray aside. "But I found it awkward to read so Bland changed it. If you ask him, he'll change yours. You don't mind not talking anymore, do you? I want to get on with this book."

No, I didn't mind. I didn't mind at all. I was excited. If I could persuade Bland to unfasten my wrist, I might reach the key. It was a thought that occupied me for the next hour.

Bland came in a few minutes before eleven o'clock carrying an enormous vase of gladioli sprays. He set it down on top of the chest of drawers and drew back to admire it.

"Pretty nice, huh?" he said, beaming. "That's for the councilmen. It's a funny thing how these guys go for flowers. The last bunch never even looked at the patients. All they did was to stand around and yap about the flowers."

He collected the breakfast-trays and took them away, then returned almost immediately. He surveyed us critically, straightened Hopper's sheet, came over and smoothed out my pillow.

"Now keep just as you are," he said. "For Pete's sake, don't get yourselves untidy. Haven't you a book?" he asked me.

"You haven't given me one."

"Must have a book. That's another of these punks' fads.

They like to see a patient reading."

He charged out of the room and returned a little breathlessly carrying a heavy volume which he slapped down on my
knees.

"Get stuck into that, baby. I'll find you something with a
little more zip in it when they've gone."

"How do I turn the pages with only one hand?" I asked,
looking at the book. It was entitled *Gynecology for
Advanced Students*.

"Glad you reminded me, baby." He took out his key. "We
keep the cuffs out of sight. These punks are soft-hearted

I watched him transfer the handcuff to my ankle, scarcely
believing my good luck. It was quite a moment in my life.

"Okay baby, mind you behave," he went on, as he tidied
the bed. "If they ask you how you like it here, tell them we're
looking after you. Don't let's have any back answers. They
won't believe anything you say, and you'll have to talk to me
after they have gone."

I opened the book. The first plate I came to made me
blink.

"I don't know if I'm old enough to look at this," I said, and
showed him the plate.

He stared, sucked in his breath sharply, snatched the
book away from me and gaped at the title.

"For crying out loud! Is that what it means?" and he went
shooting out of the room with it, returning breathlessly with
a copy of the parallel translation of *Dante's Inferno*. I wished
I had kept my mouth shut.

"That'll impress them," he said with satisfaction. "Not that
the punks can read, anyway."

A few minutes past eleven o'clock the sound of voices
came down the corridor, and in through the half-open door.

Bland, who had been waiting by the window, straightened

his jacket and smoothed down his hair.

Hopper scowled and closed his book.

"Here they come."

Four men came into the room. The first was obviously Dr. Jonathan Salzer, the most distinguished-looking of the four, a tall, thin man with a Paderewski mop of hair as white as a dove's back. His tanned face was set in cold, serene lines, his eyes were deep-set and thoughtful. A man, I imagined, on the wrong side of fifty, still powerful, his body as straight and as upright as a cadet's on parade. He was dressed in a black tail-coat, striped trousers and was as immaculate as a tailor's dummy. After you had got over the shock of the mop of hair, the next thing you noticed about him was his hands. They were quite beautiful hands; long and narrow, with tapering fingers—a surgeon's hands or a murderer's hands— they could be good at either job.

Coroner Lessways followed him in. I recognized him from the occasional photographs I had seen of him in the press: a short, thickset man with a ball-like head, small eyes and a fussy, mean little mouth. He looked what he was, a shyster who had spent all his life pulling fast ones.

His companion was another of the same breed, overfed and tricky.

The fourth man hovered outside the door as if he wasn't sure whether to come in or not. I didn't bother to look his way. My attention was riveted on Salzer.

"Good morning, gentlemen," Salzer said in a deep, rich voice. "I hope I find you well. Coroner Lessways, Councilman Linkheimer and Mr. Strang, the well-known writer, have come to see you. They are here to ask you a few questions." He glanced at Lessways. "Would you care to have a word with Mr. Hopper?"

While Lessways was gaping owlishly at Hopper and

keeping at a safe distance, I turned to look at the fourth man whom Salzer had introduced as Strang.

For a moment I thought I really had gone crazy, for standing in the doorway with a nonchalant look of boredom on his face was Jack Kerman. He was wearing a tropical white suit, horn spectacles, and out of his breast pocket a yellow and red silk handkerchief flopped in the best traditions of the dandy.

I gave a start that nearly upset the bed. Luckily Salzer was busying himself with my medical chart and didn't notice. Kerman looked woodenly at me, lifted one eyebrow and said to Salzer, "Who is this man, Doctor? He looks well enough."

"This is Edmund Seabright," Salzer told him. His cold face lit up with a smile and he reminded me of Santa Claus about to hand out a toy to a good child. "He has only recently come to us." He handed the medical chart to Kerman. "Perhaps you would be interested to see this. It speaks for itself."

Kerman adjusted his horn spectacles and squinted at the chart. I had an idea he couldn't see well in them, and knowing him, guessed he had borrowed them from someone.

"Oh yes," he said, pursing his lips. "Interesting. I suppose it's all right to have a word with him?"

"Why certainly," Salzer said, and moved to my bed. Kerman joined him and they both stared at me. I stared back, concentrating on Salzer, knowing if I looked at Kerman I would probably let the cat out of the bag.

"This is Mr. Strang," Salzer said to me. "He writes books on nervous diseases." He smiled at Kerman. "Mr. Seabright imagines he is a famous detective. Don't you, Mr. Seabright?"

"Sure," I said. "I am a detective. I've discovered Anona Freedlander is right here on this floor, and Nurse Gurney is dead and her body has been hidden somewhere in the desert by your wife. How's that for detection?"

Salzer's kind, sad smile embraced Kerman.

"He runs true to type as you can see," he murmured. "Both the women he has mentioned disappeared, one about two years ago, the other recently. The cases were reported in the newspapers. For some odd reason they prey on his mind."

"Quite so," Kerman said seriously. He studied me, and behind the thick glasses his eyes seemed to squint.

"And there's another thing you should know." I half sat up and whispered, "I have a handcuff on my leg."

Lessways and Linkheimer had joined Salzer and were staring at me.

Kerman raised his eyebrows languidly.

"Is that true?" he asked Salzer.

Salzer inclined his head. His smile was for the whole of suffering humanity.

"Sometimes he is a little troublesome," he said regretfully. "You understand?"

"Quite so," Kerman said, and looked pained. He did it so well I wanted to kick him.

Bland came away from the window and stood at the head of my bed.

"Take it easy, baby," he said softly.

"I don't like this place," I said, addressing Lessways. "I object to being drugged every night. I don't like the locked door at the end of the corridor, nor the mesh-grill over the window at the other end of the corridor. This is not a sanatorium. It's a prison."

"My dear fellow," Salzer said smoothly before Lessways could think of anything to say, "you get well and you shall go home. We don't want to keep you here unless we have to."

Out of the corner of my eye I saw Bland slowly clench his

fist as a warning for me to be careful what I said. There were a lot of things I could have said, but now Kerman knew I was here I decided not to take any chances.

"Well let's move on," Lessways said. "All this looks very good." He beamed at Kerman. "Have you seen all you want to see, Mr. Strang? Don't let us hurry you."

"Oh yes," Kerman said languidly. "If Dr. Salzer wouldn't object, I might like to call again."

"I'm afraid that would be against the rules," Salzer said. "Too many visits might excite our friends. I'm sure you will understand?"

Kerman looked at me thoughtfully.

"You're quite right. I hadn't thought of that," he said, and drifted towards the door.

There was a stately exodus, Salzer being the last to leave. I heard Kerman say, "Is there no one else on this floor?"

"Not at the moment," Salzer said. "We have had several interesting cures recently. Perhaps you would like to see our files?"

The voices drifted away, and Bland closed the door. He grinned at me.

"Didn't work, did it baby? I told you—just a nut along with a lotta other nuts."

It wasn't easy to look like a disappointed man, but I somehow managed it.

5

SALZER was talking sense when he had said visitors excited his patients. The effect on Hopper was obvious, although it wasn't until Bland brought in the lunch-trays that he showed signs of blowing up.

When Salzer and the visitors had gone, Hopper lay still, staring up at the ceiling, a heavy scowl on his face. He remained like that until lunchtime and paid no attention to any remark I made, so I left him alone. I had plenty to think about anyway, and I wasn't pining for his society. But when Bland set the tray on the night table, he suddenly lashed out, sending the tray flying across the room to land with a crash and a mess on the floor.

He sat up, and the look of him brought me out in goose pimples. His face altered so I scarcely recognized him. It grew thinner, older and lined. There was a ferocious, trapped look in his eyes you see in the eyes of the fiercer beasts in the zoo. And the way Bland skipped out of his reach was as quick as the hop of a frog.

"Take it easy, baby," Bland said, more from force of habit than to mean anything.

Hopper crouched down in the bed and stared at him as if willing him to come within reach, but Bland wasn't to be tempted.

"Just my goddamn luck," he said savagely. "He has to throw a fit just when I'm going off duty."

Laboriously he cleared up the broken crockery and piled the bits on the tray. By the time he was through he seemed to have decided to ignore Hopper, who continued to watch him with mad, glittering eyes.

"I'm going anyway, see?" he said to me. "I gotta date, and I'm not going to bust it. You'll be okay. He can't reach you, and maybe he'll snap out of it. He does, sometimes. If he starts trying to walk up the wall, ring the bell. Quell's on duty but don't ring unless you have to. Okay?"

"Well I don't know," I said doubtfully. I didn't like the look of Hopper. "How long do I get left alone?"

"Quell will be in every so often. You won't see me 'til

Tomorrow," Bland said impatiently. "If I don't beat it now, Salzer will make me stay and watch the punk. I'm the only one who can do anything with him."

An idea jumped into my mind. I didn't like being left with Hopper. It gave me the shakes just to look at him, but with Bland out of the way and the handcuff key within reach, there was a chance to start something.

"So long as someone's within call," I said, settling back on my pillow. "But I'd just as soon go with you. How about it?"

He grinned.

"My frill is screwy enough without you being around."

He took Hopper's wrecked meal away while I tried to eat, but Hopper's heavy breathing and the way he glared at the opposite wall, his face working, turned my stomach. After a couple of attempts to get the food down, I pushed the tray away. What I wanted was a cigarette. I wanted that more than anything in the world.

Bland came back after a while. He had changed out of his white uniform, and now looked so smart I scarcely recognized him. His hand-painted tie nearly made me color blind.

"What's up?" he said, looking at my tray. "Think it's poisoned?"

"Just not hungry."

He glanced at Hopper who had again crouched down in the bed as soon as he saw him and was glaring at him murderously.

"Well he won't put me off my fun," he said with a grin. "Just take it easy, baby. Don't bear down on it."

"I want a cigarette," I said, "and if I don't get one, I'll raise the alarm before you get out of the house."

"You can't have a cigarette," Bland said. "You nuts aren't safe with matches."

"I don't want a match; I want a cigarette. Light it for me

and leave me a couple more. I'll chain smoke. If I don't have a smoke I'll flip my lid. You don't want two of us on your hands, do you?"

He parted with the cigarettes reluctantly, lit one for me and edged to the door.

"Tell Quell to keep away from him," he said at the door. "Maybe he'll settle down when I've gone. Whatever he does, don't ring that bell for five minutes. Give me time to get clear."

Hopper made a sudden grab at him, but he was too far away to do more than disturb the air around Bland but the way Bland skipped through the door told me he was scared of Hopper. And so was I.

The afternoon was the longest I have ever lived through. I didn't dare attempt to get the handcuff key in the chest of drawers. I had no idea when Quell was likely to make an appearance, and then there was the problem of Hopper. I didn't know if he was likely to start something if I got out of bed. I knew I had only one chance to get at the key, and if I fluffed it I wouldn't get another. I decided the attempt would have to be made at night, when Hopper was asleep and Quell in bed. That meant I had to avoid being drugged, and I hadn't an idea how that was to be done.

As soon as Bland had gone, Hopper quieted down. He ignored me, and lay staring at the opposite wall, muttering to himself and running his fingers through his thick, fair hair. I tried to catch what he was saying, but the words came to me only as a jumble of discordant sound.

I was careful not to make any sudden movement to attract his attention and lay smoking, and when I could get my mind away from him I wondered what Kerman was doing.

How he had persuaded Lessways that he was a writer on mental diseases foxed me, and I suspected Paula had

something to do with that. At least they knew the setup now.
They knew Anona Freedlander was in the building. They
knew about the door at the end of the corridor and the mesh-
grill over the window. One or the other had to be overcome
before they could rescue me; and I hadn't a doubt that they
would rescue me. But how they were going to do it was a
problem.

Around four-thirty the door pushed open and a young
fellow in a white uniform similar to the one Bland wore,
came in, carrying tea-trays. He was slimly-built, overgrown,
and weedy. His long, thin face had the serious, concentrated
expression of a horse running a race. He wasn't unlike a
horse. He had a long upper lip and big teeth that gave him a
horsey look. It wouldn't have surprised me if he had neighed
at me. He didn't. He smiled instead.

"I'm Quell," he said, setting the tray on the night table.
"You are Mr. Seabright, aren't you?"

"No," I said. "I am Sherlock Holmes. And if you take my
tip I wouldn't go near Watson. He's in one of his moods."

He gave me a long, sad, worried stare. From the look of
him I guessed he hadn't been mixed up with lunatics for very
long.

"But that's Mr. Hopper," he said patiently, as if talking to
a child.

Hopper was sitting up now, clenching and unclenching
his fists, and snarling at Quell.

Quell may have only been in the racket a short time, but
he was smart enough to see Hopper wasn't in the mood to
play pat-a-cake. He eyed Hopper as you might eye a tiger
that's suddenly walked into your sitting-room.

"I don't think Mr. Hopper wants to be bothered with
dinner," I said. "And if you take my tip you'll keep away until
Bland returns."

"I can't do that," he said dubiously. "Dr. Salzer is out, and Bland isn't likely to be back until after midnight. He really shouldn't have gone."

"It's too late to worry about that," I said. "Fade away, brother. Shake the dust off your feet. And if you could bring me a little scotch for dinner, I'd welcome it."

"I'm afraid patients aren't allowed alcohol," he said seriously, without taking his eyes off Hopper.

"Then drink some yourself and come and breathe over me," I said. "Even that would be better than nothing."

He said he didn't touch spirits and went away, a perplexed, scared look on his face.

Hopper stared across the room at me, and under the intense scrutiny of those glaring eyes I felt a little spooked. I hoped fervently the handcuff on his ankle was strong enough to hold him if he took it into his head to try and break loose.

"I have been thinking, Hoppie," I said, speaking slowly and distinctly. "What we must do is to cut that punk Bland's throat and drink his blood. We should have done it before."

"Yes," Hopper said, and the glare in his eyes began to fade. "We will do that."

I wondered if it would be safe to try for the key now but decided against it. I wasn't sure of Brother Quell. If he caught me trying, I felt it would sadden his young life even more than it was saddened already.

"I will make a plan," I said to Hopper. Bland is very cunning. It won't be easy to trap him."

Hopper seemed to calm down and his face stopped twitching.

"I will make a plan too," he said.

The rest of the evening went by while he made his plan and I thought about what I was going to do if I got free of the cuff. It seemed unlikely that I would be able to escape from the house, but if I could locate Anona Freedlander and have a talk with her and warn her she was soon to be rescued I wouldn't waste my time. Then when Kerman showed up— and I was certain he would show up sooner or later—we wouldn't have to waste time hunting for her.

Quell looked in occasionally. He didn't do more than put his head around the door, and Hopper was too preoccupied with his plans to notice him. I made *ssh*-ing signs every time Quell appeared, pointing at Hopper and shaking my head. Quell nodded back, looking more like a horse than ever, and went silently away.

Around eight o'clock he brought me in a supper-tray and then went to the foot of Hopper's bed and smiled at him.

"Would you like something to eat, Mr. Hopper?" he asked coaxingly.

Hopper's reaction to this gave even me a start. It nearly gave Quell heart failure. Hopper shot forward to the end of the bed, his arms seemed to stretch out as if they were made of elastic, and his hooked fingers brushed Quell's white jacket. Quell sprang back, stumbled and nearly fell. His face turned the color of putty.

"I don't think Mr. Hopper wants anything to eat," I said, the piece of chicken I was chewing suddenly tasting like sawdust. "And I don't think I'm that keen either."

But Quell wasn't interested in how I felt. He went out of the room with a rush of air, a streak of white and a bang of the door.

Hopper threw off the bedclothes and started after him. He landed with a crash on the floor, held by his ankle, and he screamed. He jerked madly at the chain, bruising his ankle. Then when he found he couldn't get free, he swung himself up on to the bed and threw himself on the chain of the handcuff. He began to pull at it, while I froze, watching him.

From where I was the chain looked horribly fragile. The thought that this madman might break loose while I was still chained sent a chill up my spine. My hand went to the bell and hovered over it.

He had the chain now in both hands, and, bracing his feet against the end bar of the bed he strained back, his face turning purple with the exertion. The bar bent but held, and the chain held too. Finally he dropped back, gasping, and I knew the danger was over. I found sweat on my face. Without exactly being aware of it those past minutes had been about the worse I had ever experienced.

The purple color of Hopper's face had turned to white. He lay still with his eyes closed and I waited, watching him. After a while, and to my surprise, he began to snore.

Then Quell came into the room, carrying a strait jacket. His face was pale but determined.

"Take it easy," I said, and I was startled how shaky my voice sounded. "He's asleep. You better have a look at that handcuff. I thought he was going to break loose."

"He couldn't do that," Quell said, dropping the strait jacket. "That chain is specially made." He moved closer and looked down at Hopper. "I'd better give him a shot."

"Don't be a fool," I said sharply. "Bland said you weren't to go near him."

"Oh, but he must have an injection," Quell said. "If he has another attack it might be very bad for him. I don't want to do it, but it's my duty."

"To hell with your duty," I said impatiently. "Handling that guy is like handling a bomb. Leave him alone."

Cautiously Quell approached the bed and stood looking down at Hopper. The heavy, snoring breathing continued, and, reassured, Quell began to put the sheet back in place. I watched him, holding my breath, not knowing if Hopper was faking or not. I didn't know if Quell was just dumb or very brave. He'd have to be completely dumb or have nerves like steel to get as close to this lunatic as he was.

Quell tucked in the sheet and stood away. I saw little beads of sweat on his forehead. He wasn't dumb, I decided. That made him brave. If I had one, I would have given him a medal.

"He seems all right," he said more cheerfully. "I'll give him a shot. If he has a good sleep, he'll be all right tomorrow."

This suited me, but I was worried anyway. No amount of medals nor money would have persuaded me to get that close to the sleeping Hopper.

"You're taking a chance," I said. "The needle will wake him. If he gets his hands on you, you're a goner."

He turned to stare at me in a puzzled way.

"I don't understand you at all," he said. "You don't behave like a patient."

"I'm not a patient," I said solemnly. "I'm Sherlock Holmes, remember?"

He looked sad again and went out. Minutes ticked by. Hopper didn't move. He continued to snore, his face slack and exhausted.

Quell returned after what seemed hours and couldn't have been more than ten minutes. He carried a tray covered with a towel.

"Now look," I said, sitting up. "Suppose you take off my handcuff? Then if there's trouble I can help you. You seem to be a sensible sort of guy. If he wakes up and grabs you, I can hit him over the head."

He looked at me seriously like a horse inspecting a doubtful sack of oats.

"I couldn't do that," he said. "It would be against the

rules."

Well I had done all I could. The ball was in his corner now and it was up to him.

"Okay," I said, struggling. "At least I'll pray for you."

He charged the syringe and approached Hopper. I watched, feeling the hairs on the back of my neck rising and my heart beginning to thump against my ribs.

He was a little shaky, but his serious, horse-like face was calm. Gently he pushed Hopper's pajama sleeve back and poised the syringe. It was like watching a man fiddling with the fuse of a delayed-action bomb. There was nothing I could do but watch and sweat for him. I sweated all right, wanting to tell him to hurry up and for the love of Mike not to stand there like a dummy, but get the thing over.

He was a little short-sighted in spite of his glasses, and he couldn't see the right vein. His head kept getting closer and closer to Hopper while he peered at the white, sinewy arm. He seemed to have forgotten how dangerous Hopper was. All he seemed to be thinking about was to make a good job of the injection. His face was only about a foot away from Hopper's when he nodded his head as if he had found the vein he was after. Very gently he laid the side of the needle down on the vein.

I wasn't breathing now. My hands were clutching at the sheet. Then, just as he was going to plunge in the needle, he drew back with an impatient exclamation and walked over to the tray he had left on the chest of drawers.

My breath whistled in my dry mouth as I said unevenly, "What the hell's the matter now?"

"I forgot the ether," he said. "Stupid of me. One should always clean the skin before making a puncture."

He was sweating almost as badly as I, but he had been taught to use ether before giving the syringe and that was the way he was going to give it; come hell, come sunshine.

Hopper stirred slightly as Quell dabbed on the ether. I was half out of bed with nervous anticipation, and Quell's hand was unsteady as he began the ghastly hunt for the vein again.

Down went his head within a foot of Hopper's, his eyes intent on Hopper's skin.

Suddenly Hopper opened his eyes. Quell was too busy to notice.

"Look out!" I croaked.

As Quell looked up with a stifled gasp Hopper, moving with the speed of a snake, had him by the throat.

6

WITH one furious, violent movement I dragged the heavy sheet off my legs and threw myself out of bed. I had a crazy idea the force of my throw would wrench the bed free so I could drag it across the floor and get at Hopper. But the bed held and I only succeeded in knocking the breath out of my body.

Quell's wild yell hit the ceiling, bounced off and burst over me like shrapnel. He yelled again, and then his next yell trailed off into a blood-chilling gurgle as Hopper's hands cut off his breath.

I didn't look at them. I was afraid to. The sound of the struggle was bad enough. Instead I hoisted myself up on the bed, slid to the end and got my free leg over the bedrail and on to the floor. I was in such a panic I could scarcely breathe and I was shaking like an old man with the palsy. I stretched towards the chest of drawers. My fingertips just brushed the handles of the top drawer. Behind me came a savage growling noise—a noise like nothing I have ever heard or ever want to hear again. I strained frantically towards the drawer handle. My fingernails got a purchase. I pulled madly away from the handcuff and the skin around my ankle felt as if it was on fire.

My nails hooked into the handle and the drawer opened an inch. It was enough. It gave me just enough purchase to pull the drawer right out so it fell with a crash to the floor. It was full of towels and surgical bandages, and hanging over the rail I scrabbled madly among the junk, hunting for the key.

A sudden yammering noise behind me sent my blood pressure up, but I didn't pause in my frantic hunt. I found the key at last between two towels, and, sobbing for breath, I swung myself back on the bed, searching for the tiny lock opening in the cuff. My ankle was bleeding but I didn't care about that. I sank the key into the lock, turned it and the cuff came off.

I was off the bed and across the room in one movement. Then I stopped short, took two steps back, and gulped down a sudden rush of saliva into my mouth.

Hopper peered at me over Quells body. He showed his teeth, and I could see his mouth was coated with blood. There was blood everywhere. On the wall behind him, over the sheet, over him and Quell.

Quell lay across the bed—a dummy in blood-stained clothes. His half-open eyes looked at me in glazed horror. Hopper had bitten into his jugular vein. He was deader than a dead mackerel. "Give me the key," Hopper said in a forced whisper. "Others shall die tonight."

I moved away. I thought I was a tough guy, but not now; Malloy-the-squeamish with cold sweat on his face and a lump of lead in his belly. I have seen some pretty horrible sights in my life, but this little tableau took the prize.

"Give me the key or I will kill you, too," Hopper said, and threw Quell's body off the bed on to the floor. He began to creep down the bed towards me, his face working, the blood on his mouth glistening in the soft lamplight.

A Grand Guignol nightmare this. A dream to tell your friends about—a dream they wouldn't believe.

I began a slow, backward, circling movement towards the door.

"Don't go away, Seabright," Hopper said, crouching on the bed and glaring at me. "Give me the key!" I reached the door, and, as my hand closed over the handle he let out an unearthly scream of frustrated rage and threw himself off the bed at me. The bed rocked, but held, and his clawing fingers scrabbled at the carpet six feet or so away from me.

I was shaking. I got the door open and almost fell into the passage. As I grabbed the handle to shut it, the horrible animal sound burst out of his throat again.

For some moments I just stood in the long, silent corridor, my heart jumping and my knees knocking, then slowly I took hold of myself. With one hand against the wall to support me, I set off slowly towards the massive door at the end of the corridor. I passed four other doors before I came to the end one. I ran my hands over the surface, feeling the soft rubber cool against my hot skin. I turned the handle, but nothing happened. The door was locked as tight as Pharaoh's tomb. Well, I expected that. But if I could I was going to get out of here. The thought of going back to that charnel-house of a room gave me the shakes. I took hold of the door handle and bent my strength to it. Nothing happened. It was like trying to push over the Great Wall of China.

That wasn't the way out.

I retraced my steps to the far end of the corridor and

examined the mesh-grill window. Nothing short of a crowbar would have shifted it, and even with a crowbar it would have taken half a day to break out.

The next move was to find a weapon. If I could find something I could use as a sap I had only to hide myself near the main door and wait for someone to show up. A simple plan, but even a Malloy will get an idea sometimes.

I began to move along the corridor. The first door I tried was unlocked. I peered cautiously into darkness, listened, heard my own breathing and nothing else, groped for the light switch and turned on the light. Probably Quells room. It was neat and tidy and clean, and there was no weapon in sight or anything I could use for a weapon. A white uniform hanging on a stretcher gave me an idea. I slid into the room and tried on the coat. It didn't fit me any better than a mole-skin would fit a polar bear, so I dropped the idea.

The next room was also empty of life. Above the dirty-looking bed was a large colored print of a girl in a G-string and a rope of pearls. She smiled at me invitingly but I didn't smile back. That made it Bland's room.

I slid in and shut the door. A rapid search through the chest of drawers produced among other things a leather-bound sap with a wrist thong; a nicely-balanced, murderous little weapon, and just what I wanted.

I went across the room to a cupboard, found a spare uniform and tried on the jacket. It was a fair fit—a little big, but good enough. I changed, leaving my pajamas on the floor. I felt a lot better once I was in trousers and shoes again. Pajamas and bare feet are not the equipment for fighting. I shoved the sap into my hip pocket and wished I had a gun.

At the bottom of the cupboard I found a pint bottle of Irish whisky. I broke the seal, unscrewed the cap and took a slug. The liquor went down like silk and exploded in my stomach like a grenade.

Good liquor, I thought, and, to make sure, had another pull at the bottle. Still very good. Then I packed the pint in a side pocket and moved to the door again. I felt the fire in my belly.

As I opened the door I heard footsteps. I stood quieter than a mouse that sees a cat and waited. The hatchet-faced nurse came along the corridor, humming to herself. She passed quite close to me and would have seen me if she had looked my way, but she didn't. She kept on, opened a door on the other side of the corridor and went into a dimly lit room. The door closed.

I waited, breathing gently, feeling a lot better for the whisky. Minutes ticked by. A small piece of fluff, driven by the draught from under the door, scuttled along the corridor apologetically. A sudden squall of rain lashed against the grill-covered window. The wind sighed around the house. I kept on waiting. I didn't want to hit the nurse if I could help it. I'm sentimental about hitting women: they hit me instead.

The nurse appeared again, walked the length of the corridor, then produced a key and unlocked the main door before I realized what she was doing. I saw the door open. I saw a flight of stairs leading to a lighted something beyond. I jumped forward, but she had passed through the doorway and closed the door behind her.

I consoled myself I wasn't ready to leave yet anyway. The door could wait. I decided I would investigate the room the nurse had just left. Maybe that was where Anona was.

I eased out the sap, resisted the temptation to take another drink and walked along the corridor. I paused outside the door, pressed my ear to the panel and listened. I heard nothing but the wind and the rain against the mesh-grilled window. I looked back over my shoulder. No one was peering at me from around the other doors. The corridor looked as lonely and as empty as a church on a Monday afternoon. I squeezed the door handle and turned slowly. The door opened and I looked into a room built and furnished along the lines of the room in which I had been kept a prisoner.

There were two beds, one of them empty. In the other, opposite me, was a woman. A blue night lamp made an eerie light over the white sheet and her white face. The halo of fair hair rested on the pillow, the eyes studying the ceiling with the perplexed look of a lost child.

I pushed the door open a little wider and walked softly into the room, closed the door and leaned against it. I wondered if she would scream. The rubber-lined door reassured me that if she did no one would hear her; but she didn't. Her eyes continued to stare at the ceiling, but a nerve in her cheek began to jump. I waited. There was no immediate hurry and I didn't want to scare her.

Slowly the eyes moved along the ceiling to the wall, down the wall until they rested on me. We looked at each other. I was aware I was breathing gently and the sap I held in my hand was as unnecessary as a Tommy gun at a choir practice. I slid it back into my pocket.

She studied me, the nerve jumping and her eyes widening.

"Hello, there," I said, cheerfully and quietly. I even managed a smile.

Malloy and his bedside manner—a talent to be discussed with bated breath by his grandchildren; if he ever had any grandchildren, which was doubtful.

"Who are you?" She didn't scream nor try to run up the wall, but the nerve kept on jumping.

"I am a sort of detective," I said, hoping to reassure her.

"I'm here to take you home."

Now I was closer to her I could see the pupils of her blue eyes were like pinpoints.

"I haven't any clothes," she said. "They've taken them away."

"I'll find you some more. How do you feel?"

"All right." The fair head rolled to the right and then to the left. "But I can't remember who I am. The man with the white hair told me I've lost my memory. He's nice, isn't he?"

"So I am told," I said carefully. "But you want to go home, don't you?"

"I haven't a home." She drew one long naked arm from under the sheet and ran slender fingers through the mop of fair hair. Her hand slid down until it rested on the jumping nerve. She pressed a finger against the nerve as if to hide it. "It got lost, but the nurse said they were looking for it. Have you found it?"

"Yes, that's why I am here."

She thought about that for some moments, frowning. "Then you know who I am?" she said at last.

"Your name is Anona Freedlander," I said. "And you live in San Francisco."

"Do I? I don't remember that. Are you sure?"

I was eyeing her arm. It was riddled with tiny scars. They had kept her drugged for a long time. She was more or less drugged now.

"Yes, I'm sure. Can you get out of bed?"

"I don't think I want to," she said. "I think I would rather go to sleep."

"That's all right," I told her. "You go to sleep. We're not ready to leave just yet. In a little while: after you've had your sleep, we'll go."

"I haven't any clothes, or did I tell you that? I haven't

anything on now. I threw my nightdress into the bath. The nurse was very angry."

"You don't have to bother about anything. I'll do the bothering. I'll find you something to wear when we're ready to go."

The heavy lids dropped suddenly, opened again with an effort. The finger slid off the nerve. It wasn't jumping any more.

"I like you," she said drowsily. "Who did you say you were?"

"Malloy. Vic Malloy—a sort of detective."

She nodded.

"Malloy. I'll try to remember. I have a very bad memory. I never seem to remember anything." Again, the lids began to fall. I stood over her, watching. I don't seem to be able to keep awake." Then after a long pause and when I thought she was asleep, she said in a far-away voice: "She shot him, you know. I was there. She picked up the shotgun and shot him. It was horrible."

I rubbed the tip of my nose with my forefinger. Silence settled over the room. She was sleeping now. Whatever the nurse had pushed into her had swept her away into oblivion. Maybe she wouldn't come to the surface again until the morning. It meant carrying her out if I could get out myself. But there was time to worry about that.

If I had to carry her I could wrap her in the sheet, but if she insisted on walking then I'd have to find her something to wear.

I looked around the room. The chest of drawers stood opposite the foot of the bed. I opened one drawer after the other. Most of them were empty; the others contained towels and spare bedding. No clothes.

I crossed the room to the cupboard, opened it and peered

inside. There was a bathrobe, slippers, and two expanding suitcases stacked neatly on the top shelf. I hauled one of them down. On the lid were the embossed initials *A.F.* I unstrapped the case, opened it. The contents solved my clothes problem. It was packed with clothes. I pawed through them. At the bottom of the case was a nurse's uniform.

I dipped my fingers into the side pockets of the case. In one of them I found a small, blue-covered diary dated 1948.

I thumbed through it quickly. The entries were few and far between. There were several references to 'Jack,' and I guessed he was Jack Brett, the naval deserter Mifflin had told me about.

1/24   Movie with Jack. 7:45.
1/28   Dinner L'Etoile. Meet Jack 6:30.
1/29   Home for weekend.
2/5   Jack rejoining his ship.

Nothing more until March 10th.

3/10   Still no letter from Jack.
3/12   Dr. Salzer asked me if I would like outside work.
        I said yes.
3/16   Start work at Crestways.
3/18   Mr. Crosby died.

The rest of the diary was a blank as her life had been a blank since that date. She had gone to Crestways presumably to nurse someone. She had seen Crosby die. So she had been locked up in this room for two years and had drug shot into her in the hope that sooner or later her mind would deteriorate and she wouldn't remember what had happened. That much was obvious, but she still remembered. The horror of the scene still lingered in her mind. Maybe she had come suddenly into the room where the two girls had been fighting for the possession of the gun. She may have drawn back when Crosby had taken a hand in the struggle, not wishing to embarrass him, and she had seen the gun swing on Crosby and the shot fired.

I looked at the still, white face. Sometime, but not now, there had been character and determination in that face. She wasn't the type to hush anything up, nor would she be influenced by money. She was much more likely to insist on the police being called. So they had locked her away.

I scratched the side of my jaw thoughtfully and flapped the little diary against the palm of my hand. The next move was to get out and get out quickly.

And as if in answer to this thought there was a sudden and appalling crash that shook the building—it sounded as if part of the house had collapsed.

I nearly jumped out of my skin, but reached the door in two strides and jerked it open. The corridor was full of mortar and brick dust, and out of the dust came two figures, guns in fists, running swiftly towards Hopper's room—Jack Kerman and Mike Finnegan. At the sight of them I gave a croaking cheer. They pulled up sharply, their guns covering me.

Kerman's tense face broke into a wide, expansive grin.

"Universal Services at your service," he said, grabbing my arm. "Want a drink, pal?"

"I want transport for a nude blonde," I said, hugging him, and took a slap on the back from Mike that staggered me. "What did you do—pull the house down?"

"Hooked a couple of chains to the window and yanked it out with a ten-ton truck," Kerman said, grinning from ear to ear. "A little crude, but effective. Where's the blonde?"

Where the mesh-grill window had been there was now a

gaping hole and shattered brickwork.

I hauled Kerman into Anona's room while Finnegan guarded the corridor. It took us about ten seconds to wrap the unconscious girl in a sheet and carry her out of the room.

"Rear-guard action, Mike," I said as we swept past him to the hole in the wall. "Shoot if you have to."

"Sling her over my shoulder," Kerman said, twittering with excitement. "There's a ladder against the wall."

I helped him climb up on the tottering brickwork. A naked arm and leg hung limply near his face.

"Now I know why guys join the Fire Service," he said, as he began his cautious climb down the ladder.

Below I could see a large truck parked near the house and at the foot of the ladder I spotted Paula. She waved to me.

"Okay, Mike," I called. "Let's go."

As Mike joined me, the door at the end of the corridor burst open and the hatchet-face nurse appeared. She gave one gaping look at us and the ruined wall and started to scream.

We scrambled down the ladder and piled into the truck.

Paula was already at the steering wheel, and as we scrambled into the back of the truck she let in the clutch and drove crazily across the flower beds.

Kerman had laid Anona on the floor and was looking down at her.

"Yum, yum," he said, and twirled his moustache. "If I'd known she was as good as this, I'd have come sooner."

Chapter Five

1

A BUZZER buzzed, and the platinum blonde unwound her slinky form from behind her desk and came over to me. She said Mr. Willet would see me now. She spoke as if she were in church, and looked as if she should have been in the front row of Izzy Jacob's pretties at the Orchid Room Follies.

I followed the sway of her hips across the outer office to the inner sanctum. She tapped on the door with an emerald green nail, opened it and tucked up a stray curl the way women have as she said, "Mr. Malloy is here."

She stood aside as my cue to enter. I entered.

Willet was entrenched behind his super-sized desk and was staring dubiously at something that looked like a last will and testament, and probably was. A fat, gold-tipped cigarette burned between two brown fingers. He waved me to a chair without looking up.

The platinum blonde went away. I watched her go. At the door she managed to snap a hip so it quivered under the black sheen of her silk dress. I was sorry when the door closed on her.

I sat down, looked inside my hat and tried to remember when I had bought it. It seemed a long, long time ago. The hatter's imprint was indecipherable. I told myself I'd buy myself a new hat if I could persuade Willet to part with any more money. If I couldn't, then I'd make do with this one.

I thought these thoughts to pass the time. Willet seemed lost in his legal flimflammery—a picture of a big-shot lawyer making money. You could almost hear the dollars pouring into his bank.

"Cigarette," he said suddenly and absently. Without taking his eyes off the mass of papers he clutched in his hand he pushed the silver box towards me.

I took one of the fat gold-tipped cigarettes I found in the box and lit it. I hoped it would make me feel like a moneymaker too, but it didn't. It looked a lot better than it tasted—that kind of cigarette usually does.

Then suddenly, just as I was getting ready to doze, he tossed the papers into the out tray, hitched his chair forward, and said, "Now Mr. Malloy, let's get at it. I have another appointment in ten minutes."

"Then I had better see you some other time," I said. "We won't be through in ten minutes. I don't know how much you value the Crosby account, Mr. Willet, but it must be worth a tidy sum. Without shouting it from the house tops it wouldn't surprise me if you won't have the account much longer."

That jarred him. He stared at me bleakly, crushed out his half-smoked cigarette and leaned halfway across his desk.

"What exactly do you mean?"

"Do you want it in detail, or do you want just a quick peep at it?" I asked. "It's bad either way, but in detail it sort of creeps up on you."

"How long will it take?"

"A half an hour, maybe more; and then you'll want to ask questions. Say an hour, maybe a little longer. But you won't be bored."

He chewed his lower lip, frowning, then reached for the

telephone and cancelled three appointments all in a row. I could see it hurt him to do it, but he did it. A ten-minute interview with a guy like Willet would be worth a hundred bucks, maybe more—to him, not to you.

"Go ahead," he said, leaning back in his chair. "Why haven't you been in touch with me before?"

"That's part of it," I told him, and laid my hat under my chair. I had a feeling I might be buying a new one before very long. "I've spent the past five days in an asylum for the insane."

But I wasn't going to jar him so easily again. He made a grunting noise, but his expression didn't change.

"Before I get started," I said, "maybe you might tell me about Miss Crosby's banking account. Did you get a look at it?"

He shook his head.

"The bank manager quite rightly refused. If he had shown it to me and the fact had leaked out, he would have lost the account. It's worth a lot of money. But he did tell me the insurance money had been converted to bearer bonds and has been withdrawn from the account."

"Did he say when?"

"Soon after probate."

"And you have written to Miss Crosby asking her to call on you?"

"Yes. She'll be here tomorrow afternoon."

"When did you write to her?"

"Tuesday—five days ago."

"Did she answer by return?"

He nodded.

"Then I don't think she'll keep the appointment. Anyway, we'll see." I tapped the ash into his silver ashtray. "All right, that covers the points we made together. Now I'd better get on with my tale."

I told him how MacGraw and Hartsell had called on me. He listened, sunk down in his chair with his eyes as anonymous as a pair of headlights. He neither laughed nor cried when I described how they had beaten me up. It hadn't happened to him, so why should he care? But when I told him how Maureen had appeared on the scene his brows came down in a frown, and he allowed himself the luxury of tapping on the edge of his desk with his fingernails. That was probably the nearest he would ever get to a show of excitement.

"She took me to a house on the cliff road, east of San Diego Highway. She said it was hers—a nice place if you like places that cost a lot of money and are smart enough to house movie stars in. Did you know she had it?"

He shook his head.

"We sat around and talked," I went on. "She wanted to know why I was interested in her, and I showed her Janet's letter. For some reason or other she seemed scared. She wasn't acting—she was genuinely frightened. I asked her if she was being blackmailed at that time, she said she wasn't, and that Janet was probably trying to make trouble for her. She said Janet hated her. Did she?"

Willet was playing with a letter opener now, his face was set and there was a worried look in his eyes.

"I understand they didn't get along, nothing more than that. You know how it is with step sisters."

I said I knew how it was with step sisters.

Time went by for a few minutes. The only sound in the room was the busy tick of Willet's desk clock.

"Go on," he said curtly. "What else did she say?"

"As you know, Janet and a guy named Douglas Sherrill were engaged to be married. What you probably don't know is Sherrill is a dark horse—possibly a con man, certainly a crook. According to Maureen, she stole Sherrill from Janet."

Willet didn't say anything. He waited.

"The two girls had a showdown which developed into a fight," I went on. "Janet grabbed a shotgun. Old man Crosby appeared and tried to take the gun away from her. He got shot and killed."

I thought for a moment that Willet was going to jump right across his desk. But he controlled himself, and said in a voice that seemed to come from under the floor, "Did Maureen tell you this?"

"Oh, yes. She wanted to get it off her chest. Now here's another bit you'll like. The shooting had to be hushed up. I was wrong about Dr. Salzer signing Crosby's certificate. He didn't sign it. Mrs. Salzer signed it. According to her she is a qualified doctor and a friend of the family. One of the girls called her and she came around and fixed things. Lessways, who isn't the type to make things awkward for the wealthy, accepted the yarn that Crosby was cleaning his gun and shot himself accidentally. He took their word for it. So did Brandon."

Willet lit a cigarette. He looked like a hungry man who's been given a pie and finds nothing inside it.

"Go on," he said, and sat back.

"For some reason or other a nurse named Anona Freedlander was in the house at the time of the shooting and she saw the accident. Mrs. Salzer wasn't taking any chances. She locked the nurse up to make sure she wouldn't talk. She's been in a padded cell at Salzer's sanitorium ever since."

"You mean—against her will?"

"Not only against her will, but for two years they have been pumping drugs into her."

"You're not suggesting Maureen Crosby is aware of this?"

"I don't know."

Willet was breathing heavily now. The thought that a client as wealthy as Maureen Crosby might be charged with kidnapping seemed to shock him, although Anona Freedlander's predicament hadn't made him turn a hair.

"Incidentally, in case you're working up some sympathy for her," I said, "we got Anona out of the sanitorium last night."

"Oh?" He looked disconcerted. "Is she likely to make trouble?"

I grinned unpleasantly.

"I should think it's more than likely. Wouldn't you want to start something after being kept locked up for two years just because some rich people are shy of appearing in the newspapers?"

He fingered his chin and did some heavy thinking.

"Perhaps we could give her a little compensation," he said at last, but he didn't look very happy. "I'd better see her."

"No one sees her until she's ready to see anyone. Right now she doesn't seem to know whether she's coming or going." I crushed out the cigarette and lit one of my own. "This kidnapping should be reported to the police. If it is, then the whole sordid story will hit the headlines. It will be your job then to hand over the Crosby millions to the Research Center. They may or may not want you to handle the account—probably not."

"All the more reason why I should have a talk with her," he said. "These things can usually be arranged."

"Don't be too sure about that. Then there's this little incident that happened to me," I said mildly. "I was also kidnapped and held prisoner for five days, and also had a certain amount of drug pumped into me. That's another little thing that should be reported to the police."

"Why talk yourself out of a good job?" he returned, and for the first time since I had been in the room, he allowed himself a slight grin. "I was about to suggest an extra retainer—say another five hundred dollars."

That made my new hat a certainty.

"That tempts me. We might call it an insurance against risks," I said. "But it would have to be over and above the fee you will pay for the work we are doing."

"That's all right."

"Well perhaps we might leave Anona Freedlander for the moment and go on with the story," I said. "There's quite a bit more, and it gets better as it goes along."

He pushed back his chair and got up. I watched him cross to a liquor cabinet against the opposite wall and return with a bottle of Haig & Haig and two small glasses.

"Do you use this stuff?" he asked as he sat down again. I said I used it whenever I could.

He poured two drinks, pushed one across the desk towards me, tossed the other down his throat and immediately refilled his glass. He put the bottle midway between us.

"Help yourself," he said.

I drank a little of the scotch. It was very good, quite the best liquor I had had in months. I thought it was wonderful how a big-shot lawyer could unbend when he sees trouble coming towards him with his name on it.

"According to Maureen, Crosby's death preyed on Janet's mind," I told him. "Maybe it did, but she certainly had an odd way of showing it. I should have thought she wouldn't have felt like playing tennis or running around at a time like that, but apparently she did. Anyway also according to Maureen, Janet committed suicide about six or seven weeks after the shooting. She took arsenic."

A tiny drop of scotch wobbled out of Willet's glass on to

his blotter. He said, "Good God!" under his breath.

"That was hushed up too. As it happened Mrs. Salzer was away at the time, so Maureen and Dr. Salzer called in Dr. Bewley, a harmless old goat, and told him Janet was suffering from malignant endocarditis, and he obligingly issued the death certificate. Janet had a personal maid, Eudora Drew, who possibly overheard Salzer and Maureen cooking up this yarn. She put on the bite, and they paid her. I got a line on her and went to see her. She was smart enough to fend me off and get to Salzer, telling him I was offering five hundred bucks for information and if he'd like to raise the ante she would keep her mouth shut. Mrs. Salzer had an answer to that. She sent along an ex-gunman who was working at the sanatorium to reason with her. According to Mrs. S, he got rough and killed her."

Willet drew in a long, slow breath. He took a drink like a man who needs a drink.

"The family butler, John Stevens, also knew something, or suspected something," I went on. "I was persuading him to loosen up when he was kidnapped by six Wops who work for Sherrill. They got a little tough with him and he died, but that still makes murder. Two murders. Now we get to the third. Are you liking this?"

He said in a gritty voice, "Go on."

"You will remember Nurse Gurney? Mrs. Salzer admits kidnapping her, only according to her, Nurse Gurney fell down the fire escape and broke her neck. Mrs. Salzer hid her somewhere in the desert. That's murder, too."

"This is fantastic," Willet said. "It's unbelievable."

"It's unbelievable only because of the motive. Here we have two people, Mrs. Salzer and Sherrill, committing three murders between them, to say nothing of kidnapping Anona Freedlander and myself, to protect a girl from newspaper publicity. That's what makes it unbelievable. I think there's a lot more to this business than we know about. It seems to me these two are desperately trying to keep a very lively cat from hopping out of the bag, and I want to find out what kind of cat it is."

"It's not newspaper publicity they're worrying about," Willet said. "Look at the money that's involved."

"Yeah, but I still think there's a strange cat we haven't found yet. I'm going to hunt for it. Anyway I'll go on. I haven't finished yet . . . The punch line comes last. Maureen told me when she came into her money, Sherrill reverted to type. He turned blackmailer. He said he would circulate the rumor that because she stole him from Janet, Janet shot her father and killed herself. But if Maureen bought the *Dream Ship* for him he would keep quiet. She bought the *Dream Ship*—that's why she converted the insurance money into bearer bonds. She gave the bonds to Sherrill. Imagine how the newspapers would scream if it got out that Maureen Crosby was the backer of a gambling-ship. Wouldn't that drop the whole of the Crosby money into the Research Center's lap?"

Willet managed to look green without actually turning green.

"She bought the *Dream Ship*?" he said in a stifled voice.

"That's what she tells me. She also said she was frightened of Sherrill, and at that dramatic moment Mr. Sherrill made a personal appearance. He announced he was going to put Maureen where no one would find her and dispose of me in the same way. I was beginning to argue with him when someone from behind bent a sap over my head and I woke up in Salzer's sanatorium. We won't waste time going into what happened there. It's enough that my assistant kidded Lessways he was a well-known writer and got himself invited to the monthly visit to the asylum with the city's councilmen. He spotted me, got me out, and we took Anona Freedlander with us. What we have to find out is whether Sherrill has carried out his threat to hide Maureen away. If she doesn't show up tomorrow my bet is she's hidden away—probably on Sherrill's ship. But if she does show up, then I'll be inclined to think she's in this business with the rest of them, and she took me to her house so Sherrill could get at me."

Willet poured another drink with a hand that wasn't too steady.

"I don't believe that's likely," he said.

"We'll see. If Sherrill is holding her, have you any power to stop her money?"

"I haven't any power over her money at all. All I can do is to advise the other trustees that she has broken the terms of the will."

"Who are the other trustees?"

"Mr. Glynn and Mr. Coppley, my chiefs, who are, of course, in New York."

"Should they be consulted?"

"Not at this stage," he said, and rubbed his jaw. "I'll be frank with you, Malloy. They would follow out the terms of the will without hesitation, and without taking into consideration the girl might be innocent. To my way of thinking the will is overly-harsh. Crosby has stipulated that if Maureen gets any negative press the money goes to the Research Center. I imagine he got a little tired of her pranks, but he didn't realize he was giving an unscrupulous blackmailer a weapon to use against her. And that's what has probably happened."

"It's occurred to you we are covering up three murders?" I said, helping myself to another drink. All this talk made me dry. "So far Brandon isn't digging too deep because he's scared of the Crosby's money, but if the facts turn out that Maureen's hooked up in these murders, he'll have to forget about her money and take some action; then you and I will be out on a limb."

"We've got to give her the benefit of the doubt," Willet said uneasily. "I'd never forgive myself if by acting too prematurely we caused her to lose her money unfairly. How about this Freedlander woman? How long will it be before she can talk?"

"I don't know. Some days from the look of her. She can't even remember who she is."

"Is she in the hospital?"

I shook my head.

"My secretary, Miss Bensinger, is looking after her. I've called in a doctor but there's nothing much he can do. He says it's a matter of time. I'm going to San Francisco today to see her father. He may help her memory."

"We'll pay any expenses involved," Willet said. "Charge it to us." He lit another cigarette. What's the next move?"

"We'll have to wait and see if Maureen turns up. If she doesn't, I'll go out to the *Dream Ship* and see if she's on board. There are other angles I'm looking into. At the moment I have a lot of loose strings that need tidying up."

There was a tap on the door and the platinum blonde came in and swayed her way to Willet's desk.

"Mrs. Pollard is getting impatient," she murmured. "And this message has just come in. I thought you should see it at once."

She gave him a slip of paper. He read what was written on it and his eyebrows shot up.

"All right. Tell Mrs. Pollard I'll see her in five minutes," he said. He looked at me. "Miss Crosby won't be coming tomorrow. Apparently, she is going to Mexico for a trip."

"Who phoned?" I asked, sitting forward.

"He didn't say who he was," the platinum blonde told Willet. "He said he was speaking for Miss Crosby, and would I give you the message right away."

Willet raised his eyebrows at me. I shook my head.

"All right Miss Palmetter," he said. "That's all."

I fished up my hat from under my chair and stood up.

"Looks like a visit to the *Dream Ship*," I said.

Willet put the scotch and the two glasses away.

"You'd better not tell me about that," he said. "You'll be careful, won't you?

"You'll be surprised how careful I will be."

"She may have gone to Mexico," he went on doubtfully. I gave him a little grin, but he didn't grin back.

"Be seeing you," I said, and went into the outer office. A fat, over-dressed woman with pearls the size of pickled onions around her neck sat breathing heavily in one of the lounging chairs. She gave me a stony glare as I picked my way past her to the door.

I looked back at the platinum blonde and tried my grin on her.

She opened her eyes very wide, stared emptily at me and then looked away.

I went out, my grin hanging in space, like an unwanted baby on a doorstep.

2

JACK KERMAN was demonstrating to Trixy, my switch-board girl, how Gregory Peck kisses his leading ladies when I tramped in. They came apart a little slower than a flash of lightning, but not much. Trixy whipped to her seat and began to pull out plugs and push in plugs with an unconvincing show of efficiency.

Kerman gave me a sad smirk, shook his head sorrowfully, and followed me into the inner room.

"Do you have to do that?" I asked, going over to my desk and yanking open a drawer. "Isn't she a mite young?"

Kerman sneered.

"Not by the way she was acting," he said.

I took out my .38 police special, shoved it in my hip pocket and collected a couple of spare magazines.

"I have news," Kerman said, watching me a little pop-eyed. "Want it now?"

"I'll have it in the car. You and me are going to 'Frisco."

"Heeled?"

"Yeah. From now on I'm taking no chances. Got your rod?"

"I can get it."

While he was getting it, I put a call through to Paula.

"How is she?" I asked, when she came on the line.

"About the same. Dr. Mansell's just been in. He's given her a mild shot. He says it'll take a long time to taper her off."

"I'm on my way to see her father. If he'll take her over it'll let us out. You all right?"

She said she was.

"I'll look in on my way back," I said, and hung up.

Kerman and I rode in the elevator to the ground floor, then crossed the sidewalk to the Buick.

"We're going out to the *Dream Ship* tonight," I said as I started the engine.

"Officially or unofficially?"

"Unofficially—just like they do on the movies. Maybe we'll even have to swim out there."

"Sharks and things, huh?" Kerman said. "Maybe they'll try to shoot us when we get aboard."

"They certainly will if they see us." I edged past a truck and went up Centre Avenue with a burst of speed that startled two taxi-drivers and a girl driving a Pontiac.

"That'll be something to look forward to," Kerman said gloomily. He sunk lower in his seat. "I simply can't wait. Maybe I'd better make a will."

"Have you anything to leave?" I asked, surprised, and braked hard as the red light went up.

"Some dirty postcards and a stuffed rat," Kerman said. "I'll leave those to you."

As the light changed to green, I said, "What's the news? Find anything on Mrs. Salzer?"

Kerman lit a cigarette, dropped the match into the back seat of the Pontiac as it tried to nose past us.

"You bet. Watch your driving, this is going to knock you sideways. I've been digging all morning. Know who she is?"

I swung the car on to Fairview Boulevard.

"Tell me."

"Macdonald Crosby's second wife . . . Maureen's mother."

I swerved half across the road, missed a truck that was pounding along and minding its own business, and had the driver curse at me. I edged back to the near side.

"I told you to watch it," Kerman said, and grinned. "Hot, isn't it?"

"Go on, what else?"

"About twenty-three years ago she was a throat and ear specialist in San Francisco. Crosby met her when she treated Janet for a minor complaint. He married her. She kept her practice, overworked, had a nervous breakdown and had to quit. Crosby and she didn't hit it off. He caught her fooling around with Salzer. He divorced her. When he moved to

Orchid City, she moved too, to be near Maureen. Like it?"

"Well, it helps," I said. We were now on the Los Angeles and San Francisco Highway and I had my foot hard down on the gas pedal. "It explains quite a lot of things, but not everything. It accounts for why she took a hand in the game. Naturally, she'd be anxious her daughter should keep all that money. But for the love of Mike! Imagine going to the lengths she's gone to. It's my bet she's crazy.

"Probably is," Kerman said complacently. "They were cagey about her at the Medical Association. Said she had a nervous breakdown and wouldn't expand on it. She vomited right in the middle of an operation. One nurse I talked to said if it hadn't been for the anesthetist, she would have cut the patient's throat—as bad as that."

"Salzer have any money?"

"Not a bean."

"I wonder who promoted the sanatorium—probably Crosby. She's not going to get away with Nurse Gurney's death. When the police find the body I'm going to tip Mifflin."

"They may never find her," Kerman said. He had a very low opinion of the Orchid City police.

"I'll help them after I've seen Maureen."

We drove for the next ten minutes in silence while I did some heavy thinking.

Then Kerman said, "Aren't we wasting time going to see old man Freedlander? Couldn't we have telephoned?"

"You get bright ideas a little late, don't you? He may not be anxious to have her back. A telephone conversation can be closed down too easily. I have a feeling he'll need talking to."

We crossed the Oakland Bay Bridge a few minutes after three o'clock, turned off 3rd onto Montgomery Street, and left into California Street.

Freedlander's place was halfway down on the right-hand side. It was one of those nondescript slums: six stories of rabbit warren, a blaring radio and yelling children.

A party of kids came storming down the stone steps to welcome us. They did everything to the car except puncture the tires and drop lighted matches into the gas tank.

Kerman picked out the biggest and toughest of them and gave him half a buck.

"Keep your pals off this car and you'll get the other half," he said.

The boy hauled off and socked a kid around the ears to show his good faith. We left him booting another.

"Nice neighborhood," Kerman said, stroking his moustache with his thumbnail.

We went up the steps and examined the two long rows of mailboxes. Freedlander's place was on the fifth floor, number 25. There was no elevator, so we walked.

"It's going to make for a happy day if he's out," Kerman panted as he paused on the fourth landing to mop his brow.

"You drink too much," I said, and began to climb the stairs to the next floor.

We came to a long, dingy passage. Someone's radio was playing jazz. It blasted like a hot breath the length and breadth of the passage.

A slatternly-looking woman came out of a room nearby. She had on a black straw hat that had seen its better days, and in one hand she clutched a string shopping bag. She gave us a look full of inquisitive interest and went on down the passage to the head of the stairs. She turned to stare again, and Kerman put his thumbs to his ears and waggled his fingers at her. She went on down the stairs with her nose in the air.

We walked along the hallway to number 25. There was no

bell or knocker. As I lifted my hand to rap, a muffled bang sounded beyond the door—the sound a paper bag makes when you've blown it up and slapped it with your hand.

I had my gun out and my hand on the door handle before the sound had died away. I turned the handle and pushed. To my surprise the door opened. I looked into a fair-sized room—a living room if you judged by the way it was furnished.

I could hear Kerman breathing heavily behind me. I took in the room with a quick glance. There was no one to see. Two doors led off the room, and both were closed.

"Think it was a gun?" Kerman murmured.

I nodded, stepped quietly into the room, motioning him to stay where he was. He stayed where he was. I crossed the room and listened outside the right-hand door, but the noise from the blaring radio killed any other sound.

Waving to Kerman to get out of sight, I turned the handle and set the door moving with a gentle push, and at the same time stepped aside and pressed myself against the wall. We both waited and listened, but nothing happened. Through the open door drifted the strong, acid smell of gunpowder. I edged forward to peer into the room.

Slap in the middle of the floor lay a man. His legs were curled up under him and his hands were clenched into his chest. Blood came through his fingers, ran down his wrists and on to the floor. He was a man around sixty, and I guessed he was Freedlander. As I looked at him he gave a choking sigh and his hands flopped on the floor.

I didn't move. I knew the killer must be in there. He couldn't have gotten away.

Kerman sneaked into the living room behind me and flattened himself against the other side of the door. His heavy .45 looked like a cannon in his fist.

"Come on out!" I snarled suddenly. My voice sounded like a buzz-saw cutting into a wood knot. "And with your hands in the air!"

A gun went off and the slug ploughed through the doorway close to my head.

Kerman slid his arm around the door and fired twice. The crash of his gun rattled the windows.

"You can't get away!" I said, trying to sound like a tough cop. "We've got you surrounded."

But this time the killer wasn't playing. There was silence and no movement. We waited, but nothing happened. I had visions of the cops arriving, and I wasn't anxious to be involved with the 'Frisco cops—they were much too efficient.

I motioned to Kerman to stay where he was and sneaked over to the window. As I pushed it up, Kerman fired into the room again, and under cover of the noise I got the window open. I leaned out. A few feet away was the window of the inner room. It meant getting onto the sill, stepping across to the other sill with about a hundred-foot drop below. As I swung my leg out of the window I looked back. Kerman's eyes were popping, and he shook his head at me. I jerked my thumb to the next window, then levered myself on to the sill.

Someone fired a gun from below and the slug splashed cement into my face. I was so startled I nearly let go of my hold, looked down into the street at the upturned faces of a sizeable crowd. Right in the center was a beefy-looking cop, taking aim at me.

I gave a strangled yell, flung myself forward and sideways, lurched against the window of the next room and crashed through the glass to land on all fours on the floor. A gun went off practically in my face, and then Kerman's cannon boomed, bringing down a chunk of ceiling plaster.

I flattened out, wriggled desperately to get behind the bed

as more shots shook the room.

I had a sudden vision of a dark, snarling face peering at me over the top of the bed, and a vicious blue nose automatic pointing at my head, then the hand holding the gun disappeared with a crash of gunfire and reappeared again as a spongy, red mess.

It was my pal, the Wop with the dirty shirt. He gave a howl, staggered to the window as Kerman rushed at him. He hit Kerman with the back of his hand, dodged past him and ran out of the door, through the other room and into the hallway. More gunfire broke out, a woman screamed, and a body thudded to the floor.

"Watch out!" I gasped. "There's a gun-happy cop out there. He'll shoot as soon as look at you."

We stood still and waited.

But the cop wasn't taking any chances.

"All out!" he bawled from behind the door. Even from that distance I could hear him breathing. "I'll blast you to hell if you bring out a rod."

"We're coming," I said. "Don't excite yourself, and don't shoot."

We moved out of the room and into the passage with our hands in the air.

Laying in the passage was the Wop. He had a bullet-hole through the center of his forehead.

The cop was one of those massive men, big in the feet and solid bone in the head. He snarled at us, threatening us with his gun.

"Take it easy brother," I said, not liking the look of him. "You have two stiffs on your hands already. You don't want two more."

"I wouldn't care," he said, showing his teeth. "Two or four makes no difference to me. Back up against that wall until the wagon arrives."

We backed up against the wall. It didn't take long before we heard the wail of a siren. Two white-coated figures came panting up the stairs, together with a representative group from the Homicide Bureau. I was glad to see Detective District Commander Dunnigan was with them. He and I had done business with each other before.

"Hello," he said, and stared at us. "This your funeral?"

"Very nearly was," I said. "There's another stiff inside. Could you tell this officer we're not dangerous? I keep thinking he's going to shoot us."

Dunnigan waved the copper aside.

"I'll be out to talk to you in a moment."

He went in to look at Freedlander.

"He's a pal of ours," I told the copper who was glaring at us. "You should be more careful who you shoot at."

The copper spat.

"I was a mug not to have rubbed you two punks out," he said in disgust. "If they had found me with four stiffs maybe they would have made me a sergeant."

"What a charming little mind you have," Kerman said and backed away.

3

WE started back to Orchid City at five o'clock after a couple of awkward hours in Detective District Commander Dunnigan's office. He had done his best to dig into a case that kept snapping shut every time he thought he had worked the lid off, but he hadn't succeeded.

My story was straightforward, and more or less true. I said Freedlander's daughter had been missing for a couple of years. This he was able to check by calling the Missing

People's Bureau in Orchid City. I told him I had found her wandering the streets suffering from loss of memory, and, having taken her to my secretary's apartment had immediately got in my car to come to 'Frisco to take Freedlander to her.

He wanted to know how I knew she was Freedlander's daughter, and I said I read the Missing Peoples Bulletin the police circulated and remembered her description.

He stared bleakly at me for some minutes, wondering whether to believe me or not, and I stared right back at him.

"Should have thought you had better things to do," was his final comment.

I went on to tell him how I had arrived at Freedlander's apartment, heard a shot, broke in, found Freedlander dead and the Wop trying to get away. I said he fired at us and we fired at him, then handed Dunnigan our gun permits. I said maybe the Wop was a burglar. No, I didn't think I had seen him before although I might have. All Wops looked alike to me.

Dunnigan had a sneaking feeling there was much more behind all this than I was telling him. I could see that plainly on his big, square-shaped face. He said so.

I told him he must have been reading too many detective stories, and could I go now as I had a lot of work to do?

But he started in from the beginning again, probing, asking questions, wasting a lot of time, and finally finishing up just where he had started. He looked like a baffled bull as he sat glaring at me.

Luckily the Wop had taken Freedlander's money and his gold watch—the only things of value in the apartment, so it was a perfect setup for a routine shoot-and-run stick-up. Finally, Dunnigan decided to let us go.

"Maybe it was a stick-up," he said heavily. "If you two

birds hadn't been in on it, it would have been a stick-up, but you being there makes me wonder."

Kerman said if he worried about a little case like this, he would be an old man and retired before he got to the big cases.

"Never mind," Dunnigan said sourly. "I don't know what it is about you guys. Whenever you show your faces in this city trouble starts, and it usually starts for me. I wish you'd keep out. I've got all the work I want without you coming here and making me more."

We both laughed politely, shook hands, promised we would attend the inquest and left him.

We didn't say a word until we were in the Buick and driving along Oakland Bay Bridge, heading for home. Then Kerman said gently, "If that guy ever finds out the Wop was the one who kidnapped Stevens, I have a feeling life may be a little difficult for you."

"It's difficult enough as it is. We're now linked with Anona." I drove along for a mile or so before saying, "You know, this is a hell of a case. All along I have had the feeling that someone is trying very hard to keep a big, strong cat from getting out of the bag. We're missing something. We're looking at the bag and not at the cat, and the cat is the key to the whole setup. It has to be. Everyone who has caught sight of it has been silenced: Eudora Drew, John Stevens, Nurse Gurney, and now Freedlander. And I have an idea that Anona Freedlander knows about the cat too. Somehow we have to get her memory going again—and *fast*."

"If she knows something why didn't they knock her off instead of keeping her in that home?" Kerman said.

"That's what's worrying me. Up to now all of them have been killed more or less accidentally, but Freedlander was murdered. That means someone is getting in a panic. It also means that Anona is no longer safe."

Kerman sat up.

"You think they'll try to get at her?"

"Yeah. We'll have to hide her some place safe. Maybe we could get Doc Mansell to put her in his Los Angeles clinic, I'll get Kruger to lend me a couple of his bruisers to sit outside the door."

"Maybe you have been reading too many detective stories, too," Kerman said, looking at me out of the corner of his eyes.

I kept the Buick moving at high speed while I thought about Freedlander's killing, and the more I thought the more jittery I got.

We reached San Lucas and I pulled up outside a drug store.

"What now?" Kerman asked, surprised.

"I'm going to call Paula," I said. "I should have called her from 'Frisco. I've got the shakes."

"Take it easy," Kerman said, and looked startled. "You're letting your imagination run away with you."

"I hope I am," I said, and made for the phone booth.

Kerman clutched my arm and pulled me back.

"Look at that!"

He was pointing to a stack of evening newspapers on the magazine counter. Inch-high headlines smeared across the front page read:

WIFE OF WELL-KNOWN NATURE CURE DOCTOR
COMMITS SUICIDE

"Get it," I said, jerked my arm free and shut myself in the booth. I put the call through to Paula's apartment and waited. I could hear the *buzz-buzz* note of the ringing tone, but no one answered. I stood there, my heart thumping, the receiver against my ear, listening and waiting.

She should be there. We had agreed Anona wasn't to be left alone.

Kerman came to stare at my tense face through the glass door. I shook my head at him, broke the connection and asked the operator to try again.

While she was making another connection, I opened the door.

"No answer," I said. "She's trying again."

Kerman's face darkened.

"Let's move on. We have a good hour's run yet."

"We'll do it in better time than that," I said, and as I was about to hang up, the operator came on and said the line was in order but there was no answer.

I rammed down the receiver and together we ran out of the store. I sent the Buick whipping down the main street, and as soon as we were clear of the town I opened up.

Kerman was trying to read the newspaper but at the speed we were going he had trouble in holding it steady.

"She was found this afternoon," he bawled in my ear. "She took poison after Salzer had reported Quell's death to the police. No word about Anona. Nothing about Nurse Gurney."

"She's the first of them to get cold feet," I said. "Or else someone fed her poison. To hell with her, anyway. I'm scared about Paula."

Kerman said afterwards he had never been driven in a car so fast in his life, and he didn't ever want to go through the experience again. At one time the speedometer needle was stuck at ninety-two, and it kept there as we roared along the wide coast road with the horn blaring.

A traffic cop came after us but he couldn't make the grade. He stuck behind for two or three miles, then dropped out of sight. I guessed he would phone our description through to the next town, so I swung off the main road and went pelting along a dirt road that wasn't much wider than twenty feet. Kerman just sat with his eyes closed and prayed.

We arrived in Orchid City fifteen minutes under the hour, and that was *some* driving. We had done the sixty-odd miles in forty-five minutes.

Paula had an apartment on Park Boulevard, a hundred yards or so from Park Hospital. We roared up the broad boulevard and braked outside the apartment block with a squeal of tires like hog-day in a slaughterhouse.

The elevator seemed to crawl to the third floor. It got there eventually, and we both raced down the passage to Paula's apartment. I rammed my thumb in the doorbell and leaned my weight on it. I could hear the bell ringing, but no one answered. Sweat was standing out on my face as if I'd just come out of a shower.

I stood away.

"Together," I said to Kerman.

We lunged at the door with our shoulders. It was a good door, but we were pretty good men. The third lunge snapped the lock and carried us into the neat little hall.

We had our guns in our fists as we went through the living room to Paula's bedroom.

The bed was in disorder. The sheet and blanket lay on the floor.

We went into the bathroom and the spare bedroom; the apartment was empty, both Paula and Anona had vanished.

I rushed to the telephone and got through to the office. Trixy said Paula hadn't called. She said a man who wouldn't give his name had telephoned twice. I told her to give him Paula's number if he phoned again and hung up.

Kerman gave me a cigarette with a hand that shook

slightly. I lit it without being conscious of what I was doing and sat on the bed.

"We'd better get out to the *Dream Ship*," Kerman said in a tight, hard voice. "And get out there quick."

I shook my head.

"Take it easy," I said.

"What the hell!" Kerman exploded, and started for the door. "They've got Paula. Okay, we go out there and talk to them. Come on!"

"Take it easy," I said, not moving. "Sit down and don't be obvious."

Kerman came up to me.

"You crazy or something?"

"Do you think you'd ever get near that ship in daylight?" I said, looking at him. "Use your head. We're going out there, but we'll go when it's dark."

Kerman made an angry gesture.

"I'm going now. If we wait it may be too late."

"Oh shut up!" I said. "Get a drink. You're staying right here."

He hesitated, then went into the kitchen. After a while he came back with a bottle of scotch, two glasses, and a jug of ice-water. He made drinks, gave me one and sat down.

"There's not a damn thing we can do if they've decided to knock her on the head," I said. "Even if they haven't done it now, they'd do it the moment they saw us coming. We'll go out there when it's dark, and not before."

Kerman didn't say anything. He sat down, took a long pull at his drink and squeezed his hands together.

We sat there staring at the floor, not thinking, not moving—just waiting. We had four hours, probably a little more before we could go into action.

At six-thirty we were still sitting there. The scotch bottle was about half full. Cigarette butts mounded in the ashtrays. We were ready to walk up the wall.

Then the telephone rang—a shrill sound that sounded sinister in the silent little apartment.

"I'll get it," I said, and walked stiff legged across the room and picked up the receiver.

"Malloy?" A man's voice.

"Yes."

"This is Sherrill."

I didn't say anything, but waited, looking across at Kerman.

"I have your girl on board, Malloy," Sherrill said. His voice was gentle, it whispered in my ear.

"I know," I said.

"You better come out and fetch her," Sherrill said. "Say around nine o'clock. Don't come before. I'll have a boat at the pier to bring you out. Come alone and keep this close. If you bring the police or anyone with you, she'll be rapped on the head and dropped overboard. Understand?"

I said I understood.

"See you at nine o'clock then," he said, and hung up.

4

LIEUTENANT BRADLEY of the Missing People's Bureau was a thickset, middle-aged, and disillusioned police officer who sat for long hours behind a shabby desk in a small office on the fourth floor of Police Headquarters and tried to answer unanswerable questions. All day long and part of the night people came to him or called him on the telephone to report missing relatives and expected him to find them.

Not an easy job when, in most cases, the man or woman

who had disappeared had gone away because they were sick
of their homes or their wives or their husbands and were
taking good care not to be found again. A job I wouldn't have
had for twenty times the pay Bradley got, and a job I couldn't
have handled anyway.

A light still burned behind the frosted panel of his office
door when I knocked. His bland voice, automatically cor-
dial, invited me to come in.

There he was, sitting behind his desk, a pipe in his mouth,
a weary expression in his deep-set, shrewd brown eyes. A big
man, going bald, with a pouch and bags under his eyes. A
man who did a good job, got no credit nor publicity for it,
and who didn't want any.

The placid brow came down in a frown when he saw me.

"Go away," he said without hope. "I'm busy. I don't have
the time to listen to your troubles; I have troubles of my
own."

I closed the door and leaned my back against it. I wasn't
in the mood for a police lieutenant's pleasantries and I was
in a hurry.

"I want service, Bradley," I said, "and I want it fast. Do I
get it from you, or do I go to Brandon?"

The pale brown eyes looked startled.

"You don't have to talk to me like that, Malloy," he said.
"What's biting you?"

"Plenty, but I haven't time to go into details." I crossed
the small space between the door and his desk, put my fists
on his blotter and stared at him. "I want all you've got on
Anona Freedlander. Remember her? She was one of Dr.
Salzer's nurses up at the Sanatorium on Foothill Boulevard.
She disappeared on May 15th, 1947."

"I know," Bradley said, and his bush eyebrows climbed an
inch. "You're the second nuisance who's asked to see her file

in the past four hours. Funny how these things come in pairs. I've noticed it before."

"Who was it?"

Bradley dug his thumb into the button on his desk. "That's not your business," he said. "Sit down and don't crowd me."

As I pulled up a chair a police clerk came in and stood waiting.

"Let's have Freedlander's file again," Bradley said to him. "Make it snappy. This gent's in a hurry."

The clerk gave me a stony stare and went away like a centenarian climbing a steep flight of stairs.

Bradley lit his pipe and stared down at his ink-stained fingers. He breathed gently.

"Still sticking your nose into the Crosby's affairs?" he asked, without looking at me.

"Still doing it," I said shortly.

He shook his head.

"You young and ambitious guys never learn, do you? I heard MacGraw and Hartsell called on you the other night."

"They did. Maureen Crosby showed up and rescued me. How do you like that?"

He gave a little grin.

"I'd have liked to have been there. Was she the one who hit MacGraw?"

"Yeah."

"Quite a girl."

"I hear there was a shindig up at Salzer's place," I said, watching him. "Looks as if your sports fund's going to suffer."

"Like I'd cry about that. I don't have to worry about sport at my age."

We brooded over each other for a minute or so, then I

said, "Anyone report a girl named Gurney missing? She was another of Salzer's nurses."

He pulled at his thick nose, shook his head.

"Nope. Another of Salzer's nurses, did you say?"

"Yeah. Nice girl—got a good body, but maybe you're a mite old to bother about bodies."

Bradley said he was a little old for that kind of thing, but he was staring thoughtfully at me now.

"She wouldn't be any good to you, anyway—she's dead," I said.

"Are you trying to tell me something or are you just being tricky?" he asked, an acid note in his voice.

"I heard Mrs. Salzer tried to kidnap her from her apartment. The girl fell down the fire escape and broke her neck. Mrs. S planted her somewhere in the desert, probably near the sanatorium."

"Who told you?"

"An old lady fooling around with a crystal ball."

He scratched the side of his jaw with the end of his pipe and stared blankly at me.

"Better tell Brandon. That's a Homicide job."

"This is a tip, brother, not evidence. Brandon likes facts, and I might not be ready to give them to him. I'm telling you because you may or may not steer the information into the proper channels and leave me out of it."

Bradley sighed, realized his pipe had gone out and groped for matches.

"You young fellas are too tricky," he said. "All right, I'll give it to my carrier pigeon. How much of it is true?"

"All of it. Why do you think Mrs. S took poison?"

The clerk came in and laid the folder on the desk. He went away still at the slow, deliberate pace. Probably his brain worked as fast as his legs.

Bradley untied the tapes and opened the file. We both stared at a half a dozen folded sheets of blank paper for some seconds.

"What the devil . . ." Bradley began, blood rising to his face.

"Take it easy," I said, reached out and poked at the sheets with my finger. Only blank sheets, nothing else.

Bradley dug his thumb into the button and kept it there.

Maybe the clerk scented trouble because he came in fast.

"What's this?" Bradley said. What are you playing at?"

The clerk gaped at the blank sheets.

"I don't know sir," he said, changing color. "The file was fastened when I took it from your out tray."

Bradley breathed heavily, started to say something, changed his mind and waved a hand to the door.

"Get out," he said.

The clerk went.

There was a pause, then Bradley said, "This could cost me my job. The crumb must have switched the papers."

"You mean he's taken the contents of the file and left that as a dummy?"

Bradley nodded.

"Must have done. There was a photograph and a descripttion and our progress report when I gave it to him.

"No copies?"

He shook his head.

I thought for a moment.

"The fella who asked for the file," I said, "was he tall, dark, powerful; a sort of movie-star type?"

Bradley stared at him.

"Yeah. Do you know him?"

"I've seen him."

"Where?"

"Do you want those papers back?"

"Of course I do. What do you mean?"

I stood up.

"Give me until nine o'clock tomorrow," I said. "I'll either have them for you or the man who took them. I'm working on something Bradley. Something I don't want Brandon mixed up in. You don't have to report this until the morning, do you?"

"What are you talking about?" Bradley demanded.

"I'll have the papers or the man by tomorrow morning, if you sit tight and keep your mouth shut," I said, and made for the door.

"Hey! Come back!" Bradley said, starting to his feet.

But I didn't go back. I ran down the four flights of stairs to the front entrance where Kerman was waiting for me in the Buick.

5

THERE were four of us: Mike Finnegan, Kerman, myself and a worried looking little guy wearing a black, greasy slouch hat, no coat, a dirty shirt and soiled white ducks. We sat in the back room of Delmonico's bar, a bottle of scotch and four glasses on the table, and a lot of tobacco smoke cluttering up the air.

The little guy in the greasy hat was Joe Dexter. He owned a hauling business and ran freight to the ships anchored in the harbor. Finnegan claimed he was a friend of his, but by the way he was acting you wouldn't have known it.

I had put my proposition to him and he was sitting staring at me as if he thought I was crazy.

"Sorry mister," he said at last. "I couldn't do it. It'd ruin my business."

Kerman was lolling in his chair, a cigarette hanging from his lips, his eyes closed. He opened one eye as he said, "Who cares about a business? You want to relax, brother. There're more things in life than a business." Dexter licked his lips, scowled at Kerman and squirmed in his chair. He turned pleadingly to Mike.

"I can't do it," he said, "not a thing like this. The *Dream Ship* is one of my best customers."

"She won't be for much longer," I said. "Cash in while the going's good. You'll make a hundred bucks on this deal."

"A hundred bucks!" Dexter's face twisted into a sneer. "Sherrill pays me more than that every month, regular money. I'm not doing it."

I motioned to Mike to take it easy. He was straining forward, making a growling noise in his throat.

"Look," I said to Dexter, "all we want you to do is to deliver this case of supplies to the ship tonight. Do that, and you'll get a hundred. What's scaring you?"

"And you're going to travel inside the case," Dexter said. "To hell with that for an idea. No one's allowed on that ship without a permit. If they catch you—and they will—they'll know I had something to do with it. The least Sherrill would do would be to shut down my account. He's likely to send someone over to crack my skull. I'm not doing it."

As I refilled the glasses I glanced at my wristwatch. It was seven-thirty. Time was moving.

"Listen Joe," Mike said, leaning forward, "this guy's a friend of mine, see? He wants to get aboard that ship. If he wants to get aboard, he's going to get aboard, see? Sherrill ain't the only guy who can crack a skull. Do you do the job, or do I have to get tough?"

Kerman pulled out his Colt .45 and laid it on the table.

"And when he's through with you, I'll start," he said.

Dexter eyed the Colt and flinched away from Mike's concentrated glare.

"You guys can't threaten me," he said feebly.

"We can try," Kerman said calmly. "Give you ten seconds before we start something."

"Don't crowd the fella," I said, and took from my wallet ten ten-dollar bills. I spread them out on the table and pushed them towards Dexter. "Come on, take your money and let's get moving. Sherrill's washed up. The cops will move in by tomorrow. Cash in while the going's good."

Dexter hesitated, then picked up the notes and rustled them between dirty fingers.

"I wouldn't do it for anyone else," he said to Mike.

We finished our drinks, pushed back our chairs and went out on to the waterfront. It was a hot, still night, with a hint of rain in the sky. Way out on the horizon I could see the lights of the *Dream Ship*.

We tramped down an alley to Dexter's warehouse. It was in darkness. As he unlocked and pushed open the door the smell of tar, oil, damp clothes and rubber came out to greet us.

The warehouse was big and cluttered up with cases and coils of rope and bundles tied up in tarred paper, waiting to be delivered to the ships at anchor beyond the harbor. In the middle of the floor was a five-foot square packing-case.

"That's it," Dexter said gloomily.

We got busy unpacking the case.

"I want a hammer and a chisel," I told Dexter.

While he was getting the tools, Kerman said, "You're sure this is the thing to do?"

I nodded.

"With any luck I'll have nearly half an hour on board before they expect me to arrive. I can do a lot in that time.

When you and Mike come alongside at nine o'clock I'll start something to give you a chance to board her. After that it's each man for himself."

Dexter came over with the tools.

"Careful how you nail me up," I said to Kerman. "I want to get out fast."

Mike waved Dexter away.

"We'll see to this, pally. Just sit over there and behave."

He didn't want Dexter to see the tommy gun Kerman was taking out of the suitcase he had brought with him. Under cover of Mike's thickset body, Kerman put the gun at the bottom of the packing-case.

"You have plenty of room," he told me. "Sure you wouldn't like me to go instead?"

I climbed into the case.

"You come with Mike at nine. If there are more than one with Sherrill's boat, and you don't think you can handle them, you'll have to come alone. They'll think you're me, anyway. If you hear shooting on board get Mifflin and a bunch of cops and come out fighting. Okay?"

Kerman nodded. He looked very worried.

"Mike, you come along with Dexter," I went on. "If he fluffs his lines, knock him on the head and chuck him overboard."

Scowling ferociously, Mike said he would do just that thing.

When Kerman fitted on the lid there was room enough in the case for me to sit down with my knees drawn up to my chin. Air came through the joints in the case. I reckoned it wouldn't take me more than a minute or so to get out.

Kerman nailed down the lid, and between the three of them they got the case on to a sack barrow. The journey down to the waterfront was pretty rough—I collected a few bruises by the time they got the case into Dexter's boat.

The outboard motor started up and chugged us out to sea. The wind coming through the cracks in the case was sharp, and the motion of the boat as it slapped its way through the rollers bothered me.

Minutes went by, then Mike whispered that we were running alongside the *Dream Ship*.

A voice yelled from somewhere and there was some cross talk from the boat to the ship. Someone seemed to be objecting to handling the case at this time of night. Dexter played up well. He said he had to see a sick brother tomorrow, and if the case wasn't taken on board now they'd have to wait for the stuff until the following day.

The man on the ship cursed Dexter and said to stand by while he slung a derrick.

Mike kept me informed of what was going on by whispering through one of the air holes in the case.

After more delay the case jerked violently and rose in the air. I braced myself for a rough landing. It was rough all right. The case crashed down somewhere inside the ship and jarred me to the heels.

The man who had cursed Dexter cursed him again. His voice sounded close, then a door slammed and I was left alone.

I waited, listening, but heard nothing. After awhile I decided it would be safe to break out. I tapped the chisel into one of the plank joints and levered the plank back. It took me less than a minute to get out of the case. I found myself in inky darkness. There was a smell like the smell in Dexter's warehouse, and I guessed I was in the ship's hold.

I took out my flashlight and shone the beam around the vast cellar. It was full of stores, liquor and barrels of beer and empty silence. At the far end of the hold was a door. I went to it, slid it back a couple of inches and peered out into a narrow, well-lit corridor.

I held the tommy gun by my side. I didn't want to be bothered with it, but Kerman had insisted. He said with a tommy gun I could argue with half the crew. I doubted it and took it along more for his peace of mind than mine.

I began to edge along the corridor to a perpendicular ladder I could see at the far end, which I guessed led to the upper deck. Halfway down the corridor I came to an abrupt halt. A pair of feet, then legs in white uniform trousers appeared on the ladder. A second later a sailor stood gaping at me.

He was a big guy, nearly as big as I was, and tough-looking. I pushed the tommy gun at him and showed him my teeth. His hands went up so fast he took the skin off his knuckles against the low ceiling.

"Open your trap and I'll rip you in half," I snarled at him.

He stood motionless, staring at the tommy gun, his jaw hanging loose.

"Turn around," I said.

He turned and I hit him on back of his head with the gun butt.

As he fell I grabbed hold of his shirt and lowered him gently to the floor.

I was sweating and worried. I had to get him out of sight before anyone else showed up.

Right by me was a door. I took a chance, turned the handle and looked into an empty cabin. Probably it was his cabin, and he had been going to it.

I caught him up under his armpits and dragged him into the cabin, then shut and bolted the door.

Working fast, I stripped him, took off my clothes and put on his.

His peaked yachting-cap was a little big for me, but it hid my face.

I gagged him, rolled him in a sheet and tied the sheet with his belt and a length of cord I found in a cabin. Then I hauled him onto the bunk, left the tommy gun beside him, shoved my .38 down the front of my pants and went to the door.

I listened, heard nothing, opened the door a crack and peered out. The corridor was as empty as a dead man's mind, and as quiet. I turned off the light, slid out of the cabin and locked the door after me.

I looked at my watch. It was twenty-five minutes past eight. I had only thirty-five minutes before Kerman showed up.

Chapter Six

1

I STOOD in the shadow of a ventilator and looked along the boat-deck. Overhead a cream and red awning flapped in the stiff breeze. The whole length of the deck was covered with a heavy red pile carpet, and green and red lights made a string of glittering beads along the rail.

Beyond the bridge-deck I could see two immaculately dressed sailors standing under arc lights at the head of the gangway. A girl in evening dress and two men in tuxedos had just come aboard. The sailors saluted them as they crossed the deck to disappear into the brilliantly-lit restaurant, built between the bridge and the fo'c'sle-decks. Through the big, oblong-shaped windows I could see couples dancing to the strains of muted saxophones and the throb of drums.

Above me on the bridge-deck three white-clad figures hung over the rail, watching the steady flow of arrivals. It was dark up there, but I saw one of them was smoking.

No one paid me any attention, and after a quick look to right and left I slid from the shadow of the ventilator across the pile of the carpet to a lifeboat—and paused, listened, looked to right and left again, and then made a silent dart to the shadows immediately beneath the bridge deck.

"They keep coming," a voice drawled above me, "Going to be another good night."

"Yeah," said another voice. "Look at that dame in the red

dress. Look at the shape she's wearing. I bet she . . ."

But I didn't wait to hear what he bet. I was scared they might look down and see me. Right by me was a door. I slid it back a couple of inches and looked down a ladder to the lower deck. Not far off a girl laughed—a loud, harsh sound that made me glance over my shoulder.

"Tight as a tick," one of the men on the bridge deck said. "That's how I like my women."

Three girls and three men had just come aboard. One of the girls was so drunk she could scarcely walk. As they crossed to the restaurant I slid down the ladder to the lower deck.

It was dark and silent down there. I moved away from the ladder. The moonlight, coming from behind a thin haze of cloud, was just bright enough for me to see the deck was deserted. One solitary light came from a distant porthole as conspicuous as a soup stain on a bridal gown.

I made my way towards it, moving cautiously and making no sound. Halfway along the deck, I paused. Ahead of me appeared a white figure coming towards me. There was nowhere to hide. The deck was as bare of cover as the back of my hand. My fingers closed over the butt of my gun as I moved over to the deck rail and leaned against it.

A tall, broad-shouldered man in an undershirt and white ducks pants came into the light from the porthole, moved out of it towards me. He went past, humming under his breath, without even looking at me, and climbed the ladder to the upper deck.

I breathed heavily through my nose and headed for the porthole again. I paused beside it and took a quick look inside. I very nearly let out a cheer.

Paula was sitting in an armchair, facing me. She was reading a magazine, a worried little frown on her face. She looked very lovely and lonely. I had hoped to find her on this deck. I couldn't think where else they could hide her, but I hadn't expected to find her so quickly.

I examined the door of the cabin. There was a bolt on the outside and it was pushed home. I slid it back, turned the handle and pushed. The door opened and I went in. It was like walking into a greenhouse in mid-summer.

Paula started up out of her chair at the sight of me. For a moment she didn't recognize me in the white ducks and the cap, then she flopped limply back in the chair and tried to smile. The look of relief in her eyes was a good enough reward for that trip I had made in the packing-case.

"How are you getting on?" I said, and grinned. If she hadn't been so damned self-controlled I would have kissed her.

"All right. Did you have any trouble getting here?" She tried to sound casual, but there was a shake in her voice.

"I managed. At least they don't know I'm here yet. Jack and Mike will be out around nine. We may have to swim."

She drew in a deep breath and got to her feet.

"I knew you'd come, Vic." Then just when I thought she was going to let her hair down, she went on, "But you shouldn't have come alone. Why didn't you bring the police?"

"I didn't think they would come," I said. "Where's Anona?"

"I don't know. I don't think she's here."

The heat in the cabin made me sweat.

"What happened? Let's have it quick."

"The bell rang and I went to the door," she told me. "I thought it was you. Four Wops crowded me back into the lobby. Two of them went into the bedroom and I heard Anona scream. The other two said they were taking me to the ship. One of them threatened me with a knife. I had an idea he would use it if I gave him the slightest chance." She made a little grimace. "They took me down in the elevator and out into the street. All the time one of them pressed the knife into my side. There was a car waiting. They bundled me in and drove off. As we were driving away, I caught sight of a big, black Rolls pulling up outside the apartment. One of the Wops came out with Anona in his arms. This was in broad daylight. People just stared but didn't do anything. They put her in the Rolls and I lost sight of her. I was brought here and locked in. They said if I made a noise they'd cut my throat. They're dreadful little men, Vic."

"I know," I said grimly. "I've met them. That Rolls belongs to Maureen Crosby. Maybe they've taken Anona to her house on the cliffs." I thought for a moment, asked, "Has anyone been near you?"

She shook her head.

"I want to take a look around the ship before we go. Maureen may be on board. Think it'll be safe for you to come with me?"

"If they find me gone they'll raise the alarm. Perhaps I'd better stay here until you're ready to go. You'll be careful, won't you, Vic?"

I hesitated, not knowing whether to try and get off the ship now I had found Paula or first make sure Anona and Maureen weren't on board.

"If they aren't on this deck I'll leave it," I said, and mopped my face with my handkerchief. "Am I feverish or is this cabin overheated?"

"It's the cabin. It's been getting hotter and hotter for the past hour."

"Feels like they've put on the steam heating. Stick it out for ten minutes, kid. I'll be back by then."

"Be careful."

I gave her a little pat on her arm, grinned at her and slid

out on to the deck. I shot the bolt and began to move aft.

"What the hell do you think you're doing up here?" a voice demanded out of the darkness.

I nearly jumped out of my skin.

A short, thickset man, wearing a yachting-cap, had appeared from nowhere. Neither of us could see the other's face. We peered at each other.

"How many times do I have to tell you guys to keep clear of this deck?" he growled and edged closer.

He nearly had me. I saw his arm lash up and I ducked. The sap glanced off my shoulder. I slammed a punch into his belly with everything I had. He caught his breath in a gasp of agony then bent forward, trying to breathe. I hung one on his jaw that nearly smashed my hand.

He went down on hands and knees and straightened out on his back. I leaned over him, grabbed his ears and cracked his skull on the deck.

All this happened in a matter of seconds. I ran back to Paula's cabin and unbolted the door, threw it open, whipped around and dragged the unconscious man in and dropped him on the floor.

"I walked right into him," I panted as I bent over him. I lifted an eyelid. He was out all right, and by the pulpy softness at the back of his head he would be out for some time.

"Put him in that cupboard," Paula said. "I'll watch him." She was pale but quite unruffled. It took a lot to rattle her.

I dragged him across the cabin and into the cupboard. I had to squash him in, and I got the door shut only by leaning my weight against it.

"Phew!" I said and wiped my face. "He'll be all right in there if he doesn't suffocate. It's like a furnace in here."

"It's worrying me. Even the floor's hot. Do you think

there's a fire somewhere?"

I put my hand on the carpet. It was hot all right—too hot. I opened the cabin door and put my hand on the planks of the deck. They were so hot they nearly raised a blister.

"Good grief!" I exclaimed. "You're right. The damned ship is on fire somewhere below." I caught her arm and pulled her out onto the deck. "You're not staying in there. Come on kid, keep behind me. We'll take a quick look and then go up on the top deck." I checked my wristwatch. It was five minutes to nine. "Jack'll be out in five minutes."

As we moved along the deck, Paula said, "Shouldn't we raise the alarm? The ship's full of people, Vic."

"Not yet. Later," I said.

At the far end of the deck was a door set in the bulkhead. I paused outside to listen, turned the handle and eased the door open.

It was hotter than an oven on full blast in there, and oil in the paint on the walls was beginning to run. It was a nice room; big, airy and well-furnished—half-office, half-lounge. Big windows on either side of the room commanded views of Orchid City beach and the Pacific. A solitary desk-light threw a pool of light on the desk and part of the carpet. The rest of the room was in darkness. Overhead came the sounds of dance music and the soft swish of moving feet.

I entered the room, my gun pushed forward. Paula came in after me and closed the door. There was a smell of burning and smoke, and as I moved to the desk I saw the carpet was smoldering and smoke was coming in little wisps from under the wainscoting.

"The fire's right below us," I said. Keep by the door. The floor might not be safe. This looks like Sherrill's office."

I went through the desk drawers, not knowing what I was looking for, but looking. In one of the bottom drawers I

found a square-shaped envelope. One glance told me it was
Anona Freed lander's missing dossier. I folded it and shoved
it into my hip pocket.

"Okay," I said. "Let's get out of here."

Paula said in a small voice, "Vic! What's that—behind the
desk?"

I peered over the back of the desk. Something was there
. . . something white, something that could have been a man.
I shifted the desk lamp so the light fell directly on it.

I heard Paula gasp.

It was Sherrill. He lay flat on his back, his teeth bared in a
mirthless grin. His clothes were smoldering and his hands,
laying on the burning carpet, had a burned-up, scorched
look. He had been shot through the head at close range. One
side of his skull had been smashed in.

Even as I leaned forward to stare at him, there was a
sudden *whooshing* sound and two long tongues of flame
spurted out from the floor and licked across his dead face.

2

THE little Wop stood in the doorway, grinning at us. The
blunt-nosed automatic in his small, brown fist centered on
my chest. The dark, ugly little face was shiny with sweat, and
the dark little eyes were shiny with hate. He had come
silently from nowhere.

"Give me that," he said, and held out his hand. "What you
put in your pocket—quick!"

I was holding my gun down by my side. I knew I couldn't
get it up and shoot at him before he got me. I pulled the
dossier out of my hip pocket with my left hand. As I did so I
saw the sudden change of expression in his eyes: hatred to

viciousness. The trigger-finger turned white as he took up the slack. I saw all this in a split second, knowing he was going to shoot.

Paula threw a chair forward to crash on the floor between the Wop and me. His eyes shifted and so did his aim. The gun went off; the slug missed me by about two feet. I was firing at him before he had time to get his eyes off the chair and on to me again. The three bullets cut across his chest like sledge hammers. He was hurled back against the wall; the automatic falling from his hand, his face twisting hideously.

"Out!" I said to Paula.

She bent and snatched up the Wop's automatic and jumped for the door. As I ran across the floor I felt it give under me. There was a sudden loud cracking of breaking timber. Heat came up at me as if I were running across red-hot boiler plates. The floor sagged and gave. For one horrible moment I thought I was going down with the floor, but the fitted carpet held just long enough for me to reach the door and the deck.

There was a terrific crash inside Sherrill's office. I caught one brief glimpse of the furniture sliding into a red, roaring furnace, then Paula caught hold of my arm and together we raced down the deck.

Tar was oozing out of the hot planks and smoke was mounting.

Out of the darkness halfway down the deck, someone took a shot at us. The slug crashed through the wooden partition behind me and ruined a mirror in one of the cabins with a crash of breaking glass.

I shoved Paula behind me, conscious that my white clothes made me look like a phantom out for a night's haunting.

More gunfire. I felt a slug zip past my face. The gun-flash

came from around a lifeboat. I thought I could see a shadowy figure crouching against the rails. I fired twice. The second shot nailed him. He came staggering out from behind the boat and flattened out on the hot deck.

"Keep going," I said.

We ran on. The deck was so hot now it burned through our shoes. Somehow we reached the ladder leading to the upper deck. Above the roar of the flames we could hear yells and screams and the crash of breaking glass.

We scrambled onto the upper deck. The deck rail was packed with men and women in evening-dress, yelling their heads off. Smoke made a black pall over the ship, and it was almost as hot up there as on the lower deck.

I could see three or four of the ship's officers trying to get the panic under control. They might just as well have tried to slam a revolving door.

"Jack must be somewhere around by now," I shouted to Paula. "Keep near me and let's get to the rail."

We fought our way through the struggling mob. A man grabbed Paula and swung her away from me. I don't know what he thought he was doing. His face was twitching and his eyes wild. He clawed at me frantically and I punched him in the jaw sending him reeling, and then pushed and shoved my way to Paula again.

A girl with the top half of her dress torn off, fell on my neck and screamed in my face. Her breath, loaded with whisky fumes, nearly blistered my skin. I tried to shove her off, but her arms threatened to strangle me. Paula pulled her away and boxed her ears hard. The girl went staggering into the crowd, screaming like a train whistle.

We reached the deck rail. Spread out all over the sea and coming in all directions was an armada of small boats. The sea was alive with them.

"Hey! Vic!"

Kerman's voice rose above the uproar, and we saw him standing on the deck rail not far from us, clinging to the awning and kicking the crazy crowd away from him whenever they threatened to tear him from his hold.

"Come on, Vic!"

I pushed Paula ahead of me. We reached him after a struggle, and after Paula nearly had her dress ripped off her back.

Kerman was grinning excitedly.

"Did you have to set fire to the ship?" he bawled. "Talk about panic! What's got into these punks? They'll be off weeks before the tub goes down."

"Where's your boat?" I panted and shoved an elderly gambler out of my way as he struggled to climb over the rail. "Take it easy, pop," I told him. "It's too wet to swim. All the boats in the world are coming."

"Right here," Kerman said, pointing below him. He swung Paula up onto the rail while I struggled to keep the customers from following her. He guided her feet on to a rope ladder hanging down the ship's side, and she descended like a veteran sailor.

"Not you madam," Kerman yelled, as a girl fought her way towards him. "This is a private party. Try a little farther along."

The girl, hysterical and screaming, threw herself against him and wrapped her arms around his legs.

"For Pete's sake!" he yelled. "You'll have my pants off! Hi, Vic, give me a hand! This dame's crazy."

I swung myself over the rail and onto the ladder.

"I thought you liked them that way. Bring her along if she's all that attached to you."

I don't know how he got rid of her but as I dropped into

the boat, he came sliding down the ladder and nearly knocked me overboard as he landed.

"Take it easy," I said, and grabbed him to steady him.

Mike had started the outboard engine and the boat began to draw away from the ship. We had to pick our way. The number of boats coming out to the *Dream Ship* was something to see. It looked like Dunkirk all over again.

"Nice work!" I said, clapping Mike on his broad back. "You guys timed it about right." I looked back at the *Dream Ship*. The lower deck was on fire now, and smoke was pouring from her sides. "I wonder how much she was insured for?"

"Did you touch her off?" Kerman asked.

"No, you dope! Sherrill's dead. Someone shot him and set fire to the ship. If we hadn't spotted him when we did, he would never have been found."

"A pretty expensive funeral," Kerman said, looking blank.

"Not if the ship's insured. You talk to Paula. I want to look at this," and I pulled Anona Freedlander's dossier out of my hip pocket.

Kerman gave me a flashlight.

"What is it?" he asked.

I stared at the first page of the dossier, scarcely believing my eyes.

Paula said, "Vic, hadn't we better decide what we're going to do?"

"Do? Jack and I are going after Anona. I want you to tell Mifflin about Sherrill. Get him to come out to Maureen Crosby's cliff house fast. It's going to finish tonight."

She stared at him.

"Wouldn't it be better for you to see Mifflin?"

"We haven't the time. If Anona's at Maureen's place she's in trouble."

Kerman leaned forward.

"What is all this about?"

I waved the dossier at him.

"It's right here, and that lug Mifflin didn't think it important enough to tell me. Since 1944, Anona had *endocarditis.* I told you they were trying to keep a cat in a bag. Well, it's out now."

"Anona's got a wacky heart?" Kerman said, gaping at me. "You mean Janet Crosby, don't you?"

"Listen to the description they give of Anona," I said. "Five foot; dark; brown eyes; plump. Work that out."

"But it's wrong. She's tall and fair," Kerman said. "What are you talking about?"

Paula was onto it.

"She isn't Anona Freedlander. That's it, isn't it?"

"You bet she isn't," I said excitedly. "Don't you see? It was Anona who died of heart failure at Crestways! And the girl in Salzer's sanatorium is Janet Crosby!"

3

WE STOOD at the foot of the almost perpendicular cliff and stared up into the darkness. Moments before Paula and Mike had dropped off Kerman and me on the desolate shore, then left in the boat to go in search of reinforcements. Far out to sea a great red glow in the sky pinpointed the burning Dream Ship. A mushroom of smoke hung in the night sky.

Kerman looked at me incredulously.

"Up there?" he scoffed. "What do you think I am—a monkey?"

"That's something you'd better discuss with your father," I said, and grinned in the darkness. "There's no other way. The front entrance is guarded by two electrically-controlled gates and all the barbed wire in the world. If we're going to get in, this is the way."

Kerman drew back to study the face of the cliff. "Three hundred feet if it's an inch," he said, awe in his voice. "Will I love every foot of it!"

"Well come on. Let's try, anyway."

The first twenty feet was easy enough. Big boulders formed a platform at the foot of the cliff, they were simple enough to climb. We stood side by side on a flat rock while I sent the beam of my light up into the darkness. The jagged face of the cliff towered above us, and bulged out near the top, forming what seemed an impassable barrier.

"That's the bit I like," Kerman said, pointing. "Up there where it curves out. Getting over that's going to be fun—a tooth and fingernail job."

"Maybe it's not as bad as it looks," I said, not liking it myself. "If we had a rope . . ."

"If we had a rope, I'd go quietly away some place and hang myself," Kerman said gloomily. "It would save time and a lot of hard work."

"Pipe down, you pessimistic devil!" I said sharply, and began to edge up the cliff face. There were foot and hand-holds, and if the cliff hadn't been perpendicular it would have been fairly easy to climb. But as it was, I was conscious that one slip would finish the climb and me. I'd fall straight out and away from the cliff face. There would be no sliding or grabbing to save myself.

When I had climbed about fifty feet I paused to get my breath back. I couldn't look down. The slightest attempt to lean away from the cliff face would upset my balance and I'd fall.

"How are you getting on?" I panted, pressing myself

against the surface of the cliff and staring up into the star-studded sky.

"As well as can be expected," Kerman said with a groan. "I'm surprised I'm still alive. Do you think this is dangerous or am I just imagining it?"

I shifted my grip on a knob of rock and hauled myself up another couple of feet.

"It's only dangerous if you fall; then it's probably fatal," I said.

We kept moving. Once I heard a sudden rumble of fall-ling rock and Kerman catch his breath sharply. My hair stood on end.

"Keep your eye on some of these rocks," he gasped. "One of them just came away in my hand."

"I'll watch it."

About a quarter of the way up I came suddenly and unex-pectedly to a four-foot ledge and I hoisted myself up onto it, leaned my back against the cliff face and tried to get my breath back. I felt cold sweat on my neck and back. If I had known it was going to be this bad I would have tried the gates. It was too late now. It might be just possible to climb up, but quite impossible to climb down.

Kerman joined me on the ledge. His face was glistening with sweat, and his legs seemed shaky.

"This has cooled me on mountain climbing," he panted. "One time I was sucker enough to imagine it'd be fun. Think we'll get over the bulge?"

"We'll damn well have to," I said, staring up into the darkness. "There's no other way now but to keep going. Imagine trying to climb down!"

I sent the beam of the flashlight searching the cliff face again. To our left and above us was a four-foot-wide crevice that went up beside the bulge.

"See that?" I said. "If we got our feet and shoulders against the sides of that opening, we might work our way up past the bulge."

Kerman drew in a deep breath.

"The ideas you get," he said. "It can't be done."

"I think it can," I said, staring at the walls of the crevice. "And I'm going to try."

"Don't be a fool!" Alarm jumped into his voice. "You'll slip."

"If you want to try the bulge, try it. This is my way."

I swung off the ledge, groped for a foothold, edged my hand along the cliff face until I got a grip and started up again. It was slow and difficult work. The hazy moonlight didn't help me much, and most of the time I had to feel for handholds. As my head and shoulders came level with the bottom of the crevice the knob of rock on which I was standing gave under me. I felt it shift a split second before it went and I threw myself forward, clawing at the rock bed of the crevice in a frantic effort to get a hold. My fingers hooked into a ridge of rock and there I hung.

"Take it easy!" Kerman bawled, as hysterical as an old lady with her dress on fire. "Hang on! I'm right with you!"

"Stay where you are," I panted. "I'll only take you down with me."

I tried to get a foothold but the toes of my shoes scraped against the cliff face and trod on air. Then I tried to draw myself up, pulling the whole of my weight with my fingertips, but that couldn't be done. I managed to raise myself a couple of inches and that's as far as I got.

Something touched my foot.

"Take it easy," Kerman implored below me. He guided my foot on to his shoulder. "Now give me your weight and push up."

"I'll push you down, you fool!" I panted.

"Come on!" His voice shook. "I've got a good grip. Slowly and steadily. Don't do anything suddenly."

There was nothing else to do. Very cautiously I transferred the weight of my body onto his shoulder, then transferred my finger grip to another ridge where I had a better hold.

"I'm heaving," I panted. "Right?"

"Yeah," Kerman said, and I felt him brace himself.

I heaved with my arms and shoulders and slid up and on to the floor of the crevice. I lay there, panting until Kerman's head appeared above the ledge, then I crawled forward and pulled him up beside me. We flopped down, side by side, not saying anything.

After a while I got unsteadily to my feet.

"We're having quite a night," I said, leaning against the crevice wall.

Kerman squinted up at me.

"Yeah," he said. "Will I get a medal for that?"

"I'll buy you a drink instead," I said, then drew in a deep breath, dug my shoulders into the wall and got my feet up against the opposite wall. By pressing hard with my shoulders and feet I managed to maintain a sitting position between the two walls.

"Is that the way you're going to travel?" Kerman asked, horrified.

"Yeah, it's an old Swiss custom."

"Have I got to do that, too?"

"Unless you want to stay where you are for the rest of your days," I said heartlessly. "There's no other way."

I began to edge myself upwards. The sharp rocks dug into my shoulder-blades and it was slow work, but I made progress. So long as the muscles in my legs didn't turn sour on me, I would get to the top. But if they did, it would be a quick drop and a rocky landing.

I kept moving. I'd rather go up this way than attempt the bulge. A third of the way up I had to stop and rest. My legs felt as if I had been running for a hundred miles, and the muscles in my thighs were fluttering.

"How are you doing, pal?" Kerman called, shining his flash up at me.

"Well I'm still in one piece," I said dubiously. "Wait until I get to the top before you try it."

"Take your time. I'm in no hurry."

I started again. It was slow work, and my shoulders began to ache. I kept looking up at the star-studded sky. It seemed to be coming closer; maybe that was just wishful thinking but it inspired me to keep on. I kept on, my breath hissing through clenched teeth, my legs stiffening, my shoulders bruised. Up and up; inch by inch, knowing there was no going back. I had to get up there or fall.

The crevice began to narrow and I knew then I was passing the bulge. The going became harder. My knees were being slowly forced towards my chin. I was getting less leverage. Then suddenly I stopped. I could go no farther. Above me the crevice had narrowed down to about three feet. Bracing myself, I got out the flashlight and sent the beam along the wall and above me. A scrubby bush grew out of the rock within reach. To my right was a narrow shelf—the top of the bulge.

I put the flash back into my pocket and reached for the bush. I got a grip on it close to where it grew out of the cliff and pulled gently. It held. I transferred some of my weight to it. It still held. Then drawing in a deep breath, I relaxed the pressure of my feet against the wall and swung into space. It was quite a moment. The bush bent, but it was well-rooted. I swung to and fro, feeling sweat like ice-water running down my spine, then I swung myself towards the ledge and with my free hand groped for a hold. My fingers dipped into a crack—not enough to hold me, but just enough to steady me. I hung there, pressing my body against the wall of the crevice, my feet treading air, my right hand clutching the bush, my left hand dug into the narrow crack in the ledge. One false move now, and I would go down. I was scared all right. I've been in some panics in my life, but none like this one.

Very cautiously I began to lever down with my right hand and pull with my left. I moved up slowly. My head and shoulders came up above the ledge. I began to lean forward as my chest touched the edge of the ledge. I hung like that, nearly done, my heart pounding and blood singing in my ears. After awhile I collected enough strength to climb another couple of inches. I dragged up one knee and rested it on the ledge. Then with a frantic effort, I heaved forward and was on the ledge, flat on my back, aware of nothing but the pounding of my heart and the rasping of my breath.

"Vic!"

Kerman's voice floated up the funnel of the crevice.

I made a croaking noise and crawled to the edge.

"Are you all right, Vic?"

His voice sounded miles away—a faint whisper out of the darkness. Looking down I saw a pinpoint of light waving to and fro. I had no idea I had climbed so far and seeing that light made me dizzy.

"Yeah," I shouted back. "Give me a minute."

After a while I got my breath and nerve back.

"You can't do it, Jack," I shouted down to him. You'll have to wait until I can get a rope. It's too tricky. Don't try it."

"Where will you get the rope from?"

"I don't know. I'll find something. You wait there."

I turned around and sent the beam of the flashlight into the darkness. I was only about thirty feet below the cliff head. The rest of the way was easy.

"I'm going now," I shouted down to him. "Hang on until I get a rope."

I practically walked up the next thirty feet and came up right beside the ornate swimming pool. Above me was the house. A solitary light burned in one of the windows.

I set off towards it.

4

THE VERANDAH was deserted when I got there, and the swing lounging chair looked invitingly comfortable. I would have liked to have stretched out on it and taken a twelve-hour nap.

A standard lamp with a yellow and blue parchment shade was alight in the big lounge. The French doors leading from the lounge to the verandah stood open.

I paused at the head of the verandah steps at the sound of a voice—a woman's voice, out of tune with the still, summer night, the scent of flowers and the big yellow moon. The voice was loud and shrill. Maybe it was angry, too, and the edges of it were a little frayed with suppressed hysteria.

"Oh shut up! Shut up! Shut up!" The voice was saying. "Come quickly. You've talked enough. Just shut up and come!"

I could see her in there, kneeling on one of the big settees, holding the telephone in a small, tight-clenched fist. Her back was turned to me. The light from the lamp fell directly on her beautifully shaped head and picked out the tints in her raven-black hair. She was wearing a pair of high-waisted, bottle-green slacks and a silk shirt of the same color and made the kind of picture Vargas likes to draw. She was his type: long-legged, small-hipped, high-breasted, and as alive and as quick as mercury.

She said, "Do stop it! Why go on and on? Just come. That's all you have to do," and she slammed down the receiver.

I didn't think the situation called for stealth or super-refined cunning, and I wasn't in the mood to play pretty. I was leg-weary and bruised and still short of breath, and my temper was as touchy as the filed trigger of a heist man's rod. So I moved into the room without bothering to tread quietly. My footfalls across the parquet floor sounded like miniature explosions.

I saw her back stiffen. Her head turned slowly. She looked over her shoulder at me. Her big black eyes opened wide. There was a pause in which you could have counted a slow ten. She didn't recognize me. She saw what looked like an overgrown sailor in tattered white ducks with a rip in one trousers knee, a shirt any laundry would have returned with a note of complaint and a face that had more dirt on it than freckles.

"Hello," I said quietly. "Remember me? Your pal, Malloy."

She remembered me then. She drew in a deep breath, pushed herself off the settee and stood firmly on her small, well-shaped feet.

"How did you get here?" she asked, her face and voice were as expressionless as the ruffles on her shirt.

"I climbed the cliff. You should try it sometime when you run out of excitement," I said, moving into the room. "It's good for the figure too, not that there's anything wrong with yours."

She bent her thumb and stared at it, then she bit it tentatively.

"You haven't seen it yet," she said.

"Is the operative word in that sentence 'yet'?" I asked, looking at her.

"It could be. It depends on you."

"Does it?" I sat down. "Shall we have a drink? I'm not quite the man I was. You'll find my reflexes act better on whisky."

She moved across the lounge to the liquor cabinet.

"Is it true about the cliff?" she asked. "No one has ever climbed it before."

"Leander swam the Hellespont, and Hero wasn't half as good looking as you," I said lightly.

"You mean you really climbed it?" She came back with a long tumbler full of whisky and ice. It looked a lot more tempting than she did, but I didn't tell her so.

"I climbed it," I said, and took the glass. "To your dark and lovely eyes, and the figure I haven't seen—yet."

She stood by and watched me drink a third of it. Then she lit a cigarette with a hand that was as steady as the cliff we were talking about, took it from her red, sensual mouth and gave it to me.

Our fingers touched. Her skin felt feverish.

"Is your sister here?" I asked, and set the whisky carefully on the coffee table at my side.

She inspected her thumb again thoughtfully, then looked at me out of the corners of her eyes.

"Janet's dead. She died two years ago," she said.

"I've made a lot of discoveries since you told me that," I said. "I know the girl your mother kept a prisoner in the sanatorium for something like two years is your sister, Janet. Shall I tell you just how much I do know?"

She made a little grimace and sat down.

"You can if you want to," she said.

"Some of it is guesswork. Perhaps you'll help me as I go along?" I said, settling farther down in the chair. "Janet was your father's favorite. Both you and your mother knew he was going to leave her the bulk of his money. Janet fell in love with Sherrill, who also knew she was coming into the money. Sherrill was quite a dashing type, and dashing types appeal to you. You and he had an affair on the side, but Janet found out and broke the engagement. There was a quarrel between you two. One of you grabbed a shotgun. Your father came in at the wrong moment. Did you shoot him or was it Janet?"

She lit a cigarette, dropped the match into an ashtray before saying, "Does it matter? I did if you must know."

"There was a nurse staying in the house at the time: Anona Freedlander. Why was she there?"

"My mother wasn't quite right in the head," she said casually. "She didn't think I was, either. She persuaded father I needed looking after, and she sent Nurse Freedlander to spy on me."

"Nurse Freedlander wanted to call the police when you shot your father?"

She nodded and smiled. The smile didn't reach the expressionless, coal-black eyes.

"Mother said they would put me away in a home if it came out I had shot him. Nurse Freedlander made herself a nuisance. Mother got her back to the sanatorium and locked her up. It was the only way to keep her quiet. Then Janet insisted on me being locked up too, and mother had to agree. She sent me here. This is her house. Janet thought I was in the sanatorium. She found out I wasn't, but she didn't know where I was. I think that's why she wrote to you. She was going to ask you to find me. Then Nurse Freedlander had a heart attack and died. This was too good a chance to miss. Mother and Douglas carried her body to Crestways. Mother told Janet I wanted to see her, and she went over to the sanatorium. She was locked up in Nurse Freedlander's room, and Nurse Freedlander was put in Janet's bed. It was quite a bright idea, wasn't it? I called Dr. Bewley who lived nearby. It didn't occur to him that the dead woman wasn't Janet, and he signed the death certificate. It was easy after that. The trustees didn't suspect anything, and I came into all the money." She leaned forward to tap cigarette-ash into the ashtray, went on in the same flat, disinterested voice, "It was true what I told you about Douglas. The little rat turned on me and tried to blackmail me and made me buy the *Dream Ship.* Janet's maid blackmailed me too. She knew Janet hadn't died. Then you came along. I thought if I told you some of the story it might scare Douglas off, but it didn't. He wanted to kill you but I wouldn't let him. It was my idea you should go to the sanatorium. I didn't think you would get Janet away. As soon as I found out where she was I got Sherrill's men to bring her here."

"Was it your idea to shoot Nurse Freedlander's father?"

She made a little grimace of disgust.

"What else could I do? If he told you she had a bad heart I knew you would guess what had happened. I got in a panic. I thought if we could silence him and get her papers from the police, we might be able to keep it up. But it does seem rather hopeless."

"Janet's here then?"

She shrugged.

"Yes, she's here."

"And you're trying to make up your mind what to do with her?"

"Yes."

"Any ideas?"

"Perhaps."

I finished my drink. I needed it.

"You shot Sherrill, didn't you, and set fire to the ship?"

"You have found out a lot."

"Didn't you?"

"Oh yes. I knew he would turn on me if the police caught him. He was a nuisance, anyway. It was quite fun to set fire to the ship. I've always hated it. Did it burn well?

I said it burned very well.

We sat for some moments looking at each other.

"I'm wondering about you," she said suddenly. "Couldn't we team up together? It seems so senseless to give all that money to a lot of stuffy old scientists. There must be nearly two million left."

"How should we team up?"

She bit her thumb while she thought about how we should team up.

"You see, she's my sister. I can't keep her here for long. If they find out she's alive I shall lose the money. It would be better if she died."

I didn't say anything to that.

"I've been in there three or four times with a gun," she said, after a long pause. "But every time I start to pull the trigger something stops me." She stared at me and said, "I would give you half the money."

I stubbed out my cigarette.

"Are you suggesting I should do it?"

This time the meaningless smile did reach her eyes.

"Think what you could do with all that money."

"I'm thinking, but I haven't got it yet."

"Oh, I'd give it to you. I'll give you a check now."

"You could always stop the check when I had done it, couldn't you? You could shoot me as you shot Sherrill," I said, and gave her one of my dumb looks.

"When I say a thing, I mean it, and when I make a promise, I keep it," she said patiently. And besides, you can have me, too."

"Can I?" I tried not to sound as unenthusiastic as I felt. "That's fine." I stood up. "Where is she?"

She stared at me, her face still expressionless, but far up on her left cheek a nerve began to jump.

"Are you going to do it?"

"I don't see why not. Give me the gun and tell me where she is."

"Don't you want me to write the check first?"

I shook my head.

"I trust you," I said, and hoped I wasn't overworking the dumb look.

She pointed to a door opposite the French windows at the far end of the room.

"She's in there."

I stood up.

"Then give me the gun. It must be made to look like suicide."

She nodded.

"Yes, I thought of that. You—you won't hurt her?"

There was a blank look in her eyes now. Her mind seemed to have wandered off into space.

"The gun," I said, and snapped my fingers at her.

"Oh yes." She shivered, frowned, looked vaguely around the room. "I had it somewhere." The nerve was jumping like a frog under her skin. "I think it must be in my bag."

The bag was laying in one of the armchairs. She moved towards it but I beat her to it.

"It's all right," I said. "I'll get it. You sit down and take it easy."

I picked up the bag and slid back the clip.

"Don't open it, Malloy!"

I turned quickly.

Manfred Willet stood in the open doorway. He had an automatic in his hand and it was pointed at me.

5

MAUREEN cried shrilly. "You fool! Why didn't you wait? He was going to do it! You stupid, brainless fool!"

Willet's cold eyes shifted from me to her.

"Of course he wasn't going to do it," he said curtly. "He wanted your gun. Now be quiet and let me handle this."

She stiffened and swung round on me. There was a feverish glitter in her dark eyes.

"Weren't you going to do it?" she demanded. "Weren't you?"

I shook my head.

"No," I said, and smiled at her.

"This has gone far enough," Willet said, and advanced into the room. "Sit down," he went on to me. "I want to talk to you. And you sit down, too." This to Maureen.

I sat down but she didn't. She stood motionless, staring at Willet, her sharp little teeth gnawing at her thumb.

"Sit down!" he said and turned the gun on her. "You're as crazy as your mother. It's time you were put under control."

She smiled then and wandered over to the armchair in which her bag had been lying. She sat down and crossed her legs and went on biting her thumb.

Willet stood in front of the empty fireplace. He held the

gun level with his waist and pointing between Maureen and
me. There was a gaunt, worried look about his face, and his
eyes kept shifting from her to me.

"Where's Janet?" he asked.

Since Maureen didn't say anything, I jerked my thumb to
the door opposite the window.

"She says she's in there."

"Is she all right?"

"As far as I know."

He relaxed slightly but didn't lower the gun.

"Do you realize there is still a lot of money to be made out
of this setup if you throw in with me?" he said. "We can still
get it under control. Where I went wrong was to let her have
so much freedom. I didn't think she was quite so dangerous.
I knew she was unbalanced. Her mother was. But I thought
they were harmless. I would have acted sooner, but Sherrill
blocked me. Now he's dead it'll be easy. You are the only
obstacle now. Will you take fifty thousand and keep your
mouth shut?"

I raised my eyebrows.

"She's just offered me a million."

He made an impatient gesture.

"Look, this is a business proposition. Don't let's waste
time. She hasn't a million. She wouldn't have given you
anything even if she had anything to give. She's not in the
position to collect the insurance on the *Dream Ship*. I am."

"What's going to happen to her?" I asked and glanced
across at Maureen who gave me a blank empty look from
blank, empty eyes.

"I'll have her put in a home. She has no alternative unless
she wants to be handed over to the police and prosecuted for
murder," Willet said, speaking softly and rapidly. "It can all
be arranged quietly. Janet isn't likely to make trouble. I can

persuade her to do what I say. She will have the trust money. You and I will have the insurance on the *Dream Ship*."

"Just let me get this straight," I said. "Did you hatch this little plot from the beginning?"

"We needn't go into that," he said curtly.

"It was his idea," Maureen said. "All along it's been his idea. He's been gambling with the trust. Janet found out. It was he who persuaded mother to lock Janet up in the sanatorium. If it hadn't been for Douglas, he would have had me locked up, too."

"Be quiet!" Willet snapped, and his face hardened.

"I guessed it was something like that," I said. "Someone to do with the trust had to be in on it. I began to wonder about you when you were reluctant to report to the other trustees. Then when Janet was taken from my secretary's apartment, I knew. No one except you and me and Paula knew Janet was there."

"What does it matter?" he said impatiently. "If it hadn't been for Sherrill and this mad woman it would have worked. But I don't stand for murder. As soon as they started that game, I made up my mind to stop her. And she can be stopped. Are you coming in with me? I'll split the insurance money with you fifty-fifty."

"Suppose I don't?"

"I'm ready for a getaway," he said. "I don't want to go, but I will if I have to. I'll have to keep you both here until I collect the insurance. It won't be easy, but it can be done. But if you're smart, you'll come in with me."

I looked at Maureen.

"Haven't you anything to say to all this?"

"There's nothing she can say," Willet said impatiently. "She either goes into a home or to jail. She's too dangerous to be left free."

I ignored him and said again, "Isn't there anything you want to say?"

She smiled then, a tight, hard little smile.

"No, but there's something I'm going to do."

She must have had the gun wedged down the side of the chair all the time. The shot sounded like a thunderclap. The gun-flash set fire to the loose cover of the chair.

Willet dropped his gun and took two unsteady steps forward, his hands clutching at his chest. I saw him fold at the knees, then I threw myself out of my chair across the narrow space that divided my chair from hers. I clutched her wrist as the gun came round in my direction. It went off and I felt the gun-flash burn the side of my neck. She and I and the chair went crashing to the floor. I wrenched the gun out of her hand, gave her a hard shove, and scrambled to my feet.

"Okay, okay—take it easy," Mifflin said from the French windows, and Jack Kerman and he came into the room.

"You all right, Vic?" Kerman asked.

"Yeah. Did you hear all that?"

"We heard," Mifflin said. "Is he hurt bad?" And he started towards Willet.

"Watch her!" I shouted and jumped forward.

Maureen had made a dart towards the window. I made a grab at her, but she was too quick. She ran out on to the verandah and down the terrace steps.

"He's dead," I heard Mifflin say in disgust as Kerman and I ran out after her.

We reached the first terrace as she reached the fourth. I grabbed Kerman and held him back.

"Let Mifflin go after her if he wants her," he said.

Mifflin came thudding down the terrace steps to join us.

"Where's she gone?" he demanded.

I pointed.

She was running well and already had reached the lowest terrace. Mifflin started after her, then stopped. She ran straight towards the cliff edge. She was still running when she went over.

For some moments we stood motionless, listening and waiting. But we heard nothing. It was as if the space between the cliff head and the sea had opened up and swallowed her.

"That's the best way out for her," I said and turned back to the house. I felt a little sick. Even if she was crazy she had been beautiful, and I always feel sorry when something beautiful gets broken.

As we reached the verandah I asked, "Did you climb the cliff?"

Kerman nodded.

"I came over the bulge," he said with an exaggerated shudder. "I'm going to dream about that for the rest of my days. By the way, Paula's around somewhere."

"Where'd she go?"

"She's looking for Janet Crosby."

Mifflin came panting up, his expression grim. "Smashed herself to pieces," he said.

"Now we'll have to explain the setup to Brandon," I said. "That should be a lot of fun."

"You have no idea," Mifflin sneered. "Now come on you two smart punks, get in there and talk!"

"Take it easy, Mifflin," I said. "I need to make sure my client is all right."

"Your client!" he balked. "What client?"

"Why, Janet Crosby of course," I said, and as Mifflin stood there with his mouth hanging open, I pushed passed him and hurried into the house.

I found them in the room Maureen had indicated, Janet

in the bed and Paula standing beside her. Janet looked pale and weak, but uninjured. Paula looked worried until she saw me, then she relaxed.

I touched her cheek and said, "Are you ok?"

"Why Mr. Malloy, I didn't think you cared."

Janet was silently staring at us, her eyes glazed over, her expression fatigued.

"Are you the man responsible for rescuing me from that horrible place?"

"I had some help," I shrugged.

"I'm beginning to remember some things . . ." she said vaguely. She frowned as if it was difficult for her to think.

"It might be better to forget some of those things," I said and patted her hand.

Then Mifflin's jittery shadow fell over us.

"All right," he bawled, "enough with the reunion. I'm not done with you, Malloy. Now get in that room with Kerman and talk."

We went in there and talked.

BRUIN CRIMEWORKS

Visit the scene of the crime

www.bruinbookstore.com

David Dodge
-DEATH AND TAXES
-TO CATCH A THIEF
-THE LONG ESCAPE
-CARAMBOLA

Fredric Brown
-KNOCK THREE-ONE-TWO
-MISS DARKNESS
New **Fredric Brown**
Double Novels:
-Vol. I: THE FAR CRY &
THE SCREAMING MIMI
-Vol. II: NIGHT OF THE
JABBERWOCK &
THE DEEP END

Wadsworth Camp
-HOUSE OF FEAR

James Hadley Chase
-NO ORCHIDS FOR MISS BLANDISH
-FLESH OF THE ORCHID
-LAY HER AMONG THE LILIES – NEW!... summer 2020
-A COFFIN FROM HONG KONG – NEW!... summer 2020

Bruno Fischer
-HOUSE OF FLESH

Edward Anderson
-FEELS LIKE RAIN

C. St. John Sprigg
-PASS THE BODY
- THE CORPSE WITH THE
SUNBURNED FACE

Elliott Chaze
-BLACK WINGS HAS MY ANGEL

Paul Bailey
-DELIVER ME FROM EVA

Bruin Asylum

Make Your Reservations Today!

www.bruinbookstore.com

The Witching Night
C. S. Cody – Booking Now

A Garden Lost in Time
Jonathan Aycliffe – Booking Now

I Am Your Brother
G. S. Marlowe – Booking Now

Dr. Mabuse
Norbert Jacques – Booking Now

Walpole's Fantastic Tales, Volume I
Hugh Walpole – Booking Now

The Magician & Other Strange Stories
W. Somerset Maugham – Booking Now

The Bat Woman
Cromwell Gibbons – Booking now

The Undying Monster
Jessie Douglas Kerruish – Booking now

The Unholy Three
Tod Robbins – Booking now

Celestial Chess
Thomas Bontly – Booking now